The Body in the Web

BY KATHERINE HALL PAGE

The Body in the Wake

The Body in the Casket

The Body in the Wardrobe

The Body in the Birches

Small Plates

The Body in the Piazza

The Body in the Boudoir

The Body in the Gazebo

The Body in the Sleigh

The Body in the Gallery

The Body in the Ivy

The Body in the Snowdrift

The Body in the Attic

The Body in the Lighthouse

The Body in the Bonfire

The Body in the Moonlight

The Body in the Big Apple

The Body in the Bookcase

The Body in the Fjord

The Body in the Bog

The Body in the Basement

The Body in the Cast

The Body in the Vestibule

The Body in the Bouillon

The Body in the Kelp

The Body in the Belfry

The Body in the Web

A Faith Fairchild Mystery

Katherine Hall Page

wm

William Morrow

An Imprint of HarperCollins*Publishers*

This is a work of fiction. Names, characters, places, and incidents are products of the author's imagination or are used fictitiously and are not to be construed as real. Any resemblance to actual events, locales, organizations, or persons, living or dead, is entirely coincidental.

HarperCollins books may be purchased for educational, business, or sales promotional use. For information, please email the Special Markets Department at SPsales@harpercollins.com.

FIRST EDITION

Library of Congress Cataloging-in-Publication Data has been applied for.

ISBN 978-0-06-325253-0

23 24 25 26 27 LBC 5 4 3 2 1

We are always all in this together.

For health care workers—especially nurses—EMTs, doctors, and teachers, along with the countless volunteers everywhere dedicated to all humankind who made many sacrifices, as they cared for and protected us with selfless devotion

For Alan, past, present, and future

The artist is a receptacle for emotions that come from all over the place: from the sky, from the earth, from a scrap of paper, from a passing shape, from a spider's web.

—PABLO PICASSO

If you'd asked me ten years ago, I would have said humanity is going to do a good job with this. If we connect all these people together, they are such wonderful people, they will get along. I was wrong.

—TIM BERNERS-LEE, INVENTOR OF THE WORLD WIDE WEB (2018)

Acknowledgments

Many thanks to the following for their expert help and support: at Greenburger, my agent, Faith Hamlin, and her associate, Abigail Frank; at Morrow, my editor, Liz Stein, and assistant Ariana Sinclair, publicist Danielle Bartlett, and library liaison Virginia Stanley; Dr. David S. Page, Dr. Robert DeMartino, the Reverend Pamela Barz, techies Andrew Payne and Nicholas Hein, Barbara Page, Jean Fogelberg, Walter "Rusty" Crump, Thomas Reed, Esq., Lincoln, Massachusetts art teachers Colleen Pearce and especially Mary Sullivan for her wonderful, detailed descriptions of the challenges posed by remote classes, and Amy Catherine Mariani for her character-naming high bid at the Youth Advocacy Foundation/EdLaw's 2021 Annual Spring Celebration.

In memory of Emanuel Charles Pologe, beloved brother-in-law who was one of the virus's first casualties. Manny was a voracious reader of all genres. His enthusiasm for mine from the very first book and our chats about them always spurred me along. I wish he could read this one and tell me what he thought.

The Body in the Web

Chapter One

JANUARY 14, 2021

Faith Fairchild set her phone down with the first sigh of relief she had felt for almost eight months. She closed her eyes briefly, opening them to glance around her kitchen, bathed in the late-afternoon sun that streamed through the windows. For a moment it was an unfamiliar place, as if she were seeing it for the first time. Such was the effect of the call from her husband, Tom, the Reverend Thomas Fairchild, with the stunning news that as one of the local VA hospital's chaplains he was eligible for vaccination and was on his way to get the shot. A simple sentence, a series of words turned the room from the everyday to a rare setting she would always remember as the beginning flicker of hope.

A call from her younger sister, Hope, almost a year earlier had marked a very different feeling: the onslaught of fear. Nothing had been normal since.

Hope and Faith were close. Their shared experience as PKs—preachers' kids—had prompted a pinky swear to avoid any form of cleric, no matter how attractive the sheep's clothing, although

Faith, deeply in love, had strayed. Their paths to adult careers veered dramatically, too. Hope had gone straight from reading the *Weekly Reader* to a subscription to the *Wall Street Journal* and carried a little briefcase as a lunchbox, eventually landing a plum job as a financial lawyer at a firm where she rose faster than the elevator at the Empire State Building, pausing only to plight her troth with soulmate Quentin and produce Quentin III without missing a day of work. The baby conveniently made his appearance on a Saturday.

Faith had always been more interested in what was *in* the lunchbox, astonishing her mother, Jane, a real estate lawyer whose idea of dinner was a nice piece of fish and a salad or a salad and a nice piece of chicken. Her father, the Reverend Lawrence Sibley, did not care what was on his plate, presumably due to a mind focused on higher matters. Faith started as young as possible with courses at ICE, the Institute of Culinary Education, and unpaid stints at a number of the city's catering firms. She knew her parents, especially her mother, were concerned the moment she had started coming home with flour on her hands, not college brochures in them. "We don't want you to limit your options, dear," her mother had said, and Faith compromised, taking college-credit courses at the New School and scheduling her culinary pursuits around them. In less than two years the coursework had been abandoned for a job at one of Manhattan's top caterers. In less than four, Faith had started her own business. It became the thing to have beautiful Faith Sibley *and* her beautiful food. Have Faith, her business, was a roaring success, although she'd had to make her advertising a bit more explicit after several calls wanting an "escort" and not a few seeking repentance.

When Faith saw that it was her sister calling during working hours on a weekday, she had been alarmed.

"Hope, is everything all right? Dad? Mom?" Reverend Sibley had retired, his reluctant congregation letting him go after he suffered a mild heart attack. He'd planned to leave earlier, but the pressure on their much beloved pastor had kept him on for "just one more year" and then another.

"They're fine. But, Fay"—Hope's nickname for her since childhood, which Faith disliked but had never been able to think how to change without hurt feelings—"things are *not* fine, and they are going to get much worse. Get your iPad, I have a list for you."

Faith had a pad and a pencil on the table, and whatever Hope was going to dictate, that could serve.

"Now, Fay, Quentin and I have been talking to our contact at the CDC, and the couple of coronavirus cases we know about are the start of what she says may well be a pandemic. It's already spreading outside China in Italy and other places."

"Why does the Centers for Disease Control think it's going to spread further? Why isn't this major news?" Quentin and Hope, with their multiple law and business degrees from a swath of institutions, had contacts not just in government but in almost every other walk of life. The best plumber, the best stock tips, the best tutor for their son.

"You're right. It should be, but let's not go into the reasons. The main thing is to prepare. The coronavirus is an unknown, a highly transmissible strain that may have jumped from a rat or other animal to humans, for which we have no cure and no vaccines."

"You're making it sound like the bubonic plague!" Faith's anxiety was mounting rapidly. Hope was the calmest person she knew aside from Tom, and her sister's even-tempered sense of humor was what saved her from being a rigid know-it-all. She wasn't being funny now.

"I'm sorry, sweetheart, that's exactly what we are afraid of, a pandemic, and we all have to get ready for what could be a very long siege. Forewarned is forearmed. There's going to be a lot of panic buying when the virus begins to spread. You need to immediately head to one of the warehouse stores to fill your company van, or order from your Have Faith suppliers. Toilet paper, paper towels, antibacterial cleaners, bleach, canned goods, batteries, bottled water—are you getting this?"

"Yes, but I can't quite believe it."

"Believe it. First aid supplies, especially thermometers, staples like flour, dried beans—you know better than I do." Hope didn't cook. The housekeeper or any number of New York restaurants she had on speed dial did. "You have a big chest freezer at home as well as work, yes?"

"Yes. The work freezers are filled with Valentine's Day dinner supplies, and once that's done, we'll be preparing for Easter and Passover orders, then graduation and wedding season starts. We're booked through next December and some dates beyond."

There was a long pause. Faith had begun to think Hope, grabbed for a crucial business decision, had rung off. Instead, her sister said softly, "I'm afraid your business, food related and every other kind, is going to take a tremendous hit. The country will be in lockdown by March."

"What! We won't be able to leave our homes?"

"Fill your freezers to the brim, stack whatever is in that pantry of yours to the ceiling, and tell Pix—they still have that dog, yes?—to stock up on dog food as well as what I tell you." Next-door neighbors Pix Miller and husband, Sam, were not only parishioners but the Fairchilds' closest friends.

"Now, put these on the top of the list. I should have started with them. Masks—"

Faith had interrupted her sister. "I'm assuming you don't mean Halloween ones, but the kind in hospitals? Where would I get those?"

"Online, CVS, Walgreens. As many as you can, but you might want to get out your little Singer and make some, as essential health workers are going to need them most and we don't want to deplete the supplies. The nice woman who does alterations for me is doing fifty for us to start. I gave her a pattern, and I'll scan it and send it to you."

Faith did not have a little Singer, and sewing a button back on was pretty much the extent of her abilities as a seamstress. Pix, however, could whip up anything from her daughter Samantha's prom dresses to the old-fashioned shirtwaists her mother, Ursula, favored. And Pix was a quilter who could be characterized as a fabric hoarder. Faith had shopped with her.

"Then, hand sanitizers—all sizes—and rubber gloves, again all sizes. If the warehouse store doesn't have the big bottles of sanitizer, your suppliers will, and get to them as soon as we hang up—they may already be out. Word is spreading fast."

Faith felt as if she had fallen down the rabbit hole and not reached bottom. "Anything else?" she asked weakly.

"I'll text you the whole list. Oh, and you'd better get plenty of tipple in. Tom drinks that local Sam Adams beer, right? And you'd better get wine for yourself. Ben will come home. Our source says that Harvard is already considering closing the dorms. Get long-shelf-life milk, powdered, too. You may not be able to get fresh milk. And stock whatever Amy drinks. Cran-Apple juice, yes?"

Hope had a memory most elephants would envy.

"And, Fay," she added. "We're moving out to the Hamptons house soon for the duration and taking Mom and Dad. The elderly will be at the greatest risk, especially those with preexisting conditions. Mom didn't object. I thought she might want to stay put. Just said she would start packing."

There wasn't much to say after that except to promise to keep in constant touch. Faith didn't allow herself the luxury of brooding but immediately started dialing, beginning with her husband, then Pix, and then her main supplier, before getting into the van to head for the closest big-box store.

That first phone call had marked the rapid change in life from actual to virtual. The months since then had been filled with Zooms, live streaming, FaceTimes, tweets, emails, and many, many phone calls. In-person interactions had mostly become a memory. At first, Faith had been intrigued by the Zoom background peeks into other people's rooms—straining to read the titles on bookshelves, noting the artwork and the furniture and speculating on whether the rooms were always like that or staged. She barely took note now unless a pet wandered into the frame, an iguana in one case, and she skipped her own previous preparations except to brush her hair, put on a little makeup, and add a screenshot background of bamboo trees.

She stopped reflecting on the past and turned her thoughts to the immediate present. Tom might have some side effects, although he never did after other shots. She needed to have an especially appetizing dinner ready in case he felt like eating. His family was a meat, potatoes, and some kind of veg one. She began to assemble the ingredients for his favorite meatloaf, garlic mashed potatoes—she'd introduced him to the bulb as an addition to the very basic Fairchild family recipe—and prepped delicata squash to sheet-pan roast on high heat (see recipe, page 253) when the meatloaf came out to rest.

As she worked, she pictured the way First Parish's parsonage kitchen had looked when she arrived many years ago as a new bride in Aleford, a small town west of Boston. Head over heels for Tom, a many-generations New Englander, she abandoned her native Big Apple—home to her favorite *B*'s: Balducci's, Bloomie's, and Bergdorf's—for the land of sensible shoes, boiled dinners, and winter wear that made her look like a different *B,* Bibendum, the Michelin tire man. The move had severely tested the whole "whither thou goest" vow.

It was the sight of the kitchen that had almost sent her straight back. The linoleum was so worn, if there had been a pattern, it was undetectable, as were the cracked Formica countertops that extended on either side of the rust-marked single ceramic sink. The look wasn't shabby chic, just shabby. A row of hanging cabinets with knotty pine doors ran above an electric stove, dividing the room in half. The avocado-green refrigerator was the sole note of color. A small drop-leaf table with two ladderback chairs, possibly a donation from a parishioner's attic, constituted the only furniture. She'd opened a door revealing a pantry almost as large as the room itself, and empty save for some mason jars with botulistic-looking contents. One narrow door flush on the wall hid an ancient pull-down ironing board lacking legs. That had been the last straw, even trumping the walls that were possibly once white, now a shade even scrubbing with bleach would not restore. They had reminded Faith of curdled milk.

Tom's predecessor had been a single middle-aged man who, from the lack of much dishware, cutlery, and pots and pans, must have been dependent on the kindness of the congregation's Ladies Alliance casserole brigade for nourishment. Faith had already learned from Tom that Aleford's restaurant scene consisted of the Minuteman Café and a limited deli counter at the Shop and Save. It had become evident that the good Reverend Tillotson was probably supping outside Aleford limits when he tendered his resignation, effective immediately, and eloped with a woman whose career some of the older male members of the congregation associated with Scollay Square's Old Howard Theatre. Tillotson's consort was an actress! In fact, the lady in question was a talented seasoned thespian, her outstanding performance as Elizabeth Proctor in *The Crucible* closely matched by Tillotson's as husband John—the reverend's maiden step on the boards. He was hooked in more ways than one, and the two left Massachusetts to try their luck in off-off-Broadway. First Parish's hastily assembled search committee made a married man with no theatrical aspirations an unwritten, but much discussed among themselves, requirement. Any footsteps on boards would be trod on those at the church.

Faith mashed the potatoes with vigor. She still used the kind of masher her grandmother had, with the prongs, liking the texture.

Tasting, she also savored the news of Tom's shot. More butter. After she'd been carried over the threshold, the kitchen was the first room she attacked, gutting it, supplementing the meager budget allotted by the Vestry with some of hers. It soon reflected *her* calling. Plenty of storage for her batterie de cuisine and walls refreshed regularly with Sherwin-Williams Goldenrod. As the years went by—and they seemed to have raced, son Ben was now a sophomore at Brown and daughter Amy a senior at Aleford High School—Faith had subtly continued to upgrade. It was her favorite room in the house, and over these last at times unbearable months it had been her comfort zone, even when what she had most felt like doing was getting into bed and pulling the covers over her head until life was back to normal.

She poured a glass of water from the fridge dispenser. As she drank, she felt the hope Tom's call had given her start to ebb. Her sister's dark crystal ball had been right. There had been a brief lull after they spoke that was almost reassuring, and then events had moved with terrifying speed. People stuck on a cruise ship in California in quarantine, the first case in Massachusetts, and then, in early March, cases carried across the country from a conference of Biogen executives at Boston's Marriott Long Wharf. Governor Baker declared a state of emergency on March 10. It was still in effect. Boston-area colleges and universities were shutting down as well, and Aleford's superintendent sent students and teachers home for two weeks to assess the situation. After announcing a plan to return to classrooms in the fall, Aleford was still remote. The proposal had been upended by the late-August spike in cases and then by there not being enough staff with so many testing positive or in quarantine. It was a small school system. The two weeks for assessing had been a pipe dream.

Ben's call telling them that the university was closing its doors had come on March 12, four weeks after Hope's warning. Young people seemed to be less susceptible, but Faith and Tom had been urging him to leave earlier. When he did call, she knew he was finally taking it seriously. It had been a while since she'd heard his voice. Text was his preferred mode of communication. Amy's, too, but she was near at hand and emerged often for breaks to chat with her mother. It appeared Amy might spend her senior year without a prom or graduation ceremonies in the auditorium and with no senior slump. She was in constant virtual contact with her friends, yet Faith could tell the situation was beginning to depress her normally cheerful daughter. But these were not cheerful times, and the anxiety that she or someone she knew would get the disease preyed on her mind.

A year ago Ben had gone back to Brown early, leaving home at New Year's, to work with the biochem professor with whom he had been researching the effects of climate change on marine life. The professor was leaving for Brittany on sabbatical before the second semester, to gather data. Ben would use the time to get required courses out of the way so he could be full-time in the lab on the project when the professor returned at the end of the summer. Now, almost five months after his scheduled return, the professor and his family were still in France, unable to leave that country or enter this one.

Unlike Aleford, Brown did attempt to bring students back after Labor Day, rotating the numbers by semester, reducing the dorm and off-campus housing occupancies. It didn't last long. After a frightening sudden surge of cases, Ben was also back to remote at home. Faith could get milk now, not powdered or long-life, but Ben still went through a gallon as if it were a pint. At times she found herself treasuring this time—all four of them under one roof again, safe. They watched old movies on Netflix, played the board games much loved by Tom's family that Faith had always avoided—they were comforting now—and, when they could, drove to various outdoor places where they could keep a safe distance from others: Crane Beach in Ipswich and World's End down in Hingham, meeting Tom's parents and his sister's family there from nearby Norwell.

Yet there were other times when the parsonage walls seemed to close in on all of them and there would be a meltdown—always triggered by something small that in normal times would have stayed small. The pressure of not knowing essentially *anything* about what might happen even got to Tom. He found himself so depleted by ministering to a community that, with technology, extended beyond his congregation as people sought solace that he blew up at his wife for putting his lucky green Celtics shirt in with a bleach wash, claiming it was on purpose. Faith had wanted to use the tattered treasure as a dust rag, but the wash mistake was just that. She'd put more than his precious shirt in, so it was hardly the only casualty. As such mishaps mounted—a potholder in the freezer, the omission of baking powder from a cake—she looked online for a cause, fearing early-onset dementia. Amy saw what she was doing and grabbed the mouse, entering "signs of Covid stress" in the search engine. "Chill, Mom. Think of the banner." At the start of the pandemic, the Board of Selectpersons had strung a banner across the main road where past ones had announced Town Meeting or other dates, stating WE'RE ALL IN THIS TOGETHER. It was still there, a bit weather-beaten but intact. Pretty much how Faith herself felt.

The use of the term "coronavirus" had mostly been replaced by "Covid-19" or just "Covid," the disease the virus caused. Faith associated "Corona" with the beer and a crown, and she had immediately thought the model of the virus looked like a bath toy her children once had—a bright squishy plastic one that was some kind of hedgehog or porcupine with bright purple spikes on the blue ball. Covid—the disease, the result of the virus—was what it was. No remotely pleasant associations, only dire ones. It *was* a plague. And it was worldwide.

Hope's phone call, then Ben's. Life turned upside down. And with the third of those early calls, life changed even more. March 20. She'd been listening to the news. The National Guard had been activated, and Massachusetts had recorded the first Covid death, an eighty-seven-year-old man.

It had been Ursula Lyman Rowe on the landline, Pix's nonagenarian mother, who was like family to the Fairchilds, too. The Millers and Ursula were the ones who had urged the Fairchilds to come to Sanpere Island in Maine's Penobscot Bay, where Ursula's family, true rusticators, had been summering since before the turn of the twentieth century. Faith, dubious, agreed to give it a try before luring Tom to warmer shores, preferably on Long Island, but Cape Cod would work. Ben was a toddler. She continued to say there must have been something in the water—not the freezing bay water but the pure well water at the house they'd rented—that kept them coming back. Of course there was the postcard view across to the Camden hills and the relaxed pace of life that would surely preclude any need for sessions on a therapist's couch ever. And most of all there was the food. Besides bounty from the salt water, there were strawberries, blueberries, chanterelle mushrooms, native vegetables, and the best goat cheeses she'd ever had, even in France. Eventually they bought a small piece of land and built a cottage, adding on as the kids grew older. They hadn't been to Sanpere since the summer of 2019. Uncertainty and then restrictions on leaving and returning to Massachusetts from other states had decided them. It had been hard.

"Faith? It's Ursula." The voice was unmistakable, a combination of Boston Brahmin and Boston "pahk the cahr in Hah-vahd Yahd."

She'd known immediately something was wrong from the older woman's anxious tone of voice.

Without waiting for a response, Ursula had continued. "I'm worried about Millicent. She's not answering the phone. Pix isn't answering hers, either. She must be out walking, but I don't think Millicent would be. Will you go over and check on her? I'm afraid she may have fallen. Of course she has been known to ignore calls, but not during this awful time. I've spoken with her, but not this week."

"Maybe she's gone to get groceries? Or a book at the library?"

"The library is closed until further notice. And it's so cold today. I don't think she'd go to the store." The Shop and Save was open with masks required, one-way traffic in the aisles, and red circles on the floor six feet apart to keep people distanced on the checkout lines. Shelves that normally held paper goods and canned beans were empty.

Faith hadn't thought a dip in the temperature would dissuade Millicent Revere McKinley from any of her appointed tasks. A proud descendant of *the* Revere, Miss, "not Ms., thank you very much," McKinley lived alone in one of the small houses that dated back to that famous day and year when the town's Minutemen had confronted the Redcoats. At some point someone had enlarged the parlor window into a bay one, where a strategically placed chair had a view straight down Aleford's main street and across the green to another key thoroughfare. Whether because of the vantage point or just a very good ear to the ground, there was little that went on in town that Millicent didn't know about, often before it happened. She wasn't a member of First Parish—her parents had been Congregationalists, and a Congregationalist she would remain in name—but it was a rare Sunday that didn't find her in the second front left pew below the pulpit. Faith and she had gotten off to a rocky start both because Faith was from a place Millicent regarded as the third in a Sodom and Gomorrah trinity and because upon finding the still-warm corpse of a parishioner in the Old Belfry on top of Belfry Hill, Faith had rung the alarm bell. A bell only rung as a call to arms for the April 19 reenactment as it had been in 1776, upon the death of a president, or on the death of a descendant of Aleford's original founders. Millicent was not alone in decrying the sacrilege, and it had taken a long time before certain citizens did not noticeably move away from Faith when she was in line at the post office. She could certainly have run down the hill and screamed, they averred. With the very real possibility of a murderer lurking in the thick bushes surrounding the site, Faith had felt justified in pulling the rope to get help quickly. Ben was an infant, strapped securely to her chest in his Snugli. The instinct of Mama Bear protecting her cub had kicked in.

The relationship between the two women somewhat mellowed over time, but other incidents had been setbacks, and Faith took nothing for granted. Millicent had indicated she was in her seventies when Faith moved to Aleford, which put her over ninety, maybe late eighties. According to Millicent, however, she was still a seventy-something. In fact, she was an old woman and alone.

Faith suppressed a sigh. Tom was in a Zoom call at his office in the church, otherwise he would be a far better choice to check on the intrepid spinster. He alone was permitted to call her Millie.

"I'll go. I'm sure everything is probably fine."

Looking back on the event, Faith thought that that was probably the last time she'd uttered the words "I'm sure everything is probably fine."

"She keeps a key under the loose brick in the walk. It's on the right, three from the stoop. Please call me as soon as you know how she is."

Ursula had not said everything was probably fine, and it wasn't.

Faith knocked loudly, letting the shiny brass American bald eagle with flags clutched in its beak fall heavily several times. When there was no response, she found the key and hoped that Millicent wasn't standing on the other side ready to pounce, adding breaking and entering to the list of Faith's misdemeanors.

She stepped into the small entryway. "Millicent, it's Faith Fairchild. Hello? Millicent?" She went into the front room and called again.

Her voice echoed off the walls in the horsehair parlor suite. Millicent's chair by the window was empty. The house was freezing. "Millicent?" Faith quickly became alarmed.

She heard a faint noise coming from the floor above, almost

like a mouse scratching, and she ran upstairs. She had never been in that part of the house. The door at the top of the stairs was wide open, and she darted into the room. A motionless figure lay in a four-poster bed under layers of blankets, eyes closed. The room was completely silent. As a minister's wife—and at other very nonrelated times—she had seen death up close, and fear clutched at her heart. As she dialed 911, Faith cried out, "Dear God, no! Millicent! Not you! Please, God!" She reached under the bedding for a hand to check for a pulse. Millicent's wrist was the size of a child's and her skin like tissue paper. There was a pulse, but it was weak. The dispatcher was asking questions. Faith's own pulse was rapid as she relayed what she swiftly observed. Millicent was breathing, although it was almost indiscernible through closed lips, her mouth dry, lips cracked. No fever. Her brow was very cold, and her face was still. No overt evidence of stroke. The pillowcase was clean. "Millicent? Can you hear me? It's Faith, Faith Fairchild. Can you open your eyes? I've called for help. They will be here soon."

Aleford's fire and police departments were less than five minutes away.

"Don't need help," Faith heard Millicent whisper. She was filled with relief. The woman was down but not out. She ran to the door to let the EMTs in, and once they were in the room starting to administer treatment, she went into the hall and called Ursula.

"Unless they think she's had a stroke or heart attack or something of that nature, which calls for immediate ER, don't let them take her to the hospital," Ursula said. "If there even is a bed. Bring her here. She'll be much safer from this virus. Dora will take care of her." Dora McNeill was a private-duty nurse who had seen Ursula through a bad case of pneumonia some years ago, and "Call Dora" were the watchwords in Aleford if anyone needed care. She favored the uniform she had trained in, and her starched white cap had brought comfort into many sickrooms. Pix had called her to move in with Ursula two weeks earlier when the college student who had been the current night presence so Ursula would not be alone and who also made dinner in return for the lodging was summoned by her parents to get back to Ohio while she could.

Faith returned to the room. The EMTs were giving Millicent oxygen, and she had opened her eyes. "Her pulse is getting stronger. It doesn't look as if she's had an episode of any kind, and she keeps insisting she's fine and was just taking a nap, but I wonder when she's last had anything to eat or drink?" one of them asked. There was an empty teacup on the nightstand next to David Hackett Fischer's *Paul Revere's Ride,* Millicent's favorite book, but no evidence of further nourishment. Faith went downstairs to the kitchen and was shocked. The garbage cans had not been put out for what looked like several weeks. They overflowed with empty soup and tuna fish cans. On the counter next to the sink stood a battalion of empty mason jars bearing traces of the fruits and vegetables Millicent put up each year. The refrigerator was also empty. Faith found cabinets she'd never dare to open in Millicent's presence barer than Old Mother Hubbard's cupboards. She called Ursula again. "She's had nothing to eat or drink for quite a while, tell Dora. And there doesn't seem to be heat on in the house."

"I blame myself."

And Faith blamed herself, too. When she got home, she washed her hands for the requisite twenty seconds, humming "Happy Birthday" twice. They'd been trying to come up with replacements since the song would never sound the way it should on actual birthdays.

She called up to Ben and Amy, who were in front of their screens, too long these days, to come down, and she told them what had happened. Tom was off his Zoom and left a voicemail that said he was at the bedside of a dying parishioner. It wasn't Covid but cancer, and the man had recently refused any further treatment, telling Tom, "There wouldn't be any point to it. No one lives forever, and no one could have had a happier life than I've had, with the best wife in the world and wonderful friends." The man's wife had died of breast cancer the year before. The man himself was only fifty-six.

The kids came down and sat at the round kitchen table. Faith put out steaming mugs of the split pea soup she'd made the day before, some bread, and the last wheel of buttery, soft Four Fat Fowl cheese. She'd thought, as usual, that food was needed, comfort food. Her children were close to Millicent, a kind of great-aunt, and she was demonstrably fond of them, even bestowing hugs.

It was Amy who identified the problem *and* came up with the solution. Faith had congratulated herself on never having the teen-daughter/mother wars she'd observed, but the issue of college choice had put a strain on their relationship. It was déjà vu as Faith heard herself say to Amy what her own mother had said to Faith all those years ago—a conversation she had never revealed to her daughter. "Keep your options open." Amy was determined to work in a restaurant kitchen and open her own restaurant someday. She'd had a taste of it filling in as a sous chef in a restaurant on Sanpere the summer before, and she'd been spending as much time as possible at her mother's side in the catering kitchen where she could safely acquire knife skills, stirring batters before that. She did not see the point in pursuing any other subject. "I've had plenty of math, history, and science and speak what my teacher says is fluent French. I've got some Spanish, too. I can always take a course in something I get interested in, and I know I'll need business courses besides culinary work. I can get all that plus other courses if I decide I want to learn some psychology, which I could use right now with you, Mom, at a place like Johnson and Wales."

What Amy pointed out that day was obvious. "Miss McKinley doesn't really live in the twenty-first century. It's been a few years since Ben showed her how to look up her ancestors on the laptop she had him get, but I'll bet she hasn't used it for anything else since. So, she wouldn't know she could order food online for delivery or even call the Shop and Save to do it. She doesn't have a television, so what she knows about what's happening now would be from the radio, and it has to have scared her. After she ran out of things to eat, she probably decided to go to bed and not get up again."

Faith had never considered that Millicent could be immobilized by anything, especially fear, but it turned out that Amy was right.

"She'll be okay at Ursula's, but there have to be others in town in the same situation. Elderly people have a high rate of food insecurity even without Covid."

Faith was impressed by her daughter. Amy talked excitedly as the plan in her head quickly took shape.

"We can offer dinners delivered, Mom. The catering kitchen is a safe preparation site, and we can put a notice on the *Aleford Crier* plus maybe send out some kind of mailing. We can't assume everyone has a computer. You've got a ton of supplies, and we can make it 'pay nothing or what you think you can afford'—like what people do when they pass a hat at charity things." The *Aleford Crier* was an online news source started by a resident disgusted by the lack of local coverage in the newspaper that served several area towns.

Ben immediately got with the program. "We can offer help in other ways, too. Miss McKinley always paid me by check. I'll bet her house was so cold because she hasn't got any kind of automatic fuel delivery set up and the company may have thought she'd moved or . . ." He stopped at the next word.

And she almost had died, Faith thought.

"I know she has a post office box, because she asked me to mail a letter and told me she didn't have a mailbox. That I'd have to put it in one in the center. So even if the company had been sending her bills, she wouldn't have received them, since she wasn't going out," Ben said, on a roll now. "We need to call ourselves something. Think of a logo. And I can set up a site where people can tell us things like allergies. I'd stick to a simple set menu, Mom, say three times a week. Of course, since stuff has tanked for you, you might want to offer delivering more expensive dinners with wider choices as a separate option. With twenty-four hours or more notice."

Ben's use of "tanked" described what had happened perfectly. The cancellations, hopefully postponements, had started even before the restrictions on the size of gatherings had.

While they finished the soup and all the cheese, Have Faith Delivered was born, and it had been going strong since. The pay-what-you-can scale—Ben had devised a program to keep track of costs and profits—worked extremely well, serving those who couldn't afford much and those who often overpaid more than generously, despite Faith's protestations. Ben and Amy had come up with a spin-off soon after, named Ben and Amy's Delivery Service after one of their favorite Miyazaki anime films, *Kiki's Delivery Service,* offering other help.

Millicent went back to her own house when things began to look better in early June. Ben had set up autopay for all her bills and online banking and showed her how to keep track. He bookmarked the town's Covid site, which updated citizens daily with information. He'd provided similar services for others, putting a notice in the Council on Aging's newsletter, which went to every household by mail. Amy sourced a plain white mailbox and post, painting the box with Betsy Ross's flag. The two then installed it only a few steps from the front door. Tom convinced Millie to wear a Medi-Alert necklace.

Deciding that the flag represented the extent of her artistic abilities, Amy suggested asking Ms. Richards, her middle school art teacher, to design a logo for each business. Faith had become friends with Claudia Richards after discovering that besides being a printmaker, she was also a gifted calligrapher and started hiring her for individual menus, place cards, and other features for Have Faith's clients. As the years passed, the two women had become very close, often making trips together to various museum and gallery shows. Beyond the shared interest in art, there had been an almost instant recognition that they shared views on most other things, as well as a sense of humor that sent them into gales of laughter at the world's foibles when they took walks together. Not being in-person with Claudia had been a hardship for Faith.

Beside the logos Claudia created—a dinner plate with wings and the two company's names in type that looked like icing in its center—Claudia drew simple illustrated instructions for the food boxes. The graphic designs were such a success that Faith and she were planning to collaborate on a cookbook in graphic novel style.

Feeding people had always been an expression of love, a way of caring, for Faith, and its importance was amplified by the pandemic not just for her but for everyone as the country turned to cooking at home and sourdough starters became symbols of hope.

Preparing and delivering the dinners had helped to keep them from what could only be called despair from March through summer and fall into very kind different kinds of holidays, especially for Tom with a Zoom Christmas Eve service. Now, in January, always the worst month to get through in New England, it was hard to maintain any equilibrium. Millicent had gone back to Ursula's in October. Despite all the support that allowed her to stay in her own house, she had felt isolated and unsafe.

Again Faith pulled her thoughts to the present, and the news that her husband would be coming home with a sore arm brought a smile to her face. She headed upstairs to tell her children.

Meanwhile, next door at the Millers', Pix was answering her phone.

"Hello? Oh, it's you. I have to get used to 'Zachmantha' being what comes up on my screen."

Samantha Miller had married Zach Cohen on Sanpere the summer before last on a perfect Maine day. They lived nearby in

Somerville. Working from the apartment had not been a problem for Zach, who was in IT. Samantha's work proved harder to do remotely. She had left a fast-track Manhattan job to work in Boston for a nonprofit the fall she met Zach. Although, as he was fond of pointing out, they had met at the Fairchilds' holiday party when they were in high school. Zach had attended Mansfield Academy as a boarder, and when Faith became enmeshed in a crime there while teaching a short winter break class for the boys, "Cooking for Idiots," Zach and she became successful sleuthing partners. Zach liked to crow that he'd spotted Samantha and fell in love at first sight before she even noticed him. Samantha had a vague recollection of him, pointing out the terrible haircut and an attempt at a goatee as reason enough to have forgotten.

"Mom, I don't want you to worry, but we have to leave our building. Zach just discovered that three people here are positive cases and one is at Mass General on a ventilator. We've been so careful, barely leaving, but the person who told Zach just now has been in close contact with one of them. And Zach spoke to one of the others earlier this week. He's scrubbed himself raw and doused in sanitizer, but he and I both think we need to leave. We're almost done packing. Even if we can get tests, it may be too early to show up. We don't have a cough or sore throat, and I know my sense of smell and taste are fine. I'm eating like a horse."

All the other calls Pix had received recently paled in comparison, including the one from Sanpere telling them that their good friend Freeman was battling the virus for his life. Samantha and Zach were young and healthy. But yes, they had to get out of that lethal Petri dish.

"We have to find a place where we can quarantine for ten days to be sure no matter what. It can't be at Granny's or with you and Dad. I know he's okay, but his heart surgery was just in November."

"It will be fine. We'll keep him separate from you the whole time, and he's gotten a clean bill of health. I can leave trays at your bedroom door, and you have a bath down the hall from your room that no one uses since Dan left for Colorado."

The youngest Miller, working remotely, had decided to quit his job just after Labor Day and head for ski country, accepting an instructor offer from a resort he knew well. Programming, while he was very good at it, had never grabbed him the way slopes of freshly fallen powder had. "Now's the time to go for it. Who knows what's going to happen?" he'd told them, sounding extremely happy. They'd agreed, although Pix did ask why he couldn't go to Vermont instead, so much closer. He'd told her he'd text and was out the door.

Samantha took a deep breath, then said in a measured tone, "Dad's checkup was telehealth. He hasn't had recent tests or seen the doctor in person! It's too risky for him to have us, and even getting food from Have Faith Delivered makes too much work for you." Her tone changed rapidly. "Plus, we've been waiting a few more weeks to tell you to be sure everything was fine." She paused. "Well, Mom, we're having a baby. So, this is very, very serious. Zach wants us to leave right away. He's loading the car now. Maybe Faith knows someone whose house is empty because they left at the beginning of the pandemic, or there are those garden apartments near Lexington. We could rent one. I mean I *do* want to be home after the quarantine is over and we test negative, but not now. Mom, are you listening? Zach may have been exposed to a carrier and that means me, too!"

"Oh, darling, I'm going to be a grandmother!"

Chapter Two

The large square stone pillars she'd been told to look for on either side of their driveway had been easy to spot, but Claudia hadn't expected the drive itself to be such a long one the first time she went to the house six years earlier.

It was May, and banks of rhododendrons in lush purple, fuchsia, and bright white spilled out on either side, with tall oaks, pines, and an occasional birch grove grouped behind. She felt as if she'd stumbled into a picture book, and her fingers itched to sketch it all.

The printed notecard on the bulletin board at MassArt had stood out—thick square stock like an invitation, as it would prove to be. She immediately noticed the font—Lucida—one of her favorites.

House sitter sought for the months of June, July, and August. MetroWest. Will need own car. No pets, nonsmoker. Remuneration: 215-248-0245.

Claudia had copied the number. Her job didn't start until the week before Labor Day, and the prospect of spending the summer in the stuffy apartment she shared with two other students on Boston's Mission Hill was not a pleasant one. She hadn't needed a car in Boston, but she would for her job and she might as well search for one now on Craigslist. That is, if she was deemed house-sitter worthy. Otherwise, she'd put it off.

She'd entered the number on her phone immediately.

"Hello, my name is Claudia Richards, and I'm calling about the house-sitter job."

"You're the first. I just posted it thirty minutes ago. I assume you are a student?" It was a woman; her voice was soft and pleasant.

"Yes, well, I have been. I've finished my coursework and will be starting a full-time position teaching art at a middle school in Aleford."

"Kismet!" the woman had exclaimed. "We live in Aleford. If you're free today, why don't you come to my office? My name is Patricia Sinclair. I'm a librarian here at MassArt, although only for a few weeks more, as I'm retiring. My husband, Edward, beat me to it and left three years ago. He taught painting and drawing."

That would have been before Claudia arrived, but the name was familiar.

"I am free, and anytime would work."

"Edward will be picking me up at four, so come then. You can meet the two of us at once."

With both librarian and artist stereotypical appearances in mind, Claudia had been surprised that Edward was wearing not rumpled corduroys and a denim work shirt with a splash or two of paint but what she was sure was a bespoke Turnbull and Asser shirt, knife-point navy linen trousers, and an old-school tie. His voice was purely this side of the pond, however, and similar to his wife's, low and warm. His thick white hair was short, and bright blue eyes shone behind tortoiseshell glasses. Patricia was the bohemian, long silver-gray hair drawn back, held in place at the nape of her neck with a handcrafted clip. She was wearing a vintage Marimekko dress featuring large black and white windowpane checks, striped tights, and ankle boots that instantly brought Pippi Longstocking to mind. A simple silver necklace of thin interlocking rings and matching earrings completed the look. Claudia had smiled to herself. Not every woman Patricia's age could pull it off, but she did—with aplomb.

And what had the Sinclairs seen seated almost at ease in front of them? A slender young woman in black tee and jeans, student garb, with short dark brown hair that fit her head like a feathered cap—she'd cut it to look more grown-up—a face with smooth skin, high cheekbones, and a wide mouth. Her eyes were a shade lighter than her hair and as round as marbles. People called her striking, occasionally beautiful. She herself avoided any labels.

She'd introduced herself and given a short bio—brought up in Connecticut and New York City, spent the last year at MassArt to complete the courses required for Massachusetts teacher certification and also fit in some in her own field—printmaking. She had a BA from the University of Connecticut but hoped to get an MFA someday. She was single, no pets, didn't smoke, and would be getting a car. Could provide references. She hadn't told them anything that wasn't true—but she hadn't told them everything.

"We bought one of your prints at the student show last fall," Edward had said. "The etching of the robin's nest with the blurred photo of a city skyline superimposed where the blue eggs should have been." Claudia was into environmental statement art at the time, and still was to some extent but had broadened her perspectives.

"Oh yes," Patricia had said. "You'll see it on the wall in the living room. The nest is so exquisitely done. Like an Audubon illustration, which you transported to this century with the photo."

Patricia had gone on to explain that the house was her family's, built by her grandfather in the early twentieth century when Aleford was a much more rural community. Originally it had been a summer retreat from their home on Marlborough Street in Boston's Back Bay, but her parents decided to move into it year-round after their wedding, and Patricia had grown up there. "And I seemed to have stayed. Happily, Edward liked it as much as I did. When we were first married and my parents were still alive, we lived in the carriage house. It had an apartment for the chauffeur during my grandparents' day, and we made some changes. When my parents died, we moved to the big house and raised our son there. He lives in California now."

"And I'm afraid he's a West Coast guy for good," Edward had interjected somewhat sourly.

Patricia had jumped back in, saying, "Of course he comes to see us often, especially in Maine at the farm. That's why we need a house sitter. We spend three months at a saltwater farm six hours north of here on the coast."

The job sounded like an easy one. She'd need to keep the house clean and aired out, but she would have plenty of free time for her artwork and "to ramble the grounds—seven acres." They were kept in shape by a lawn service that specialized in pollination gardening. Claudia sensed it was going to look much different from the manicured lawns and specimen plantings she'd grown up with in Greenwich.

"If you want it, the job is yours," Patricia had said. They'd obviously decided even before meeting her. Was it her print? "As soon as you have wheels, come out and we'll walk you around."

When she finally reached the end of the drive that spring day, she fell in love with the house instantly. If it hadn't been designed by H. H. Richardson, it had been by someone influenced by him. Part was stonework—including a two-story turret—and the rest dark brown shingles interrupted by windows of all sizes, a few stained glass. When Claudia pulled up to the front door, the couple had been waiting on the wide wraparound veranda sitting in the requisite wicker furniture overlooking spheres of sapphire-blue hydrangeas in bloom. Inside the house, some of the walls retained the golden oak paneling, but others had been replaced, and lightened, by ivory plaster, bringing the house into the present without sacrificing the past. A mix of furniture and art echoed the plan. An Eames chair stood at ease next to a Biedermeier secretary, a Chihuly glass sculpture faced a Parian marble Greek bust, and her own small piece hung on a wall with other works including folk art portraits, a Marsden Hartley seascape, and what Claudia had recognized as a Henry Horenstein photograph of a whale's tail.

They took her, with obvious pleasure, through the entire house, and she had her pick of all save the master bedroom, selecting one that looked out over the perennial garden and a small pond in the rear. The bathrooms and especially the kitchen seemed to have been updated recently.

"Edward is the chef, and when he retired he wanted a new kitchen and it made sense to do the baths, too," Patricia explained.

Claudia's most important job was to make sure the alarm system was always armed. "Even if you think you are only going for a short walk, dear. Aleford is not immune to evil, and over the years we've had several attempts at burglary. My grandparents had live-in help plus the chauffeur in the carriage house. You can see the roof from the window here—it's alarmed, too," Patricia had pointed out. "But since my parents moved in and then when we did, we've always had a state-of-the art system. It was just serviced. It isn't the loss of our treasures so much as the sense of being violated."

Edward tapped his wife playfully. "It *would* be the loss, my dear, although the idea of people touching our stuff and stripping the place makes me sick."

Claudia promised faithfully. She was familiar with alarm systems. She was familiar with loss, too, but kept that to herself.

She left with a folder containing information on how to reach them in Maine and details about the house—"The back door sticks when it's humid"—and the feeling that she had not only new landlords but new friends. Friends! "Feel free to invite your friends out," they said. *Not a problem,* she'd been tempted to reply. *I don't have any.* She smiled and thanked them.

That first summer was idyllic. She explored the surrounding towns, met with the Aleford superintendent. Claudia had chosen teaching as a way to support herself. She hadn't expected to become so enthusiastic about the prospect during her practice teaching. She was an only child and had never had any experience with children. She'd relished the energy and creativity that flowed from the kids—maybe a little too much energy at times, but she'd managed it well, going for fair and firm. As she'd ordered supplies for her classroom and made lists of projects that summer before she took her place in Aleford's school system, she'd felt a peace she'd not known for many years.

The Sinclairs came down to Aleford for a wedding in July and asked her if she would like to rent the carriage house "at a peppercorn rent." They had decided to stay in Maine until Columbus Day and go back in May. Claudia had peered in the windows of the carriage house, but it was hard to see what was there. When they took her in, she felt at home. Much as she'd liked being the "lady of the manor," the carriage house was more her scale and style. The ground floor had originally consisted of three bays, and Claudia imagined the Pierce-Arrow, a Packard, some kind of roadster that the chauffeur would keep polished, vehicles that had so quickly replaced carriages. Arched heavy wooden double doors remained, with the same kind of stone used for the main house in between them, however the newlywed Sinclairs had leveled the interior and put weather-resistant double-paned glass where once the cars had exited, adding a front entry. The space later became solely Edward's studio, and opening the outside wooden doors provided perfect north light. Before going in, they opened what amounted to shutters, and the three of them stepped through the front doorway into an open-plan room, most of which was filled with Edward's supplies, which included easels and, to Claudia's delight, a good-size press. A galley kitchen took up one wall, and there was a seating area with a couch and armchairs facing a wood-burning Franklin stove. "You won't need it for heat," they said, "but we always like to sit in front of a fire." One of the first things Claudia had noticed on the main house was the abundance of chimneys, all sizes and shapes. There were fireplaces in almost every room.

Upstairs was the carriage-house bedroom, with a high ceiling and windows on three sides. The bathroom had the original claw-foot tub, and the chauffeurs must have been large men. Claudia, tall as she was, could almost swim in it. "We couldn't resist keeping it," Edward said, "but the rest is this century."

Claudia had been worried about finding a place to live near Aleford within her means and not a long commute—her time in Boston had introduced her to winter in Massachusetts, much harsher than Connecticut's or New York's. So far she hadn't found anything, and time was getting short. Aleford had few rentals. The carriage house was a perfect solution, and she accepted on the spot.

"But I don't want to turn you out of your studio," she protested, and Edward replied, with more than a little regret, stretching out his gnarled hands, "My painting days are over. I can barely hold a brush now, because of my arthritis, but I've had a good run." Having seen his work in the house and online, Claudia had been impressed by his career, and how modest he was about it.

At the start of the pandemic the Sinclairs had closed the big house and left for Maine. Now, close to a year later, they were still there and did not plan to return anytime soon. She had been used to being alone when they were gone for extended summers, but this stretch was different. When they'd left in March 2020, the notion that she would still be teaching her classes remotely, ordering food and other necessities online, and only venturing out to a few places—always masked, always socially distanced—was an inconceivable one. Prior to that she had made friends among her fellow teachers—especially her high school counterpart, Brian Kimball—and some people in town, most especially Faith Fairchild, whom she met when Amy Fairchild was in one of Claudia's first classes at the middle school. On Parent

Night, attendees had listened to Claudia's little speech and then made tracks for the "important" subjects. The ones in which success led to Ivies and the like. Faith and her husband, Tom, had stayed behind to look at the artwork displayed and talk to Claudia herself. When Faith discovered that the calligraphy on some of the notices was Claudia's, she had quickly offered her work at Have Faith hand-lettering menus, place cards, and invitations. It had led to further work in town. The Fairchilds knew the Sinclairs. Before long, Claudia was to discover that in Aleford everyone knew everyone due to the town's overlapping circles of churches, the historical society, Friends of the Library, town committees, and the garden club. She hadn't realized how many people *she* knew until the spring 2019 reception for her show at the Clark Gallery in nearby Lincoln was standing room only. She was especially touched that the Sinclairs had come down from Maine for it. That night Claudia looked around at everyone, especially her landlords and the Fairchilds, and silently said to herself, *It's true. Friends are God's apologies for family.*

In late August 2020 as Covid suddenly ramped up its numbers, spreading fear and wild speculations, the Sinclairs' son had appeared at the carriage house. The only cars that had come down the long drive had been Have Faith Delivered vans with dinner, a godsend for Claudia, who didn't like to cook; Brian Kimball's Mr. Bean Mini Cooper for an occasional socially distanced walk; and Faith, to walk as well as talk about illustrations for their possible cookbook, plus the instructions for the current delivery boxes. The car she saw pull in was a generic one with Florida plates, and Claudia immediately thought it might be a rental. The driver parked by the big house and looked at it face on for a while before turning and walking with a purposeful stride straight to the carriage house. He pulled a mask from his pocket and put it on, but not before Claudia had a good look at his face. So like Edward Sinclair's that he had to be his son.

He knocked, and as she opened the door, also masked, he said aggressively, "I assume you're Claudia Richards," and stepped into the room, forcing her to move several yards backward.

"Yes. And you are?"

"Christopher Sinclair. Patricia and Edward's son. I've been up in Maine with them and thought I'd check in on things." He was wearing a polo shirt with the crocodile logo, chinos, and a visor embroidered with the name of a San Diego country club. Not exactly a Down East look. He took another step forward, forcing her farther back, and glanced around the room.

It was a mess. Claudia had been working on a series of etchings of arachnids and their webs. Photos of spiders of all types and webs were pinned to the walls. She'd made her own intricate webs with thin string and hung them from the beams. Soon after she'd moved in, the kitchen and the studio had merged almost by osmosis, and she liked it that way, although now the remains of breakfast, a mug of very old coffee, and other bits of food next to a zinc etching plate she'd been working on were not creating a good impression. Her printmaking and other art supplies were on shelves, but the ones she'd been using recently lay within reach on the long metal-topped table she'd found at a house sale her first fall, installing it with the Sinclairs' enthusiastic permission. Patricia and Edward had encouraged her to go further with her blend of the natural and unnatural worlds.

Christopher was instantly making his opinion of Claudia clear. His face was a thundercloud, but as he opened his mouth, she spoke first.

"I'm not very tidy. Never have been," she explained. "I have a good clear-out and cleanup every so often. Otherwise, it's what you see."

"And my parents know this?"

"Yes, when they were here, they'd drop by often to see what I was working on or just to visit. I haven't spoken to them this week. Is all well? I think it's wise for them to stay in Maine where the case numbers are so low."

"Oh, you do, do you? I imagine you take quite an interest in their health."

Claudia was taken aback by his confrontational tone. She was very much aware of being far away from anyone should he escalate what was fast becoming a frightening encounter. She spoke in an even voice. "I don't know what you are suggesting, but I think you'd better leave."

"I don't think you have the authority to throw me out of my own property."

"As a renter, I do, and have your parents given it to you? I wasn't aware."

"I know what you're paying, and I could have you arrested for taking advantage of two elderly people. Abusing them." He'd almost spat the words out, while ignoring her question.

"It sounds to me as if *you're* the one abusing them! Patricia and Edward are both fully functioning adults, older, yes, but you must think very little of them if you think they aren't capable of making their own decisions. I know it's a low rent for the area, but they are paying for peace of mind about the other house and the grounds. Plus, I've made them take a higher rent over time, as well as gifts of my artwork."

"Artwork? This crap?"

"And you're a noted art critic? In fact, what is it you do? Besides not visit them here."

"My work is on the West Coast, and it's hard for me to get away. I'm a property developer, mainly golf courses. Not that it's any of your business, nor is how often I see my parents."

"Ah, it's all clear now. You're afraid I'll bring undue influence on them to add restrictions so when you inherit you won't be able to turn this into some kind of club and greens. Aleford doesn't have a golf course, so the 'fairway' is wide open. There's even the pond for a water hazard."

He looked at her appraisingly. "You sound like someone who plays."

"Played. And if you don't have any more opinions to express on my art, my friendship with your family, or anything else, I'd like you to—as I said—leave."

He did, with one parting shot. "I'm not taking my eye off the ball, and you very well know what I mean."

"Mother!" Samantha Miller shouted, not her usual "Mom." Pix's joyous exclamation had been followed by several sentences all running together: "How are you feeling? Morning sickness? When is the baby due? Where is your doctor?"

"Mother! Stop! I shouldn't have said anything about the baby yet! What matters right now is that you *have* to find us a place to stay! Is Millicent still staying with Granny? Although her house would be a last resort even if she would let us stay. I'd be a nervous wreck."

Millicent's parlor, dining room, and other areas were filled with innumerable fragile family heirlooms spread out on mazes of tilt-top tables, revolving bookcases, and lowboys; the dining room table was covered with vases and dinnerware that didn't fit into the crammed china cabinets, and was surrounded by spindly Windsor chairs that had not stood the test of time.

Pix, a bit chagrined at having been overly distracted, snapped back to the reality at hand, while the reality to come moved pleasantly to the back of her mind. She had to get them out here and safe. "Millicent's would really not be suitable. I'm sure we can find another place. I'll call Faith, and Dad might know of one, too." Sam Miller was on the Planning Board, and Aleford's real estate was embedded in his mind. "Don't worry—and tell Zach to try not to. I'll call as soon as we've located a spot for you. I'll call Dr. Kane, too. He may want you both to get tested."

"I told you. It wouldn't show up yet. That's why we have to quarantine. Unless we start to have symptoms, we have to find a place and stay put." Pix could hear the sob in her daughter's voice. "I can't believe this is happening, Mom. They have the vaccine. Why can't they just start giving it to everyone?"

"I don't know, sweetheart. But they have to begin with the most vulnerable and the health care workers. There isn't enough now for everyone, but there will be soon." Pix had entered the world as an incurable optimist, her mother always declared, and even though the pandemic had cast dark shadows, she remained a person who looked on the bright side even these days, despite several losses.

"Maybe pregnant ladies will get moved up to an earlier phase," she added. The Massachusetts governor had outlined the various phases for eligibility. Samantha and Zach's young ages plus their lack of underlying health conditions put them at the end of the line, along with the rest of their cohort. Sam would be eligible before Pix, but she hoped there would be a spot for her anyway and planned to go with him. Dora was trying to get shots for Ursula and Millicent after their doctor and other PCPs she'd called told her they didn't have the vaccine and had no idea when or if they would get a supply. Gillette Stadium in Foxborough was soon opening as a vaccination site, Fenway Park, too, but the bitter January cold would be a deterrent. Even with an assigned time, the two elderly women couldn't stand outdoors in a line.

"I'll call the doctor and see if he knows about pregnant women eligibility after I make the other calls," Pix said. "May I tell Faith your news, about the baby, I mean?"

Samantha sighed. Telling the Fairchilds was fine, but she knew her mother, and before long, once Samantha was able to go out, all Aleford would be commenting on how it must be a boy because she was carrying low, or vice versa. One good thing about Covid was that no one would come close and touch her bump when she began to show.

"Faith, and her family, Dr. Kane, but no one else, please. I want to tell Granny myself in person when I can. And I don't know exactly when I'm due. I only took the test last month. I thought my periods were odd again."

Samantha had had very irregular periods from the start, and while birth control pills helped, she didn't like the side effects and, once married, stopped them. They had assumed it would take a while to get pregnant. When they told Pix that, she was dubious. "All you had to do was lay a pair of trousers across the bottom of the bed, and that did it for me, but I know things are different now. It seems to take longer for couples."

"I'll also ask Dr. Kane to recommend an ob-gyn. Mine—and Faith's, too—was great but retired ages ago."

"Mom . . ."

"I know, I know. I'll find you a place right away!"

Faith was delighted about Samantha's pregnancy news—they would be wonderful parents—but very worried about Zach's exposure. "You don't know for how long or how close he was? We know now that it's most contagious airborne, droplets, and there's very little risk from surfaces, but he was in contact with one or more of the cases in their building, yes? And Samantha, too?"

Faith thought back to the elaborate way she'd sanitized her groceries, washing fruit in soapy water for twenty seconds, removing the packages of cereal and other things from the boxes they came in, and taken other precautions during the early months of lockdown. Would she smile about scrubbing broccoli someday? She thought not.

"I'll get on this right away," she told Pix over the phone. "If they need a place temporarily, the church is heated and has a full kitchen. There are camping cots stored in the youth group closet for their trips. Call her back and tell them to bring their sleeping bags just in case." Like the rest of the Miller family, Samantha and now Zach were lovers of the great outdoors, considered sleeping under the stars better than Faith's preference for sleeping in a four- or five-star room. "Poor Samantha. She has to be so stressed by this news, and her hormones must only make things worse."

"She did sound a bit high-strung," Pix said. "More than a bit." Her normally calm daughter had been verging on panic.

Faith thought of her own relatively uneventful pregnancies. If there had been significant news headlines, she didn't remember any now. When she spoke to Samantha, she'd advise her to avoid the news and anything else on TV except bingeing on rom-coms.

"I'll make calls. Best not to tell Ursula and Millicent until we have a place, although Dora might know of someone who's left their Aleford house for a spot to wait this all out. A second home or with close relatives in a pod."

Like the food washing, the notion of a pod had come to mean something other than "peas in a" or aliens. Because of Sam Miller's heart surgery, the Fairchilds hadn't formed one with them and also because Pix was seeing her mother and Millicent, although not as much as she wished. The Fairchild parsonage and the Millers' large Federal brick house were next to each other, but a thick stand of Canadian hemlock served as a privacy hedge. After the two families had become close, Tom and Sam created a trellised opening so their wives, in particular, could run back and forth easily. Since Hope's alarming call and the lockdown that followed soon after, Faith and Pix had met in all kinds of weather, far enough away from each other to create a safe zone. Their phones, even FaceTime, were in constant use, but they needed to see each other in person, no matter how distanced.

"Samantha wants to tell her grandmother the news herself, but no one is more discreet than Dora, so let's ask her."

Faith, Pix, and Dora had made calls to no avail before Pix talked to her husband, who had been in court representing a client remotely.

She hadn't dared disturb him until she was sure he was finished. She told him the quarantine news first.

"And they're having a baby, but we have to find a place now." She'd learned her lesson, and all the fruitless leads had pushed due dates and morning sickness away. Now she just wanted to get them sequestered.

Her husband had leaned back, and she knew he was mentally roaming the town. His broad smile indicated his joy at the baby news.

"The Sinclairs. I'll call them. They've been in Maine since last March. One of the school art teachers is in the carriage house, but that's a good distance from the house. She's probably seeing to it, but I'm sure a week or more of occupancy at a higher temperature and using the appliances would be a good idea to keep the place in shape."

Patricia and Edward's farm in Brooklin, Maine, was close to the Millers' on Sanpere Island. The two couples sailed together and had many friends there in common.

"And they were at the wedding!" It seemed a very long time ago but would only be two years in August. Pix remembered how elegant the Sinclairs had looked, both in pearl-gray outfits—Edward in a linen suit and Patricia's long dress a pleated column that looked like a Fortuny. As she thought back to that halcyon day, Sam was already calling Edward on speakerphone. Within a few minutes it was all arranged to everyone's satisfaction.

"I think Samantha may know our tenant, Claudia Richards," Patricia said. "We'll call her now. She can tell them everything when they're there, even if she can't walk them through the house. The alarm system, the furnace. I'm so glad we can help."

"And, Sam," Edward said. "I have my eye on a new boat. I'll call you another time to get your advice. You know I'm a wooden boat man, but I'm also an old one and I'm thinking of something easier to maintain. But let's get off and get the youngsters into the house right away."

"We can't thank you enough, as they will, too," Pix said. "And since they will be house sitters in effect, I have to tell you, although not for public consumption yet, they are going to be parents, too!"

Sam shook a finger at his wife, still beaming. This was one of those secrets that didn't need to be kept for long. He hung up.

"I'll call Faith and Dora to tell them we found a place after we tell the kids," Pix said. "And I'll get Whole Foods to deliver essentials for now, and tomorrow they can make a list of groceries they'll need."

"And I'll open a bottle of champagne, okay, Grandmama or whatever you want to be called? I'll be Pop; Granpop if the little one prefers."

By late afternoon that day, the young couple was installed in the Sinclair house, FaceTiming with Claudia, who was happy to have them as neighbors for however long. She went over everything they needed to know immediately and told them to call back at any time if they had questions.

Not only had the market delivered what looked like food for the entire quarantine, but Ben, the Have Faith Delivered delivery person, dropped off dinner for both houses. Tonight's offerings seemed to have been selected with exactly what the couple needed: comfort food. Succulent-looking smothered pork chops with onions and green bell peppers, more than enough for two; mashed sweet potatoes; a mixed-greens salad; and a stack of flourless cookies Amy had dreamed up when that basic ingredient was scarce. They were now the most requested ones (see recipe, page 255).

Samantha and Zach lit a fire in the living room fireplace and were soon asleep in each other's arms, waking later, wondering aloud for a moment where they were, and then, ferociously hungry, heating the meal before heading for bed. "It's going to be all right, isn't it?" Samantha said anxiously—and drowsily. She had the feeling that being tired was going to be a new constant.

"It's going to be more than all right," Zach murmured, planting soft kisses on her neck until he reached her mouth. Lifting his head slightly, he laughed. "I can't wait to tell my mom she's going to be a bubbe." Alexandra Kohn was sitting out the pandemic in her apartment in Paris with meals delivered from La Tour d'Argent and other favorite restaurants. Zach's parents had divorced when he was four, and his father had remarried, pretty much vanishing from his son's life. Alexandra's involvement was sporadic, and Zach was sure much of it was due to the fact that she would have had to have given birth to him as a child herself in order to match the age she said she was at various times. Besides shaving years off, at some point she became Kohn instead of Cohen. Being a grandmother was going to be a tough pill to swallow, but she'd get her doctor to give her one to help get over the shock.

Taking a walk, Claudia smelled the woodsmoke and saw the lights, not on timers as usual. She hadn't thought she was lonely, but the activity gave her a pang. In-person contact had been very infrequent, and much as she loved living in the carriage house, she was far from any other homes. Teaching remotely was harder and kept her more busy devising activities than she'd ever had to be in her classroom, with materials to hand out and contact with her students. Weekends were filled with her own work that she hadn't been able to squeeze in during the week. Sitting in front of her screen, even with breaks to get up, was more tiring than she could have predicted. At the end of the day all she wanted to do was collapse.

Brian Kimball had been a lifeline in terms of support—he was going through the same thing, although with older students—and companionship. She found herself looking forward to the Skype time they scheduled just to talk, have a drink, and decompress. She'd never had a male friend like Brian, one who made her laugh and always lifted her spirits—vodka tonics in her case. Their happy hours had become longer and happier, her drink refilled often during and after, as the pandemic dragged on. His wife, Margaret, was a commodities trader with an international company that had an office in Boston. She was used to working remotely at all hours even before the pandemic. She was, as Brian put it, "the big cheese," making far more money than he did. Three years earlier they'd moved from Boston's South End to a midcentury modern house in Aleford when Brian took the teaching job. Claudia had gone to a party there, and when she complimented Margaret on the décor and authentic furnishings, Margaret's face had shone. "It's my baby. Every time I source something online it's like Christmas. We have photographs of how it looked originally, and I'm trying to replicate it. The Gropius House in Lincoln is my inspiration. Brian thinks I'm a little nuts, but it's his thing, too." He'd walked over at that point.

"What's my thing, besides you two beautiful women?" Margaret *was* beautiful, light blond hair, pulled back in a high ponytail that exposed her long neck and shoulders—it was a warm night, and she was wearing a strapless teal sheath that brought out her green eyes, with a Bauhaus-inspired geometric steel pendant. Brian was blond, too, a shade darker, and his casual silk shirt matched her dress. They were a very attractive couple.

There hadn't been any parties since, and Claudia knew from Brian that Margaret was totally immersed in her job, obsessed with the markets, and fearful for the future.

Margaret's drink of choice was her work, and that had left Brian free to help Claudia, especially at the start of the pandemic when she'd suddenly had to teach not just the middle school kids but K–5, when that teacher had to replace a math teacher who got Covid. There was much shuffling of teachers throughout the system as each day brought new and often calamitous surprises. Claudia assembled kits including drawing paper, a folder, pencils, crayons, and a Sharpie—and even putting those few supplies together had been hard. Brian had a similar one for his students, fewer, and had helped her deliver hers to each home, taking a portion of her list. What she hadn't expected and should have was that the kits would be used for other things around the house and not stay intact. Soon she had kids drawing on scraps of paper and Post-its. It was important to get the kids outdoors, so she sent them outside to draw what they saw—landscapes, birds, flowers, butterflies, pets. She asked her older students to measure a large circumference in their backyards and as the seasons changed document what happened within the circle. Paper sculptures for all ages were a hit as she showed them what they could make without scissors or glue, tearing any paper, even newsprint, to make whole pop-up cities. The app the school system used, Seesaw, had a drawing component, and that worked best for some kids. Early on in the pandemic she'd decided the way to cope with the anxiety all the kids were experiencing was to make each class fun, an escape. She could read their faces, and what she saw made her feel so helpless. There was no way to reach across the World Wide Web and comfort them, so she taught them how to do Zentangles, a combination of relaxation and drawing—filling in small squares or overlapping circles with patterns drawn with a sharp pencil or fine-point pen. The patterns filled the entire spaces, and concentrating on what was essentially doodling filled the mind—the Zen part. She'd found herself using the technique, created by a monk and an artist, in her own work as a way to relax herself.

But how long could this continue? She missed her students. She missed life.

Faith sat at the kitchen table waiting for her husband to come home. There had been a beautiful sunset, deep red with streaks of gold. The kids had eaten the meatloaf, potatoes, and squash and immediately headed upstairs for what had become combination bedrooms/classrooms over time. There was plenty of food left, and she wanted to eat with Tom.

It had seemed a particularly long day—the call from Tom followed by Pix's and that drama, plus more calls of all sorts. Figuring out the meal-box schedules and offerings. Assembling the boxes at the catering kitchen. Talking to her sister about her parents, still well, but she longed to see for herself.

And then waiting.

Tom came in as the night turned velvet dusk, and they kissed, locked close together until he spoke. "Just a slightly sore arm, and what's for dinner?"

For now, she thought, *it doesn't get better than this.*

Chapter Three

"One step forward, two steps back; one step back, two forward." Tom sat up in bed awakened by words he'd been muttering in his sleep. His arm hurt. He'd tried sleeping on his back, not on either side as usual, and had been tossing all night. Next to him, his wife was sleeping soundly. Exhaustion had an unintended benefit, and she tumbled into bed each night instantly embraced by Morpheus's arms. Tom wasn't as lucky and knew that he had to get up or he'd lie wide awake until dawn. Warm milk and honey or mint tea sometimes worked. He slipped on his robe. The house was chilly. They turned the heat way down at night—it had taken Faith years to get used to this New England custom—no, rule was more like it—and one he couldn't break. Like calling a frappe a milkshake or rooting for the Yankees, not the Sox. She'd taken to flannel nightgowns in defense, pretty ones from some company with a woman's name. Arlene West? Eileen?

Turning the overhead kitchen light on brought the room into stark relief. He quickly opted for tea and sat nursing the mug, warming his hands, at the kitchen table. He could see the Millers' garage light, the only beam in view. Aleford's streetlights were few and far between. You weren't supposed to be up that late, let alone driving. He both cherished and chafed at all the shibboleths he'd grown up with and very occasionally felt a stab of guilt for inflicting them on his Bright Lights, Big City wife. The early years had made for some dicey moments over these, but she had mostly given in, or maybe he had.

What would he have done these last months without her? And what had he been dreaming of that had resulted in those words about taking steps? Getting vaccinated today, or rather yesterday, was a step forward, but he had to be honest with himself. It also meant somewhat backward. Soon, with the second shot, he'd be safe to take on increased burdens—in-person calls, meetings, picking up the threads of his "before" ministry.

Threads. Much to his surprise, thread was one of the first shortages, close on the heels of paper goods. Pix had put out a call when she ran out so she could continue to make the hundreds of masks she was distributing, particularly to health care workers. Now it seemed those early colorful ones had not been very safe and the hunt was on for N95s, prices for them soaring as the pandemic created yet another division between the haves and the have-nots.

He got some of Faith's shortbread from a tin on the counter and sat down again.

Despite the weather outside, sleet, he forced himself to think of spring. If, as the governor was saying, we could all get at least one shot—or jab, as the British said—First Parish could have Easter services together, in person, although probably outdoors. It had been almost a year since he'd shut the sanctuary doors after a service with pews filled; the next Sunday he'd preached in an empty church to a congregation watching the video Ben had taped and streamed. His tech-savvy son, patient always with his father's lack of skill, had soon set up Zoom software, upgrading for what became a larger congregation online than in person. He installed an enormous flat-screen TV at the rear of the sanctuary so his father could preach to those Zooming in, sharing his screen so that in a way they were worshipping together. In the beginning the order of service with readings and words to hymns was posted, and when Tom stood at the pulpit hearing his own voice echoing atonally from the high beams, he felt anguished. He tried to picture those at home, wondering whether they were silent or bravely raising their voices. The music director Zoomed from her home, pounding her upright piano instead of the church organ.

The religious-education director Skyped right away with Tom to suggest that they not try Zoom Sunday school. "Our kids are going to be in front of screens for hours during the week and need to be outdoors on weekends, doing things with their families where possible." She suggested game nights for the whole family, playing Pictionary and Mad Libs. Christmas 2020 was like none other, and she'd created a lovely Advent booklet, each week labeled—Hope, Peace, Joy, and Love—with simple instructions on how to make the Advent wreath, poems and readings from the Bible to recite as each candle was lit, and carols. Claudia Richards, an art teacher at the middle school, illustrated it. She had not joined the church but had frequently attended services and was delighted to be part of the project. Tom sensed that she was searching for something and had hoped to speak with her when she first started to come, but then the in-person opportunity was lost—for the foreseeable future, he feared. She seemed lonely, according to Faith, who had become her friend, but Faith added that it might just be because she was an artist and by nature needed only the company of her art, her imagination.

The tea soothed Tom, and he rinsed the mug at the sink, putting it on the dish drainer.

Being at the hospital today had brought home even closer some aspects of the pandemic. There wasn't a single bed available, and staffing was an issue. Unable to be there in person, just as with his First Parish family, he had FaceTimed or Zoomed with the burned-out doctors, nurses, and staff, who kept the hospitals running and were often taken for granted. People assumed that they would be there on duty and nothing could change it. Tom had consoled patients at the end of life, taken off ventilators with nurses in hazmat clothing holding a phone toward an ear. Not telehealth but teledeath. Then later he talked to their loved ones left bereft, unable to squeeze a hand, kiss a dear face. He became used to giving blessings this way at all times of day and night and never stopped feeling how inadequate it was.

Zoom. He hated Zoom, even though it had helped him, and he sensed it helped those seeing one another's faces even more. But still, he hated it. Faith did yoga on Zoom and was wishing the class would stay that way. She was a more reliable attendee than when she had to drive to the Wellness Center in Concord, especially in bad weather. Tom would be happy to never see the Zoom logo and spinning circle again.

Ben was in his element with all these techie adaptations, though he would have much preferred to be in the lab. Even if he could be back at the university, his professor was locked down in France. Ben, whose French was excellent, except perhaps to a Parisian, had proposed going there—the professor had access to a lab and was using it—but as soon as the *idée* left his lips, both parents had said in chorus, *"Absolument non!"*

He found consolation in watching movies on the church's big TV. Whatever he wanted and whenever.

Tom turned out the light and headed for the stairs, tempted to go up one and back two, then the reverse. The words had to have meant something, and it would become clear as his mind became clearer. He got into bed and said a prayer, asking to stay the course, to avoid self-pity and despair, despair, that great enemy. Aloud, softly, he said, "Oh Lord, open my heart and my hands to help—and to step forward, however many steps at a time."

Four years earlier Faith had asked her longtime assistant, Niki Theodopoulos—Niki Constantine when she had first started—if she would be interested in co-owning Have Faith. "I'm not ready to throw in my toque, but I'd like to start spending summers in Maine and, if I can get him to ever take time off, do some traveling with Tom now that the kids are almost out of the nest," she'd said. Niki accepted. She had known it was coming, but she laughed and said, "Aren't you the woman who told me when Sofia was born that you never stop raising your kids, even if the nest is empty?" Faith admitted she had said it but neglected to admit that she had cribbed it from Pix when the Fairchild children were toddlers and reading *Pat the Bunny* pretty much solved all problems.

Sofia, now three, had been joined in February 2020 by Alexander. Niki's husband, Philip, had been her mother's goal for her—well educated, bright future, close-knit family—and Greek. Therefore, Niki had resisted, as she had for years, bringing numerous swains to the house ranging from bikers to Hare Krishnas. When she met Philip at a cousin's wedding, she turned down his requests for dates until, finding that she was looking forward to the calls where he'd ask her out in such funny ways, she finally gave in. That first date led to another to another until the Big Fat Greek Wedding of her mother's dreams came true. Faith had followed each step with the avidity of someone hooked on the soaps.

Niki had texted early this morning and asked if Faith was free to get together at the kitchen. Faith called back.

"This isn't a dinner-box night, so I'm just going to be doing some prep work. Come anytime. Whatever works with the kids. Can't wait to see them—and of course you, sweetie."

"Eleven would work. And can you believe the latest? No cream cheese. I get the ketchup shortage—everybody pours it over everything in this country, but unless you're sourcing it for bagels and lox or that horrible combination of cream cheese and jelly, what's up? I've turned down more orders than I ever baked, I'm beginning to think."

Niki had a knack for desserts, much to Faith's initial delight, especially cheesecakes in all sorts of flavors: traditional New York, praline, chocolate macadamia, Amaretto, s'mores, and most requested—pomegranate with a raspberry liqueur glaze. Eventually, and possibly due to Niki's mother's word-of-mouth praise of her daughter's skill reaching households in Greater Boston on up to New Hampshire, Niki started a separate business offering just the cheesecakes, working out an agreement with Faith to use the catering kitchen.

"Even if I could get cream cheese, there would still be a problem delivering them or having people come get them. It's not as if I've been doing them since all this started, but I'd like to think I could."

"I'm so sorry," Faith said. "But things will sort themselves out."

"That's what you say," Niki responded, and hung up.

It wasn't like her friend to be so abrupt, and Faith wondered what was going on. The Constantines had lost Niki's beloved father, Dimitri, four years earlier. He was older than his wife and had suffered from multiple health issues. Niki, the only daughter, had definitely been Daddy's little girl, and he'd never said a word about any of the men she brought home, unlike her mother, who would walk out of the house. Until Philip, of course. Philip the perfect match who showed them photos that he carried in his wallet not only of his nieces and nephews but of his parents. When Niki told Faith about him, she had pretended to gag, but Faith knew his love of family was important to Niki, almost, as Niki kept saying, as important as his drop-dead handsomeness.

Niki took her father's death hard, and it still upset her that he never would know his two new grandchildren, but time had blunted the grief, although she often told Faith there was not a day when she didn't think of him in some way large or small. Maybe today was a large day. Niki's voice had sounded strained.

She arrived on the dot of eleven, and it took a while to get the kids out of their snowsuits, boots, hats, scarves, and mittens—Faith didn't miss those days—and settle them in the area Faith had created for her own kids when they were little so she could safely bring them to work with her. Alex immediately fell asleep. "He's totally programmed when it comes to naps," Niki said. "Just not sleeping at night."

Faith got out paper and crayons, and soon Sofia was settled, too.

"Okay, let's have some coffee." They could keep an eye on the kids but be by themselves at the far end of the room. They were both masked, and Faith reflected that at some point when they didn't have to wear a mask anymore, her face would feel naked. Niki had let her dark curls grow, and they swirled around her shoulders as she leaned over her cup. She had always been a pretty girl, and now she was a beautiful woman, maturity adding interest to her features. Faith's thick blond hair had gotten long, too, and Tom wanted it to grow to Rapunzel length, but Amy kept it trimmed to an in-between compromise, while Faith cut her daughter's. Amy's hair was also blond, but lighter and straight, hanging like a silken curtain to the middle of her back. Faith and Amy had watched several YouTubes on cutting men's hair to keep Tom and Ben from getting shaggy, but their efforts did not come close to the skill of their barber in Newton.

Her coffee was almost gone. They were sitting on stools at the long counter well apart, and Faith waited for Niki to say something. Anything. She guessed it was up to her to start.

"Are you hungry? I have some Portuguese caldo verde going for tomorrow's boxes. If I don't tell certain people the soup has kale besides the sausage and beans, they lap it up. I don't know when or why kale started getting such a bad rap."

Niki shook her head. She'd taken her mask off to drink her coffee, and now Faith noticed that her lips were trembling.

"Please," Faith said. "I know something's wrong! You know you can tell me anything."

"Philip's leaving me."

"What!"

Niki nodded and burst into tears.

Faith was shocked. Over the course of the pandemic, she'd heard that the strain of being in lockdown had caused several breakups, notably neighbors on the other side of the Millers' house. The couple's children were scattered across the globe, and after thirty years of marriage, closeness had not made their hearts grow fonder; rather it shattered them. The wife had been the one to leave, heading for California, where she'd grown up and seldom been since. Her husband preferred the White Mountains.

But Philip and Niki! How could this be happening?

Niki was digging in the diaper bag and pulled out a packet of Princess Elsa tissues.

Faith waited for Niki to blow her nose and mop her tears.

She took a deep breath. "He's not divorcing me, but he's leaving. Today or tomorrow. His parents are at their house on the Vineyard, and he's moving to the Hartford one, which is empty. He says he can't take the chaos in our house anymore. That he's not getting any sleep and the kids are out of control, running all over—well, Sofia is. It's impossible to work, and I'm not doing anything about the situation. That I'm a bad mother."

"No! I can't believe he said that!"

"Maybe not in those exact words, but that's what he means. I know he grew up with parents who expected perfect behavior from their kids. God forbid they should make a fort with the couch cushions or a mess in the kitchen. It's too cold for me to take them outdoors for long, and who knows if Sofia's day care center will ever reopen. As for playdates, I can't even remember what they are. I'm keeping my kids, and us, safe. What more does he want?"

"But he has an office. Can't he just shut the door, put headphones on?"

"That's what I said, and it didn't go over well. You know how small the house is. He says even with headphones he can hear the racket. It was all we could afford in Belmont, and we wanted to be there because of the schools. It's worth way more than we paid for it now with the shortage of housing stock. No one's budging. I thought we could find an office rental, but all those buildings are shut, his downtown included. And the library—all the town buildings are closed. I even called our church, but that's off-limits, too."

"Okay," Faith said, "I'm getting out the double fudge brownies I baked this morning for Have Faith Delivered. Desperate times call for chocolate. Sofia is still busy drawing and Alex is sound asleep, so sit where you are and I'll get them—and more coffee. The most important thing for you to understand is that Philip is *not* leaving you. He adores you, and the kids. He's leaving a situation he can't handle anymore, and I'll bet he feels guilty as hell."

"Ha," Niki said. "I'll bet he feels free as a bird."

Returning from the pantry with a platter of brownies, Faith said, "You're saying that because it's what you'd like, too. Been there, done or at least have thought of doing that. What mother hasn't? Going to get groceries or gas and thinking, 'I could just keep driving.'"

"Maybe you're right."

"I know I am. And when did you last get a night's sleep yourself? But what we have to figure out is where Philip could go to work other than Connecticut. Weaning Alex off his naps to sleep through the night comes next."

Niki started to tear up again. "Phil would get stuck there. Connecticut is on the list of states where he'd have to be tested to come back, so even if he did go for the workweek, he couldn't come home weekends. He'd have to find a test. Impossible, and if he got one, it would take too long to get the result."

"And he knows all this?"

"He knows it," Niki said bitterly. "And he may not cook the way I do, but he can put together a meal, so he wouldn't even miss me for that."

Thinking he would miss his wife for other reasons, Faith said firmly, "We can solve this. We've tackled worse. Right away I'm thinking he could go to Vermont to Craig's, Tom's brother. Remember he owns Pine Slopes, and the resort is shut down. Staff are living there, and some of the condos are occupied by owners who fled their other homes for the safety of Vermont. It won't be a problem to get him a place, and since the state has the lowest number of Covid cases in the country and is not on the list of places we can't go and return back, that would work."

Niki brightened. "It's a long drive, but he could come home more easily than from Connecticut. He says he would Skype with the kids so they wouldn't forget him, but they need to get hugs from him. He didn't say anything about Skyping with me." She savagely bit her brownie.

"He's not himself. You know that. He must be behind in work, and I'll bet that's what's causing all this. He may be worried about losing his job."

"I wish we could come up with someplace closer."

Faith filled her in about Samantha and Zach. "It was hard enough to find a place for them, although we only looked in Aleford. But, Niki, why can't he go work at your mother's in Watertown? She's rattling around that big house alone."

"Don't think that wasn't my first thought, but picture it. She'd be interrupting him every five minutes with baklava or something she heard on the news. She'd drive him crazier than we are."

"Hmm," Faith said. "Wait. How about instead of Philip leaving you, you leave him?"

"What did you put in these brownies? Are you nuts?"

"No nuts, too hard to get. Listen. We should have thought of this immediately. It will mean a major sacrifice on your part. But as a very biased observer, I'd say your marriage is worth it. You pack up everything and move in with your mother. She'll be in heaven, and yes, you will get more child-rearing and other advice than you could ever want, but think of conjugal visits back in Belmont while she takes care of the kids."

"That *is* an incentive, but what if I totally lose it and kill her, or worse? I'll be in one of those tacky jumpsuits, not a good look for me, and the kids motherless," she said, unable to suppress a smile. "It's the only solution. You're right, Faith. The reason I didn't think of it straightaway was, well—it's my mother."

"Why don't you call Philip now? Go into the office and I'll sit with the kids."

It was a long talk, and Faith was beginning to think Connecticut was on the horizon. Sofia had demolished a brownie and two juice boxes while relating *Frozen* scene by scene. Alex, awake now, sat on Faith's lap, intently listening to his sister while gnawing on Zwieback Faith had found in the diaper bag.

"It's okay," Niki announced as she crossed the room. "Could you help me get the kids dressed? And call Ben? Since he's not delivering food tonight, maybe he could move us? It's amazing how much stuff two small children seem to require. I can pack in five minutes—jeans, some tops, underwear, socks, and my toothbrush. For them I need a steamer trunk."

Her—and Faith's—relief was palpable. "You were right, you know. He's way behind at work, and while no one has said anything yet, he's been waiting for the ax to fall any moment. And he's sorry. Very sorry that he had such a meltdown. I told him I'd make sure to make his apology memorable. When we can schedule it."

"And your mother?"

"Over the moon and 'I told you so' combined. She's already started cooking, enough for us and him. I may end up putting on the baby weight I lost."

Sofia gave Faith a hug and promised to finish telling her the rest of the movie next time, Alex waved both chubby fists bye-bye, and they were out the door.

"I'll call you," Niki said. "And thank you."

"No need." Faith smiled. "If he had gone through with this idiotic plan, tell him, I would have had to come by and slap him sillier."

Faith finished getting the meal-box contents ready to assemble the next day for delivery. Besides the soup and brownies, there was a round of soft goat cheese from the local farm store and rolls. Claudia had added an illustration of frolicking goats along the bottom of the instructions—simple ones that indicated all the diner had to do was heat the hearty soup. As she closed the refrigerated unit, her phone rang. The caller ID told her it was Ellie Porter.

Hope and Ben had been right about the fate of food-related businesses. Many restaurants were able to serve outdoors the previous summer into the fall, but caterers had the problem of number restrictions, so even if she could have catered an event under a tent, the numbers would be, of necessity, small. The cancellations and postponements had come in fast and furiously. Once Have Faith Delivered started, there were a few more elaborate dinners than the boxes ordered, but not many. Birthdays, baby showers, holiday parties crossed out hurt, but the weddings were what broke Faith's heart—and the hearts of the couples and their families. Several had canceled outright and, in some cases, used the money for a down payment on a house or to rent an apartment with a quick stop at the justice of the peace to start married life, possibly with the prospect of a celebration later. Much later, as it turned out. She returned deposits, merely subtracting what had been spent. It only seemed fair. Niki had offered small tiered wedding cakes for these sparse ceremonies with the newlyweds, their parents, maybe a best man and maid of honor. Some clients had sent photos with bridal-themed masks and the few attending spread far apart. You couldn't see smiling faces, but Faith knew they were there.

Since the start, she'd had calls from brides trying to decide what to do, and there were a few dates for June 2021, although Faith was almost certain the kind of wedding they were considering—anywhere from forty to four hundred guests—wouldn't occur.

But the bride who called the most often wasn't figuring out a date. At least not for the wedding. A date for a baby.

Ellie Porter was not a bridezilla. Faith knew the Porters from the Ganley Museum in town. Ellie's mother, Nina, was a longtime Board of Trustees member, and Nathan Porter, Ellie's father, had been instrumental early on in pursuing grants for the small contemporary art and sculpture park. The Porter nuptials were set in stone, planned more than a year ago to the last sugared almond, starting with the ceremony at the museum performed by Nathan's brother, an ordained priest residing in Washington State. Three hundred guests would nibble on hors d'oeuvres on the terrace overlooking Aleford's water supply, a picturesque reservoir. No swan ice sculptures, but local artists had created designs that would be carved to decorate the cocktail hour buffet. The sit-down dinner inside would offer a choice of butter-poached lobster, individual beef Wellingtons, or a medley of wild mushroom risotto with truffle oil, followed by dessert and dancing on the grounds near the Jim Dine double-hearts sculpture. A large fantasy version of a medieval tent with a sturdy floor would be erected. Bride and groom were lovers of all things Arthurian, and Ellie's dress would have suited Guinevere perfectly—no white tulle veil, but a diadem that sparkled on Ellie's long chestnut locks. Niki had used the theme as the inspiration for the cake, complete with an edible silver Excalibur extending from the top layer.

The only hitch was the date. June 13, 2020.

Ellie's older sister had eloped with her swing-dance partner—"Daddy is still sorry he encouraged her to take lessons. I mean she has always been pretty shy and he thought she could meet a nice cheerful group of people, only Sean turned out to be teaching her some very new steps," Ellie had told Faith when they first started planning the wedding a year and a half earlier. "Happily married, they are still 'dancing'—one kid and one on the way. My sis picked right up on a new kind of rhythm. And both my brothers married ladies from places not well known to Daddy—Indiana and South

Dakota. Really. Blame OkCupid. So, none of my parents' friends and few of our family made those, although the South Dakota one was a hoot. The bride rode to the altar, which was in their barn, on a bedecked stallion. And that wasn't the groom. Mom was fine with all three weddings, but I know she's with her dear Nathan on this one, so pull out all the stops, Faith."

Faith had. Claudia used what looked like aged parchment for her beautifully calligraphed Save the Dates and invitations, creating bright crests for the families. The parents of Adam, the groom, lived in Maine, and his father owned a seafood shipping company—he called for a lobster dish as one of the entrées—and was "as happy as a dog with two tails" to have an escutcheon, using it for the business. They had a round dining table in their house, so he figured that qualified them.

The Skype with the Porters in late March when the stay-at-home order was announced was terrible. The decision to put off the wedding that had been looming ever closer was finally made definite. Faith would never forget seeing Nathan's sad, still face—and the tears that streamed down it.

In the months to follow he was the most adamant about re-scheduling for 2021 or even 2022.

Before accepting her wedding event, Faith had met Ellie at various times, especially since Ellie had gone to Wellesley and knew Samantha Miller as a fellow alum, so Miller parties had often included her. Planning Ellie's wedding had been great fun. They were often joined by one or both parents, and Ellie would make everyone laugh by suggesting outrageous ideas like mini fake fire-breathing dragon centerpieces for each table, a real tour-nament, and an authentic Arthurian menu featuring venison pies, turkey legs, pottage, and mead, and peacocks roaming the Ganley grounds.

Ellie wasn't laughing today, although as she often said on these calls to Faith, "At least I haven't lost my sense of humor, just my mind."

The call started as usual. "Hi, Faith. It's Ellie. And I don't think I can go on much longer. Daddy isn't budging, even though I think maybe Mom has come over to Adam's and my side. His parents, too. Daddy calls it 'the dark side,' and fortunately Adam's parents are Mainers and expect people from away to be strange, so they aren't taking it the wrong way, which of course it is. I mean. Wrong. He makes it sound like we are all in league with the devil. I'm at the point where I'm going to jump Adam's bones, get the bun in the oven, and to hell with the wedding."

This was about par for all the calls from Ellie since the decision to postpone had been reached. Aside from her sense of humor, she had a gift for mixing metaphors.

"Honestly, Faith, if I was living at home, I wouldn't put it past Daddy to pin me down and strap a chastity belt on, like *Robin Hood: Men in Tights*. Somewhere in his head I know he knows that ship has sailed. Adam and I moved in together before the pandemic, thank goodness, but me walking down the aisle with a baby bump or even an actual baby is light-years away from his comfort zone. I mean he likes all this modern art and is a broad-minded guy, but first comes marriage and *then* the baby carriage."

"Where does that even come from?" Faith said. "I think we used to jump rope to it."

"Well, whoever dreamed it up did not take into account biological clocks, and mine is a speeding stopwatch. I can't skip a year or more of fertility just to please my father. Or can I? Should I? What if I do and then it takes years and we need to do the whole in vitro thing, which costs a fortune, and I'll have to take all these drugs and look so horrible, Adam will divorce me."

Faith was in total sympathy with Ellie, much as she understood how Nathan felt. So many dreams had vanished or been put on hold over the last year plus. Ellie was twenty-eight and more than ready to look under cabbage leaves. But Nathan had categorically refused the idea that the couple get married now and have the wedding celebration when it was safe to go through with the original plan.

Ellie's suggestion that it would simply mean one change—a flower girl or ring bearer—did not go over big.

"What should I do? What would *you* do?"

"Oh no you don't, missy. You've tried this before. Think of me as Switzerland without that gooey fondue. Completely neutral."

"I can't elope. That would really break his heart. We'd have to tell him what we were going to do. Adam has all the information on getting a license, and we could get married at Waltham's city hall. Twenty dollars for the license and one hundred for the justice of the peace. Because of Covid, we might have to do the ceremony part on the front steps. The whole thing is a bargain."

"Love you to pieces, but I have to go. Tom was able to get vaccinated at the VA yesterday as one of their chaplains and he says he feels fine, sore arm but nothing else. Still, I want to see for myself that he's still doing all right."

"That's wonderful news! My parents will get their shots long before Adam and I do. If it all sped up, we might be able to have the wedding in June, but there's the travel problem. My uncle would be coming from the West Coast, and the guests are all over the place, too. I just have to bite the bullet and tell Daddy we're going to do it. Both things." She sighed. "Or maybe not. I have to think some more about it all. But a baby, just think . . ."

"Good-bye, Ellie. Talk to you soon. Go interrupt Adam's work and have a glass of wine."

"While I can," she said cheerfully.

Driving home, Faith thought how complicated this wedding cancellation/postponement was compared with the others. None of the event changes or deletions had been easy for any of those involved, and there was still one, like Ellie's, that refused to be resolved. Persis Wald's plans for her husband's eightieth. The woman was an immovable force. Turning into the parsonage driveway, built when cars were much narrower and always a tricky maneuver, Faith decided not to think about Persis now. Or later.

It was a busy weekend. Like all of them. Saturdays usually meant Tom was "putting the polishing touches" on his sermon or, as often as not, starting over and writing a whole new one. Sunday now meant the Zoom service and what that involved, although with Ben taking over, all Tom had to do was preach. At one point he'd suggested Faith organize a Zoom coffee hour as some congregations were doing or even a Zoom book group. She'd told him as nicely as she was able—holding back the steam that wanted to escape from her ears—that she did not have time to do either, what with the food deliveries, foraging, and keeping the family on track, whatever that was these days. This included both sets of parents and close friends.

The food-box orders had picked up in the late fall. People were able to get out and about during the summer, and cooking had become a new hobby for many. Faith was bombarded with all sorts of concocted recipes—peach chili was one of the more interesting notions. Chocolate chip corn and beet soup one of the least. Ben made the deliveries Monday, Wednesday, and Saturday, which meant prepping the day before. No, she wouldn't be hosting coffee klatches. Fortunately, others in the church and elsewhere did. Their friends Patsy and Will Avery hosted the most popular one in town, combining cooking their native New Orleans dinners with a book discussion around the virtual table as they ate it afterward. They posted the dinner menu and necessary ingredients and the selected book a week earlier. Faith had marveled over how innovative people had become in creating communities in isolation and attended when she could. Which reminded her that she hadn't finished this week's selection, Paule Marshall's classic *Brown Girl, Brownstones.* She'd take it to bed but knew she wouldn't get past a paragraph before her eyes closed.

It was after two in the morning. Amy hadn't been able to sleep, and now it was Tuesday. The light was on in Ben's room. She could see it under his door. She didn't know what to do. Was no closer to a decision than she had been hours ago.

She got out of bed and put on her bathrobe. The house was cold. Outside it was pitch-dark. Her room was at the front of the house, and she hadn't heard a single car go by since she'd come upstairs.

Switching on the hall light, she went into her parents' room. Her father slept on the side nearest the door. They teased him that he was instantly awake if one of them so much as coughed, but it was true, and he sat up now.

"Honey, having trouble sleeping? Come down to the kitchen, and I'll make you a snack and something warm to drink."

His words woke her mother.

"Amy, are you okay?"

"Ben's not in his room or anywhere else in the house. I went over to the church, thinking maybe he was there watching TV, but he wasn't. The van and cars are here."

She took a deep breath.

"He's missing."

Chapter Four

Benjamin Fairchild was in love. Deeply in love. It was the real thing. What those sappy Hallmark movie ads called "forever love," but the words were ringing true. When he was just a teenager, he'd thought Mandy Hitchcock was it. They met while working at the lodge on Sanpere. She had grown up on the island in pretty terrible circumstances, really no family at all, and Ben, the rest of the Fairchilds, too, became her family. She was almost three years older and wouldn't take him seriously for a long time, but eventually she did, and it had seemed they were meant to be. Then she went to Bates College on a scholarship and gave him the "always best friends" talk, even as he persisted. Looking back, he realized it was not love but an infatuation. He'd been trying to make up for the life she'd had, and also, he had to admit, she was beautiful and smart. Her being an older woman was part of the allure, too.

Now was something else entirely. He knew right away, actually after a couple of hours, that he would never meet anyone he would want to spend the rest of his life with except Catherine. It was love—and certainty.

She was the same age and a sophomore, but their paths hadn't crossed until recently. They were in different dorms and had different majors, different friends. And then it happened. Brown had called back a limited number of students for in-person classes in fall 2020. Ben was crossing the green in front of University Hall, his laptop case slipping from his shoulder about to knock the iced coffee he'd picked up at Dunkin' when a girl looking at her phone bumped into him, sending the liquid flying.

"Oh my God, I'm so sorry! I never do this. I mean look at my phone and don't watch where I'm going. Or spill people's drinks, either. What was it? I'll go get you another one."

"It was a caramel iced macchiato, and I don't need one. I drink far too many. They should put me in a commercial." He knew he was smiling, a big smile.

"We could do it together," she said, laughing. "That's all I drink, too. I hope I didn't spill any on your clothes."

"Or yours?"

They checked each other out. Their clothes and more . . . He was a few inches taller than she was and had short sandy-blond hair. He pointed to the tee shirt he was wearing with jeans—it sported Thoreau's quote BEWARE OF ALL ENTERPRISES THAT REQUIRE NEW CLOTHES. "I take this pretty literally. My dad is even worse. He's still wearing a Brown sweatshirt from when he was here, although the elbows are kind of torn."

She had jet-black hair that reached far down her back, and when he looked straight at her face, he noticed there were tiny flecks of gold in her brown eyes—and a few sun freckles across her nose. If she was wearing makeup, it didn't look like it. Her lips were naturally crimson, he was sure, and suddenly he wanted to talk to her, get to know her. Get to know her enough to kiss those lips. He felt as if he was coming down with a cold. Kind of shaky. He'd just been tested on campus. It wasn't Covid. This was something else, something new.

"How about I buy you one and you buy me one and we sit

for a while? We may not have these sunny days much longer," she suggested.

A while stretched out to several hours and dinnertime. They arranged to meet at the library after classes the next day. Besides her name—Catherine Mariani—he'd learned she was the oldest of five. "Kind of your basic typical large Italian family. My grandparents emigrated from southern Italy to Brooklyn, where a cousin had a job waiting for Nonno at his grocery. The grocery expanded to a couple of stores, specializing in Italian foods, and the family expanded, too. I have forty-five first cousins. Zoom Thanksgiving and Christmas are going to be wild. My parents met in high school, and as soon as she could my mother convinced my father to head for the Island. Long, that is. Big house, statue of Michelangelo's *David* in the center of a fountain on the front lawn. You either love it or hate it—and I haven't told you about the plastic-wrapped living room furniture. I love it."

That was when Ben fell head over heels. "I love it." He replaced the "it" with "you," and after a very short time, that happened. Catherine was equally as, even more maybe, crazy about Ben. They had almost everything in common, from the iced coffee to their research. She had created an environmental studies major focusing on climate change. Large posters of Rachel Carson and Greta Thunberg were blue-tacked to her wall. Their goals after graduating were virtually the same, as was the passion behind them.

Soon they were alternating from his room to hers. Life was good. And then came the announcement that the campus case numbers had spiked and the university was closing again. Catherine was headed south and Ben north. They couldn't believe how unlucky they were.

Ben had planned to go home when the semester was over, knowing that operating Have Faith Delivered and Ben and Amy's Delivery Service depended in part on his being there. Also essentially running the church services for his dad. Going home was different for Catherine. She was worried about being able to go remote again in the noisy household. "Fun, hugs all around, but even in my room I can barely hear myself think. It was terrible last spring. Plus having me right there, I'm everyone's tutor."

When they parted, they were both teary, but they knew FaceTiming and Skyping would have to do for now. "After the vaccine, we'll be able to see each other no problem," Ben said confidently.

But the prospect of a shot retreated further and further away, like looking in the wrong end of a telescope. What also got behind for Catherine was her coursework, and in early December her parents found a small apartment in Providence through a cousin of a cousin or some other Italian connection, and she moved there in order to keep up with her classes, hoping they'd be in-person by spring. It was tantalizing to be so close to Ben, but it might as well have been Mars, he said, complaining. As a Massachusetts resident he couldn't leave the state without quarantining on his return.

"I just want to see you! I have to see you!" he said.

"Oh, my love, me too. Me too!"

"Amy, do you have any idea where Ben is?" Tom asked.

She pulled her robe around herself tightly. What to say?

"I don't exactly."

"Get under the duvet, you look freezing," Faith said. "We know he had dinner with us and went to his room afterward. I saw the light under his door when I went to bed." She was thinking out loud.

"It was on when I got up to get a glass of water about one."

What Amy didn't add was that she'd gone back to bed and couldn't sleep. The light was on in her brother's room, but she hadn't heard any noise, no typing, none of the sci-fi audiobooks he listened to very late at night. Finally, she'd gone to his door and opened it a crack to listen better. The room was silent. She'd opened it wide. Silent—and empty. The covers on the bed were pulled to the side, but the pillow was smooth. No dent where his head would have been. He wasn't in the bathroom they shared.

Maybe he'd gone to the kitchen for a snack. She'd crept softly, avoiding the stair that sometimes creaked. But he wasn't in the kitchen, either. He wasn't anywhere downstairs. She'd put on her parka and boots and gone to look in the garage. The van was in the driveway parked behind the car the two of them had bought last April for the business. It was a clunker, but they were only using it around town. The family car was next to it as usual. She'd checked out the church.

When she'd gone inside, she decided she had to tell her parents he was gone. Ben and she were close. They'd never had the kind of sibling stuff she'd seen in other families. They might tease each other, but it was almost always good-natured. She'd heard her mother tell Aunt Hope that she wanted her kids to have the relationship they had, and the Miller kids, that she wasn't going to put up with anything else. Now Amy was going to squeal on her brother, and it was making her feel sick. But this wasn't Ben. There must be something very wrong. He wouldn't just take off. Except . . .

Her mother was reaching for her phone. "Don't bother, Mom. He has his turned off. You'll get his voicemail, and his text is silenced, too. I've been trying."

Tom asked again, "Can you think where he might have gone? Normally we'd call friends of his, but not these days."

Amy took a deep breath. "He's been depressed. And he FaceTimes a lot with Catherine. You know, the girl he met when Brown returned to in-person last fall."

"I remember he mentioned he had met someone and that they had similar majors. That she was from Long Island," Faith said.

Amy knew that it wasn't just wanting to save the earth that they had in common. It was much, much more. He'd been moony ever since he came home. It was the way he had been about Mandy Hitchcock years ago, but what was different this time was that he was quiet about it. Before, he couldn't stop talking about Mandy. Now it was as if he wanted to keep what he had with Catherine—and Amy was sure it was intense—all to himself.

"I think he may have gone to see her."

"What! To Long Island?" Faith exclaimed.

"Catherine is back in Providence." That much Ben had told his sister.

Tom got up and pulled some clothes from the closet. "You two try to get some sleep. I'll wait downstairs."

"As if," Amy said, leaving the room.

"As if," Faith said, reaching for her own clothes.

Catherine and Ben had been developing the plan for weeks with the precision of a military campaign, thinking of every possibility, any out-of-the-blues. They had scouted locations online and made lists of what could go wrong. They had come up with what they thought was responsible, masked and six feet apart at the rendezvous. But they could look into each other's eyes and hear each other's somewhat muffled voices in person. That was what mattered.

The roadblocks were many. Ben couldn't go to Rhode Island. He'd have to quarantine, maybe get tested, as soon as he crossed the border back. Catherine did not have the restriction, but she also did not have a car, so couldn't meet him. And where? Outdoors was safest, but the weather was unpredictable. They'd have to abort if a nor'easter came pummeling, and even without snow, current temperatures were punishing. They had to meet at a time when Ben would not be missed, which meant late night or very, very early morning. It couldn't interfere with his food delivery.

At last it was a go—they'd perfected it all. A short time together, but so worth it. Catherine would take the train from Providence that left at 12:25, arriving at 12:58 at Route 128 Westwood in Massachusetts, where Ben would be sitting in the Amtrak station's huge waiting room, resisting the urge to leap up and hug her as she stepped onto the platform. At that time of night, they were sure the space would be empty, or near enough. It was the last train to Boston, so even if people did get off, they wouldn't linger, but head for the car park. No crowds.

Earlier, but not too early, Ben would leave Aleford, borrowing his friend Glenn's car. Glenn and his family had headed for Montreal to self-isolate with his mother's family, especially to care for her sister, who had cancer. Glenn had given Ben his keys and asked him to start the car every once in a while so the battery wouldn't die. He'd said to use it as well whenever he liked. Glenn's house was a short walk from the parsonage.

Ben left the house, being sure to make his room seem occupied, and drove to the station. When Catherine walked through the door of the waiting room, the bleak place was transformed into a palace. And she looked like a princess to him, even in her bright green MAKE EARTH COOL AGAIN bobble hat. She ran toward him and measured six feet with the tape she brought, sinking into the chair in tears.

"What's wrong? Did something happen on the train?"

"No, you silly. These are tears of happiness. I can't believe we're actually here together. It's seemed years, not weeks."

They talked and talked, gazed and gazed. Too soon, Ben had to leave to get home before anyone was up and he was missed. His father, in particular, was an early riser. The drive to Aleford took twenty minutes, shorter at this time of night, but he allowed thirty, and after a farewell that included a promise from each of them, a promise of yes, he drove back, entering the kitchen at 2:47.

A light was on over the table. Three chairs were occupied. Amy was asleep, her head resting on folded arms. His parents were very much awake.

"So, son," his father said, using a tone of voice Ben had never heard before—beyond serious, beyond anger—"would you care to tell us where you've been?"

Across town, at Brian and Margaret Kimball's house, another drama was playing out. Also in the kitchen. Margaret had been working for twenty-four hours with a brief three-hour nap in the middle. She kept a Keurig in her office, subsisting on K-Cup coffee and KIND energy bars. The deal was crucial and the negotiations across several time zones. At last it was a wrap, and wearily she made her way out of the room to eat a proper meal. She was thinking of one of the meals from MAX Ultimate, her favorite caterer; she ordered MAX @ Home meals regularly and stowed them in the freezer. Maybe their Thai coconut chicken soup and then some of their heavenly rosemary-braised lamb shanks. Or something else of theirs tucked away for a time just like this. They were worth the price and so was she. Brian's studio light was shining from under his door, but he often fell asleep on the couch there if he'd been working late. During the pandemic, he'd started creating digital art, moving his easel and canvases to the garage.

She yawned and stretched, walking into the open-floor-plan kitchen area while reaching to turn on the lights, expecting to see them reflected on the quartz countertops and gleaming farmhouse sink. Instead, the sink was filled with dirty dishes and pots, despite the dishwasher next to it. The counters were covered with opened jars and cans, scattered strands of uncooked linguine, boxes of crackers and assorted half-eaten cheeses on their slate cheese plate. The stove top was caked with spilled spaghetti sauce, and a large frying pan revealed remnants of sautéed ground beef and onions.

"Brian!" she yelled, heading for his studio and flinging the door open. As she'd suspected, he was sound asleep. She shook his shoulder and yelled his name again, more loudly this time and directly into his ear. "What the hell! I've been busting my ass working for so many hours, I scarcely know what day or time it is, and you've been doing what? Judging from the mess, you've been cooking, and there better be several dinners waiting for me!"

He jumped up, rubbing his eyes. "Honey, I'm sorry. I guess the kitchen is a little messy. I cooked some stuff for myself. I'll make something for you now."

She strode out of the room, and he followed, still apologizing. "I meant to clean up tonight, but I must have fallen asleep. Why don't you sit down and I'll make dinner for you and then I'll clean up?"

"You clean, and I'll find something myself, thank you very much." She went to the freezer for the soup, thinking that a hot mug of it would go a long way to calming her down.

There wasn't any soup. Or the lamb shanks. Or any other entrées or soup. Or bread. Or ice cream. Or much of anything.

"What? Did you have a party while I was working? With my headphones on all the time I wouldn't have heard a thing! No, even you wouldn't have a party now. Just same ol' same ol' inconsiderate behavior that's been your norm the entire time we've been stuck inside all these months. It's *my* job to keep food stocked. House cleaned. Pretty much everything that needs doing. While you play around on your computer when you don't have the small amount of teaching required to keep your job, and of course there's those long intimate chats with your girlfriend Claudia. Maybe you made your special linguine with Bolognese sauce and dropped it off at her house far back in the woods. Far from prying eyes!"

Brian didn't move. He was stunned by the intensity of her rant. "Look, you're the one losing track of time, and I probably should have asked if you wanted some of what I made, but you've told me not to disturb you unless it's an emergency! So there's no reason to be blaming me now for getting hungry and making myself food. Look, I'm sorry. Okay?" He *had* made the sauce, which took several pans, but he'd eaten it all himself.

Margaret grabbed a dirty cup from the sink and threw it against the eco-friendly bamboo-matted wall, where it crashed, sending the pieces skittering over the custom travertine flooring.

"Oh, sweetheart, your favorite Russel Wright cup. The Ripe Apricot one. It was so hard to find a pair."

She grabbed another. A Seafoam Blue one, and threw it at him. He deftly caught it.

"Don't you sweetheart me. I'm going to bed. And don't even think about opening the door. It's going to be locked!"

"Be reasonable, Margaret. Don't do this. Let's sit down and talk."

She walked over to him and he smiled. She gently took the cup from his hand and smashed it on the floor next to his bare foot. He stopped smiling, but she gave him a big grin and left the room.

Her father's words woke Amy up. "Ben, don't be mad at me, please. I got scared. Everything's so scary now. I had to tell them. It was getting so late."

"You have nothing to apologize to your brother about. You did the right thing. And I'm still waiting to hear what he did, and I'm assuming it wasn't the right thing, unless he's been strolling the streets of Aleford looking up at the sky for hours."

Tom was never sarcastic. Faith felt more than shocked. Remarks like this were her department. It was almost as if they had an agreement. Good Cop, Bad Cop. Her relief when Ben walked in the door had been so overwhelming that all she wanted to do was hug him, give him a warm drink, and tuck him into bed. But Tom was right. And it was Bad Cop time for both of them.

Ben looked wide-eyed at his parents and Amy. He cleared his throat and tried to say something. Instead, standing absolutely still, he started to sob, to his and everyone's surprise. And it all came out.

"You have no idea what it's been like! Worried about people getting it. People dying from it. And no normal life. I was supposed to be doing the research that was going to get published with my professor. Instead, months of remote learning and not getting anywhere with what I want to be working on." He wiped his face on his sleeve. "And what about Amy? She's missing the best part of high school, senior year, and the closest she gets to her friends is on a computer screen or maybe once in a while a walk where you have to speak through a mask and can't really be heard.

"Yes, I went to see my girlfriend tonight. But we did it completely safely. And our carbon footprints were as small as we could make them. She took the train from Providence after midnight to the Amtrak Route 128 station. She could leave Rhode Island. I didn't break the law and cross the state line. I did borrow Glenn's car to drive to the station, which he *said* I could, and we met there. We sat six feet apart, masked, didn't share or even bring food, and then I came straight back here. You would never have known I was gone. I *had* to see Catherine. I knew it would help both of us not feel afraid about what's happening, even if we were just together for such a short time. She's alone, and I've been worried about how depressed she sounds."

He started sobbing again, deep sobs, tears running down his face onto his neck.

"You have *no* idea how bad it has been day after day not to see each other in person. We love each other very much, and I'd do what I did tonight again in a heartbeat."

Faith handed him a dish towel, and everyone was quiet for a minute while Ben buried his face in it.

"Obviously we did not know about your feelings for Catherine—"

Ben interrupted his father, shouting, "And she has the same feelings for me!"

Tom continued, his tone serious but different from before. "You two have taken excellent precautions and planned with care for yourselves and others, but you do know, son, that you have to quarantine now for ten days after contact with anyone from another state."

"I thought that was only if you were in contact with someone who had tested positive." Ben was almost whispering, and lowering his voice even more, he said, "Oh, shit."

It took more than a minute for Brian to clean up the kitchen and go online to place food-delivery orders from Margaret's preferred purveyors. They'd been married almost six years, but he figured it must be less if you counted actual face-to-face time. She'd always been blunt about how much her career meant to her, and he admired her drive. The money was nice, too. It meant vacations at places he could never afford on a teacher's salary and the occasional sale of a painting. It also meant this house. Planning it, watching the renovations, the hunt for the perfect furnishings had been the happiest they'd ever been together, save the heady first dates, the sex. She was as passionate in bed as she was when she was going for a bonus. He got hot just thinking about it as he turned off the lights. A faint dawn's winter light was creeping up on the horizon. He grabbed a pointed nail file from a compartment in one of the kitchen drawers where she kept some makeup and a small brush. Margaret would never be caught unawares without looking perfectly groomed. Upstairs outside the master bedroom, he let his clothes fall into a heap and opened the push-button lock with the file. He'd had to do it before when they'd had a fight. In the past her quick temper had always dissolved into hot make-up sex.

She was asleep. He pulled the sheet and blanket down on his side and slipped in, appreciating the quality of the linens—the fine cotton felt almost like satin. Her hair was down and spread out on the pillow. She always slept naked, too, and the warmth spreading from her body excited him so much, he wasn't sure he could hold off. It was like being a teenager. He closed his eyes and ran his hand down her side, caressing her breast.

"Go sleep with your whore," she said softly. The only part of her body that moved was her foot, and the kick was swift. Her aim was dead-on. He limped to the guest room, cursing. Not softly.

"Same time. Same place." Faith read the text from Pix. And replied, "Yup. Bring a large coffee. Much to talk about."

It was relatively warm for January, but she still put on the Canada Goose coat that Hope had given her. With the hood up, it encased her entire body, and her boots were the warmest Uggs made. She grabbed an insulated travel mug and filled it with hot coffee. She'd been a coffee drinker back in her salad days in Manhattan, but the consumption then paled in comparison with what she imbibed in Aleford. She'd learned immediately that upon entering someone's home, she'd be offered a cup and would be expected to offer the same at hers. It had nothing to do with the time of day. It was a ritual.

Pix was framed by the spiky Canadian hemlock trained on the arched trellis. The low temperatures had produced a kind of *Game of Thrones* effect. Her mask was pulled down low enough that she could sip her coffee, and Faith did the same with hers.

"What's going on?" Pix asked. "You need to put a smiley face on a text like that, or I'll worry."

"Good point. It's nothing to worry about now and I'll start at the beginning, but at the moment we have three in quarantine—your two and Ben! I mean, what are the odds?"

"Excellent," Pix said ruefully. "I'm assuming Ben doesn't have it or you wouldn't be so calm."

"He doesn't. Or not yet. Like Zach and Samantha, it's too soon for symptoms."

Faith shook her head and quickly filled Pix in on last night. "But they were being very cautious, and I do like the sound of her, what little I know, that is."

"Men! Ben isn't a boy anymore, so can't say that, but men! When Samantha was in love or even had a little crush, we knew all about it, plus everything about him down to his shoe size."

"Ben did go off the rails a little over Mandy, remember, but he was definitely a boy then. A teenage boy. He didn't talk about being in love the way he did last night. And he snapped, Pix. Right after he walked in the door. I guess we must have seemed like some kind of star chamber waiting to lock him up in the Tower of London. The last time I can remember seeing him cry was in third grade when the class bunny died. He was holding back tears until he got off the bus and then started sobbing like last night. I thought it was a teacher or classmate, not Pookie."

"Where have you put him? Sequestered in his room? Thank goodness Tom got his first shot, so it's somewhat safe for him to interact, bring him food," Pix said.

"More like thank goodness you and I brainstormed for Zach and Samantha. Until Sam thought of the Sinclairs, the church was the best option. The room the youth group uses has a couch, so he doesn't have to sleep on one of the cots. The parish hall has a full kitchen. He's not at Amy's level, but he can cook. Tom picked up food I ordered and stocked it. Amy is delivering the dinner boxes, so she'll bring him those, which covers three nights. And there's a full bath off the Minister's Robing Room. You've seen it."

When Tom gave his fiancée a tour of the church all those years ago, announcing what the small room off his church study was, she had burst out laughing, thinking it was a joke. Or some quaint New England term. But while her beloved did smile, he told her quite seriously that it was exactly what it said. Where he put on his vestments. Over the years Faith had made sure to leave a few clean collars and socks without holes that also matched in the large Sheraton dresser. She still wondered what impulse was behind the shower in the bathroom, though. Cleanliness is next to godliness?

"What does Amy have to say about Catherine?"

"You know how tight Ben and she are. I think she feels it's up to him to tell us about Catherine. She did say that he's shown her some photos on his phone and Catherine is very pretty. Oh, and he's very, very serious about her, which we gathered from what he said last night about being in love. Judging from what we could make out between the sobs, they'll be following each other's carbon footprints forever. Tom and I are concerned that they're very young to be so involved."

"And you weren't? I met Sam my last year in college. He had already graduated. We were married almost as soon as the ink dried on my diploma."

"Things are different now. Couples wait longer to be sure. Even so, the divorce rate is high."

"Maybe they *are* sure. Our grandchildren could grow up together!"

"Speaking of which—and I still think Ben is too young to make this kind of commitment, but will let it go for now—how is Samantha feeling?"

"Dr. Kane referred her to an ob-gyn at Emerson Hospital, and they have an excellent birthing center there. She had a telehealth visit yesterday with the doctor and will go in person as soon as she's out of quarantine and tests negative. But everything seems fine. She doesn't even have morning sickness. Just feels tired. I like the sound of the doctor. Very sensible. Told her to get outside and walk when the weather permitted, that her diet sounded excellent, but maybe add more protein, and what else? Warm baths to relax. Zach found an app that teaches massage for pregnant women, and it sounds as if they're having fun. Samantha did say that the quarantine was already dragging for Zach. That he was restless. Work is slow and he needs a project. I guess she's it."

"No thought of moving back to Somerville once they're both vaccinated and things are safe?"

"This is one of those 'cross that bridge when' things. Right now she wants to be here. All three kids were born at Emerson. I think as soon as she saw the double line on the pregnancy test, she wanted to come home. Even before the rush to leave the building because of the virus. That apartment was not much larger than a dorm room. If she is in her first month, the baby will arrive at the end of the summer. They can have the house to themselves if we can go to Sanpere in the spring. Before that they have the top floor all to themselves. Sam and I have been talking about it. I don't know which of us is more tickled. We'd love to have them here. And trying to find a short- or even long-term rental in town will be tough. Once little Beanbag—that's what they're calling it so far—makes an appearance, they'll have figured out where they want to be. Just so long as it's close!"

"No problem with deciding which in-laws for holidays. Can you imagine Alexandra as a grandmother?"

"I have a problem imagining her as a mother!"

They both laughed and Faith said, "This isolated quarantine is going to be hard on Ben. The month of January is a project term, and his professor has him doing some literature searches, but that's it. Catherine may be more involved with whatever she's doing. He can't do the food deliveries or the other jobs unless he can walk the person through whatever the matter is online, sharing their screen. Amy is bored with school and very bored with waiting to hear whether she's been accepted anywhere, so she's happy to take everything over. Maybe Zach can think of a project he and Ben can do together. Design some kind of new site."

Pulling her mask up and stepping back toward her house, Pix said, "No matter the consequences, I'd say Benjamin Fairchild is very happy today. Love, sweet love."

Stepping back into her house, Faith found herself humming the tune, hearing Dionne Warwick's voice. Yes, love, sweet love, is what the world needs now.

On Monday, Claudia got a call from the alarm company. They were getting a low-battery signal from the system in the carriage house and asked her to check by arming and disarming the system. She did, repeated it as instructed, and they said the battery was in fact low. "Nothing to worry about. It's working, but we need to replace it. It's been a few years since that was installed."

Probably before she came, Claudia thought.

"We can have someone out there Tuesday or Thursday. It won't take long, and all our service people take every precaution, suited up completely, and the area will be sanitized afterward."

"Tuesday anytime works better than Thursday. I'm a teacher and will need to be on Zoom with students much of the day."

They offered eleven o'clock and told her she would have to vacate the premises. "We suggest clients sit in their cars. When the technician leaves, wait an hour for the sanitizer smell to dissipate. It's not unpleasant but a bit strong."

"Do you need to replace the battery in the other house?"

"No, that's fine. It was done recently enough."

She hung up and decided to tidy the downstairs after she ran the press over the plate she had just finished inking. She was eager to see how the new lines she'd added to an intricate spiderweb that covered almost the entire surface looked. A space in the center waited for the spider, and she wasn't sure yet what form this one would take. Two of the editions she'd created were arachnids with human faces. She liked the idea of a storybook figure for this one. A reference to Scotland's King Robert the Bruce? His spider. The one he watched thinking all was over, lying in a rude shed, the sixth battle for Scotland's independence from England lost. The spider was losing hers, too, attempting to weave her web in the ceiling just above his head. Six tries and none reached across the beams, but she persisted, and the seventh delicate thread was a success, as, inspired, so was he. She had been creating such dark prints. She'd give Bruce's spider a go.

The finished print satisfied her critical eye, and she cleaned the zinc plate. After the alarm company left, she'd have all day to work on a Scottish spider.

Christopher Sinclair had gotten under her skin with his remarks about her housekeeping, her art. She had almost dismissed the art criticism from a man who probably thought nothing more lovely than an uninterrupted green sward, but she took the other harder, trying to keep her mess in control since his unwanted visit. Tidying up, she made sure the chemicals she used and stored in clear glass bottles were off the table, the inks and turpentine, too. She put the used rags in a special container and gathered all the scraps of paper left over to burn in the Franklin stove later. She pinned the impression she'd just made to the line of others on the wallboard that she'd installed behind the long table.

Putting her work aside, she made a quick call to Samantha and Zach to let them know a van from the alarm company would be coming to check her system, not theirs. She cherished a hope that after the quarantine they would stay in the house for a while. It had been so long since she'd been with people, except Faith's occasional distanced visits and walks. And Brian. They mostly Skyped. But their walks had been special. Lately he seemed depressed, but then, everyone was.

The next morning she moved her car and sat in the back seat with a drawing pad and pencils. Almost precisely at eleven a van with the logo pulled up and someone got out. The hazmat suit made it impossible to tell whether it was a man or a woman. The technician raised a hand in a wave and went in the door that, as instructed, she had left unlocked, the alarm off. She felt a slight wave of panic watching this creature, something from a *Ghostbusters* or nuclear attack movie, amble into the house. *What times we are living in,* she thought, *when the surreal is real.*

She started making notes on the pad, illustrating them. Aleford had a Town Meeting every spring, but also something called the State of the Town at the end of January. Similar to the president's State of the Union address, it was a presentation of what had been accomplished the prior year, what needed work, and future projections. Claudia's remote classes had received extremely positive feedback from parents and administrators. Part of the evening would be devoted to how students had fared under this difficult kind of instruction. The superintendent asked Claudia to explain what she had done and the reasoning behind it. She'd looked at the agenda, which was already posted on the town website, and saw she wouldn't have much time. She'd wanted to show an animated short her middle schoolers had made, but there would have to be a link instead. She continued to make notes and a list of the artwork she could show. It was all going to be a Zoom—a huge audience.

Claudia hated Zoom.

Chapter Five

"I've finished the next four box instructions," Claudia said. "I had some free time. I'll leave them at my front door for you—and the new Madeleine Wickham I just finished for you, my fellow Anglophile! Or Ben can pick them up tonight when he drops my box off. I think knowing what's in them ahead of time makes them even more delicious."

"Ben is out of commission for a while, but I can do it," Faith said. "It's a bit icy for a walk, but we can bundle up and chat in the gazebo by the pond unless your free time is gone." The Sinclairs had expanded the original gazebo into a screened-in summer house. The furniture was put away for the winter, but the built-in benches made for a good meeting place in the Time of Covid—a phrase that was on everyone's lips.

It was on Claudia's now. "Oh, Faith, he doesn't have the virus, does he? You sound okay, so it's something else?"

"It's something else, but related," Faith said, and told her the tale of true love run slightly amok.

"I can't match that, although I did have someone suited up in Covid protective gear arrive. The alarm company had to replace the battery this morning, and my free time was spent in the car. It was replaced quickly, but I had to wait an hour for the smell to disappear of whatever was used to clean afterward. To be sure, I gave it an extra thirty minutes. Finished working on my wretched Zoom presentation and then had fun doing some Have Faith Delivereds."

"I've been saving them all and want to frame them. There are so many now maybe we could have a raffle for the Boston Food Bank or something else. They are truly works of art, and I'm excited about doing the cookbook. Amy wants you to animate some of it for a YouTube. She also thinks the two of us could live stream walking people through some preparations I do for the food they then heat up with the drawings as a background."

"You have very creative children, Ms. Fairchild. They definitely think outside the box," Claudia quipped. "I'm sorry you have the bother of picking the sheets up each week, but my scanner/printer would never do as nice a job as the one you have."

"That's Ben's doing, and I don't even want to know how he got such a good deal on the new one. I'm afraid it's the cyber equivalent of falling off a truck."

The word "truck" reminded Claudia of the alarm company van. "It was eerie watching the technician. I couldn't tell anything about who was underneath. It looked like a creature from a very scary science-fiction film. I've seen health care workers on the news in the same kind of garb, but this was real. A creature walking in and fortunately out of the house. What would the chauffeurs of yesteryear have thought? Not the kind of livery they wore."

Although Claudia was making light of the experience, Faith thought she must have been shaken by it. The carriage house was well off the beaten path, and despite the upsetting sight, Faith was glad the company had made sure the alarm was in working order. "Why don't I come by and deliver your dinner? Amy and I are splitting the route. I'll save yours until the end, around four, and we can at least have a quick visit outside."

"Perfect. See you then."

Faith Fairchild wasn't Claudia's idea of a minister's wife, not that she had known many. Her childhood had been spent in Greenwich, and going to church on Sunday was something people like her family did, just as the girls went to Greenwich Academy and then transferred to Miss Porter's, her mother's alma mater, too, starting in ninth grade, coming home on weekends. The rector's wife looked like Claudia's mother and her mother's friends. Pastel suits with their pearls in spring and summer; shades of brown or navy the rest of the year, Hermès scarves, and heels, but not stilettos. Handbags matched their shoes. They all smelled like Arpège.

Besides the Greenwich house, the family owned a townhouse on Manhattan's East Side. It was where Claudia's mother had grown up, and Claudia often took the train to spend time with her grandparents there, especially with her grandmother after her grandfather died. Claudia had her own room and liked hearing the sounds of the city, so different from the Greenwich estate. Their church in New York was Saint Thomas on Fifth Avenue, and she wasn't sure who the reverend's wife was. The Saint Thomas women blended together, too, although in winter their fur coats were richer looking than their Greenwich counterparts' outerwear.

Claudia's grandmother had been baptized, confirmed, and married there, as had her only child, Claudia's mother. Claudia, too, had been baptized and confirmed beneath the High Gothic vaulting surrounded by stained glass that rivaled Rheims.

Her grandmother's funeral had been at Saint Thomas. And so had Claudia's mother's, the two so close to each other, the flowers needn't have been changed. But of course they were. Claudia was fifteen. By then she could hardly remember her mother as the active, energetic woman who won mixed doubles at the club each year, gave elegant dinner parties in both homes for her husband's law partners and other contacts, and hosted the legendary Greenwich Jingle Party, the most fun gathering of the season, inviting a few artists and musicians to, as she put it, "jazz up the mix." Claudia would be allowed to stay up for the beginning in a red velvet dress from Jacadi, Mary Janes, and white socks with a lace frill. Her long, thick hair was held back with a green velvet-covered headband. The outfit never varied, just the length of the dresses and the store, and the socks were replaced by tights.

She couldn't remember a time when she hadn't drawn pictures, and while she wasn't overly praised—it could go to her head—she felt encouraged. When asked what she wanted to be when she grew up, she said, "An artist." Her mother quickly corrected her. "Nice, dear, but you'll be a wife and mother first. Always remember. That's what a woman should be." Her grandmother used to whisper, "You can be all three," and that was their private joke.

She was allowed to use an empty servant's room for her "studio," as she called it, "her mess," her mother and the housekeeper said. There wasn't as much time as she wanted to draw and eventually paint, what with tennis lessons, dancing school—not ballet, but proper dancing and etiquette—golf and sailing at the club, besides school activities. She didn't mind being at an all-girls school. She felt shy with the boys at the club dances and other events. She was so much taller than most of them until her late teens, and even then she always wore flats.

Her father generally stayed in the city, coming home to Greenwich on weekends. She grew up in a world of women. His interactions with her consisted of questions about whatever sport was in season—her golf, tennis, or sailing, and once in a while school. When he was there, her parents had a life apart from hers, as she assumed most children did. It started with cocktails, the two of them or a gathering, which she knew not to interrupt, before going out to the club or dinner parties. Her mother went into the city on opera nights—they had season tickets. There were also benefits to attend; her father was on the board of a number of charitable institutions. Claudia had proudly shown him some of her drawings when she was younger, but he'd told her to concentrate on her other skills, "not scribbles." When her mother's cancer was diagnosed and the side effects from the treatments meant she spent most of the time in bed, her father started to come home weeknights more. Soon there were private-duty nurses, and Claudia's time with her mother was always cut short. "Don't tire her, dear." She was at Miss Porter's by then, and the weekends never came soon enough. Her mother was fading away before her eyes, as was her grandmother in her own bedroom in the city, unable to communicate after a stroke, which was followed by a major one that took her instantly when she was told of her daughter's death.

Friends of both women told Claudia they would be there for her, invited her to concerts or the theater, and then that faded away, too. She had friends at school, but death is frightening for teenagers, who believe it will never happen to them, and the girls, even her roommate Suzie "with a Z" told her she needed to get over it. That her mother wouldn't have wanted her to "mope." It was her art teacher who provided the comfort and understanding Claudia desperately needed, offering her extra time in the well-equipped studio and often appearing with a thermos of cocoa and cookies. She encouraged her to work on a portfolio and apply to art school or one with a strong art department. Slowly Claudia began to heal. Even when her father flatly refused to consider an art school and told her he'd decide on what college she would attend, she was determined to pursue the career she'd always wanted. He just didn't need to know. She was seeing him more the summer between her junior and senior years. The townhouse was undergoing a major renovation, and he was living in the Greenwich house, which he had planned to put on the market as soon as the work was completed on the Manhattan one. She became his tennis and golf partner on occasion, and he took her to several club dinners. He asked one of her mother's friends, Bitsy Hamilton, to take her shopping for appropriate clothes and to get her hair styled. People would stop by their table and say what a beautiful daughter he had. She knew it was important to him, a handsome man himself.

That was the summer she met Bitsy's son, Charles, and she was flattered by the attention of an "older" man. He was going into his second year at Yale.

Her father's choice was the University of Connecticut, and that was fine with Claudia once she saw the programs in art and art history. Her art teacher had agreed that it was a good choice and took her to see the facilities. Claudia did not mention her major to her father, and he didn't ask. Storrs wasn't that far from Yale in New Haven, and she continued to see Charles from time to time there and in Greenwich. His father had died when Charles was thirteen, and he understood what she was going through. He also told her her artistic work was "gifted," although she teased him that he said this as an excuse to go up to her studio at home in Greenwich, where she had a large futon, which they made use of as the relationship developed. They were a good-looking couple. He was a few inches taller, blond, and his athletic activities had produced a body straight from a J.Crew ad. Claudia was slim, her high cheekbones and thick, dark, wavy hair made for a striking contrast when the two were together. She wasn't interested in fashion, preferring practical jeans and tee shirts unless she was seeing her father—or Charles—who both preferred her to "look like a girl." She treated it as a joke and humored them.

Waiting for Faith this afternoon, she was wearing a denim jumper over a bright turquoise turtleneck and striped tights, a style copied from her landlady, Patricia, as was the bright color. She noticed there was a large smudge of black ink on her sleeve. It would be covered by her coat, and anyway, Faith wouldn't care.

Early on in their friendship, Faith had asked her about her family, and Claudia had answered, "I don't have one. My mother died when I was fifteen. My father and I aren't close. No sibs." Since then, she had been tempted to tell her what had happened. Why she was in Aleford. The thought continued to occur to her over the years, and it entered her mind now. How would she feel? Better or worse? If she ever did tell anyone, it would be Faith . . .

As Claudia Richards, about to become Claudia Hamilton, slipped out of the limo parked at a side entrance to the church and looked up at the bright cloudless June sky, for a moment she cherished being alone with her happiness. Her father had gone up the imposing front stairs into the Gothic church, and she'd meet him in a room at the top before the walk down the aisle.

She had never imagined getting married would be so much work and take so much time. When Charles proposed the Christmas Eve the year before, it had felt right and she'd accepted immediately. He had quaintly already asked for her hand from her father. Both he and Charles's mother were delighted with the match. Claudia did *want to get married at Saint Thomas's, but not until after her graduation the following year. She wanted to continue the tradition, picturing an intimate ceremony with their closest family and friends. That idea was greeted with indulgent smiles. Now, opening the outside door to step into the area below the sanctuary, she could almost feel the pressure of the pews overhead filled with more than four hundred guests, and that when she went down the front steps in a shower of rose petals, the sidewalk would be crammed with onlookers. The wedding of the year, a return to the good old Gilded Age days when Consuelo Vanderbilt was the bride. Charles wasn't a duke, or British, but he did favor Savile Row for his clothes, including the morning suit he was wearing today.*

His mother's wedding present had been the house in Greenwich, "much too big for someone called Bitsy for a reason," she'd joked. She had already moved into a nearby condo that was actually quite large. Charles could commute to law school at the City University of New York, and Claudia would, well, she supposed, be a wife, artist, and someday a mother.

But those four hundred plus guests! All turned her way. The day that lay ahead felt as long as the aisle had during the rehearsal.

Endless tasks had filled her last year of college. Showers, not just one, lunches, teas—all so she could meet the right people who would be her friends, women friends. Ones with whom she would shop, go to an occasional concert or show at a museum. Some in the city, some in

Connecticut. Then there were the meetings with the wedding planner that took up so much time, she began to miss classes, until she eventually turned it all over to Bitsy. Claudia was more than happy to leave the choice of table linens—shell pink or old rose—up to her. Bitsy cared about things like this. And Charles had definite opinions as well, particularly about food and drink. As for the dress, that had been the most difficult of all. It had to be Vera Wang and custom. After numerous consultations, Claudia was surprised to get her own way. A dress that fit her willowy frame and height, a heavy pure-white satin with long sleeves ending in points that emphasized her elegant hands, which she had struggled to keep pristine in these last weeks as she finished her studio work at UConn. There had been no argument about the veil. It had been her great-grandmother's and worn by her daughter, granddaughter, and now great-granddaughter—Alençon lace from France. The tiara that held it in place on Claudia's elaborate hairdo had been made for the first bride by Tiffany. The precious fabric billowed softly behind her as Claudia stepped into the building. She caught it to keep it from catching in the door and headed for the stairs. The Big Day was starting.

She was stopped by the sound of voices from the restroom on one side. She knew those voices. The door was open, and she walked toward it with a smile. But the first sentence she heard froze her in place, and she backed against the wall.

"Hurry up, Suze, we don't have much time." It was Charles and Suzie, her maid of honor, former roommate.

"Oh, Chipster, always in a hurry. No one's going to think you're not going to show up for a deal like this. Now, is this good, or how about this? I know what you like . . ."

Claudia heard him moan, "Faster, faster. Oh God!"

"And what's Miss Prim like?"

Charles let out a deep breath. "Nothing like you, honeybun, I've told you. Think fish, a very cold fish."

"But what about those scales? Those golden scales."

He snorted. "That's what I do think about. Close my eyes and picture scales weighted with gold bars."

Claudia's entire body filled with such an intense anger, it felt as if she would explode out of the dress. She shot through the open door, screaming, "You shit, Charles! Both of you! I hope you'll be very happy together. Just cross my name off the license, and you're good to go." She wrenched the $464,000 Cartier engagement ring from her finger and threw it at them. Charles's striped trousers and underwear were puddled around his ankles. Suzie was kneeling, wiping her mouth with what Claudia recognized as one of the lacy handkerchiefs she had given all her attendants.

"Now, sweetie, this isn't what it looks like," Charles said, struggling to stand up while reaching down to pull up his clothes.

"It isn't? Then what exactly is it? Oh, don't bother answering. I'm leaving."

"No!" He blocked her way to the outside door. "You are not *doing this to me. We are getting married today whether you like it or not."*

Claudia had started to laugh and realized it would soon become hysterics. She ran up the stairs, her veil looped over her arm, with Charles close behind. Her father and Bitsy were waiting at the top.

"What is going on? People are beginning to wonder where you are, Charles," his mother said.

Flushed, Claudia faced her father. "The wedding is off. Telling you what I caught them doing downstairs will make me sick."

James Richards looked at Charles, Suzie cowering behind him. "I don't care what they were doing, although I can imagine. This marriage has been arranged, and it's going forward. Now pull yourself together, Claudia, and you, Charles, go around to the altar. Your best man is about to have kittens by the look on his face."

Bitsy reached out and patted Claudia's arm. "I'm sure whatever it was, it was just a last little peccadillo. Now come with me and I'll fix your hair."

Claudia was wide-eyed in disbelief. "No! It wasn't so much what he was doing as saying. Father"—her voice was shaking—"he's marrying me for the money. He doesn't love me. You can't want me to marry a man like him!"

"It's a good match. I gave my approval. Now go with Bitsy quickly. I don't want people starting to think that something may be wrong."

"But something is *wrong. Very wrong!" Claudia started toward the door and the impressive outside stairs to Fifth Avenue past all those surely disapproving statues of saints.*

Bitsy blocked her way. She echoed her son. "You are not *doing this. You're behaving like a child!" The look she gave Claudia was one of pure hatred.*

Claudia appealed once more to her father. "You can't want this for your daughter!" His look was more controlled than Bitsy's but filled with cold dislike. "You will cease to be a daughter of mine unless you walk up to that altar and say your vows. I will not allow you to disgrace me, shame our families."

Charles suddenly found his voice. "Nor will I. I told you it was nothing. I'm going to get in place. Your father is right. You will not humiliate us in front of everyone."

Although stunned, Claudia found her voice, too. No longer shaking.

"Oh yes I will."

She darted past Bitsy, who tried to grab the veil, ran down the steep entrance stairs, unaware of the shots taken and videos made that would soon go viral, into a cab in front that a late guest had just left, pulling the door shut.

"Changed your mind?" the cabbie said.

"Absolutely," she answered, and gave the townhouse address, adding, "Please step on it."

Years ago, she had hidden a key in one of the topiary urns that stood on either side of the townhouse's front door in case she forgot hers and was coming home late. She got out. "I'm sorry. I don't have any money, but I'll be right back," she told the cabdriver.

"No problem, miss. The meter's running."

The key was there and she raced up to her room, back in seconds with the fare and a big tip. "Good luck," he said, and pulled away.

In her bedroom, still with the Laura Ashley décor she had selected with her mother when she was in sixth grade and had never wanted to change, Claudia dumped the trousseau contents of the suitcase packed for the Paris honeymoon onto the floor and filled it with what she normally wore and her toiletries kit. As she packed, she took off her dress and veil, leaving them on the bed. In her bathroom, she scrubbed her face and undid her hair, raking a brush through what had been an elaborate chignon and gathering her curls into a messy bun. She grabbed her leather messenger bag and filled it with her laptop, phone, and a file she kept in her desk with her birth certificate, diploma, and a photo of her mother and grandmother. Her mother was holding baby Claudia on her lap. Her passport, credit cards, and wallet with some cash in it were in her purse. "Hurry, hurry," she said aloud. She emptied the purse into a smaller one and put it into the bag. She left the pearls Charles had given her as a wedding gift—after many hints, she'd given him the Rolex Cosmograph Daytona she knew he wanted—and replaced diamond earrings from her father with simple gold hoops. Most of her jewelry, inherited from her grandmother and mother, was in the bank, and it would stay there. After changing into light-wash jeans, a navy tee, a long oatmeal cotton cardigan, Keds, and a New York Yankees baseball cap, she stopped and glanced around the room. She knew she'd never be back. The last item she took was her honors portfolio in its large zippered black case.

She left the key on the bed next to her wedding finery. At the last moment, she took her veil, stitched to the tiara, and put it in the suitcase. She needed to have those women with her always.

Out on the street she was relieved to see that no one had caught up with her. Or probably no one was chasing after the persona non grata of the moment. It would be lowering themselves to her level. And who would it have been in any case? Definitely not her father. Instead, she pictured Bitsy and the wedding planner leading everyone across the street to the Saint Regis for the reception. "The bride is indisposed." Had they said something like that?

Her bank had a branch on Madison that was open on Saturdays, and it was the one she used most frequently. First stop. Greeted cordially, she filled out a slip for a cashier's check for fifty thousand dollars and another for a thousand dollars in cash. Once she'd turned twenty-one, she had complete access to both her grandmother's and mother's bequests. Prior to that she'd had to go through the trustee, their lawyer. It was quickly done with a smile. If the tellers were surprised to see her there instead of at her well-publicized wedding, they were too discreet to comment.

This was the last withdrawal she'd make. As soon as she got wherever she was going, she would have to find a job.

Had Charles been waiting until she was of age to pop the question? She was sure of it now.

From Madison, she headed across Park to Lexington and walked downtown. Lexington was not a street her family or Charles frequented. Next stop. She went into the first place advertising all-day breakfast, spreading out in a booth. She was ravenous. A short stack, two eggs over easy, bacon, hash browns, toast, and coffee.

"Visiting?" the waitress asked.

"No, passing through," Claudia said, and asked for more maple syrup.

Mopping the plate with the last of the toast, she thought of her father's words. Had she ever been his daughter? And there had been that word. "Arranged." It had all been arranged. By him? His to-do list? Marry off daughter? And Charles. He'd arranged it, too. His mother's face had been filled with hatred; Charles's had more than a touch of desperation. Claudia had planned to go to his Yale graduation, but he'd said it would be a madhouse. Did he graduate? He never seemed to do much work, mostly telling her about the good times he was having with his buddies. He'd gotten drunk at the club dances a few times and apologized for his behavior with flowers the next day. And what about those summer internships? He told her her father had arranged—that word again—prestigious ones, but were they? And he wasn't at Yale Law as his father had been and Claudia had assumed he'd be. Was everything she'd been told a web of lies?

She'd disabled the GPS tracking on her phone and, ignoring the texts from almost everyone on the planet, sat nursing a last cup of coffee while she transferred the contacts she wanted to save to a notebook she kept in her bag. There weren't many. She removed the SIM card and left the phone on the floor.

Afterward, she dropped the card into a storm drain, walked down to Penn Station in the still-beautiful June day, and looked at the departures. Last stop. The next train she could easily catch was going to Boston.

So, Boston it was.

Faith was running late and only had time to pick up the illustrated instructions with a promise to come back for a walk soon. "I need a real walk. At the moment it feels like I'm on a perpetual treadmill and no matter how fast I go, I don't get anywhere."

"I wish I could help you, but I'd be hopeless in the kitchen, and anyway, it wouldn't be safe to have me there. Brian told me he'd heard teachers and day care workers are going to be in phase two for vaccinations, which could be early March. I could at least help you deliver food then."

"You're taking an enormous load off my shoulders with the artwork. Everyone loves them, and more to the point, they need them to prepare the food. Now go do your own work. I want to see the new stuff next time."

"Think tangled webs. Very tangled."

"Good. Spiders bring good luck. I don't know why people are afraid of them, except those brown recluse ones and tarantulas. Regular spiders dangling from a web are a sign of money and joy. Ben did a project on them in fifth grade, so ask me anything."

"I've read everything I can find, books and online. You're right, they are lucky. I was intrigued by the artistry of the webs, but the more I learned, the more fascinated I became with the creators. *Charlotte's Web* was my favorite book growing up. Maybe still is."

"'It is not often that someone comes along who is a true friend and a good writer.' Change 'writer' to 'artist,' and that's us," Faith said. "Consider the line a virtual hug from me, and E. B. White, too."

After Faith drove off, Claudia poured herself a large vodka tonic and leaned back in her chair staring at the wall of webs and spiders. White's Charlotte *was* an artist, the web she wove to save Wilbur the pig a masterpiece. The glass was soon empty, and before she opened the dinner box, she poured another. It always helped.

When Faith saw her sister-in-law Betsey's name, she answered the phone immediately.

"Everything's okay, don't worry. I mean of course things are not okay, but Mom and Dad are fine."

The new normal meant starting a phone call this way and ending it with "Stay safe."

Both Marian and Dick Fairchild, Tom's parents, were over seventy-five, and Dick was diabetic. They had been living with Betsey for many months of the pandemic.

"Good to hear," Faith said. "Everyone else? The boys and Dennis?"

"Yes, yes. But I'm going out of my mind. Mom and Dad clearly qualify for vaccination in phase one—Dad's preexisting condition and age. But there are no appointments anywhere, and I've been calling locations all over the state. We've all been very careful, but you know as well as I do how contagious it is, and all it takes is a droplet and they'll get it. Think of your aunt Chat."

Faith couldn't go there. It was much too painful and just like Betsey to bring it up, but she was right. Chat, short for Charity—generations of Sibley women were named Faith, Hope, and Charity. Faith's mother had decided to stop at Hope. Charity was Faith's father's youngest sister and had had a legendary public relations firm in New York City, retiring much to her friends' surprise to Mendham, New Jersey—Jersey a more foreign country for them than any on the globe—to raise miniature horses and dogs. It was one of the dogs that knocked her over, breaking her hip, in February 2020. She went into an excellent assisted living complex to recover, and the virus tore through it despite all the precautions. She died that April. Alone, listening to their voices on the phone the nurse held up for her as she slipped away.

Pausing to swallow hard, Faith said, "I don't know what advice I can give you. Tom, as you know, was able to get his shot as a VA chaplain. When he gets the next, he'll be able to safely visit."

"They don't need a visit; they need the shots!"

This was raw anguish, and as tried as Faith often was by her sister-in-law, her pain hit hard. And Faith was worried about her parents-in-law, too. Her sister had already gotten their parents a first shot of course. Things were easier in New York State. What Betsey was saying was what Dr. Kane and every other PCP Faith had heard about was saying. They didn't have the vaccines.

"Are there waiting lists? Can you put their names on several?" Faith asked.

"No. And everything is automated. I keep getting these stupid messages, even from the state. I filled out their online forms for them and got a message on the phone that when a slot was open, they would be informed."

Automated. The word filled Faith's mind.

Ben was in quarantine still. So was Zach. They needed a project.

"Bets, I just had an idea. If anyone can break through those automated systems to schedule appointments—legally, I mean—Ben can, Zach, too. I'm going to hang up and call both of them now."

"You think there's a possibility?"

"If they can't, no one can," Faith said with a confidence she hoped was real.

She started to text the two of them—she wasn't sure she'd ever heard Zach's voice on the phone—when hers rang again. It was Ellie Porter. She could wait. Each call proposed a new, more outrageous plan. The last involved having the baby and pretending it was a friend's until after the wedding. Her hefty appearance would be explained to her parents as stress eating.

Faith's lengthy text brought immediate results from both Zach and Ben. Faith had heard from Pix that Samantha spent most of the time either napping or reading *What to Expect When You're Expecting* and other pregnancy and parenting books, even how to raise a happy teen, which was an oxymoron if Faith ever heard one. So, Zach was all for the project, mentioning that both Ursula and Millicent needed appointments.

Twenty minutes later the two of them called, much to her surprise, and filled her in.

"Easy peasy. What you have to do is sign up as soon as the appointments are released. It's different days, not just for the two chains but all the individual stores. The one constant is that they get posted around two A.M. We hop on at the dot, not too soon or we'll get locked out, and keep refreshing our screens. Each of us should be able to cover at least a dozen locations. Looking just now, those nearest to us fill up right away. No matter how fast we might be or how long we keep at it. So we're thinking of starting in the middle of the state and along the border with New Hampshire, lower population densities. Once we get them for Grandma, Grandpa, Ursula, Millicent, and Dora, too, we're going to offer it as one of the options from Ben and Amy's Delivery Service. As more people become eligible, it's going to get harder and harder."

Zach added, "Aside from protecting our family, the only way to get on top of the virus, especially with the variant they're talking about, is to get as many people vaccinated as possible. Of course, we won't charge and the shots are free, but people could donate to the Red Cross or other health care organizations."

"I'll call Betsey and Dora now. Fingers crossed."

"Oh, ye of little faith," joked Zach. "Ben is a star, and as you know, I'm not half bad."

Faith had depended twice on Zach's skill, once years ago and more recently, to dive into what was a darker side of the web and help solve two murders.

"Very cute. Now you two get to work!"

She made her calls, and as she was leaving the kitchen to tell Amy the latest, the landline rang. There were very few people who called on it, and the ring always startled her. She had a feeling who it might be, and she hadn't talked to her in a while. Caller

ID was a boon, but she had been feeling a little guilty at avoiding Persis. Persis Wald, half of Aleford's most notable power couple. One would think that the mover and shaker would be younger, one of the vocal parent community, one or both names in famous IT start-ups past and present, or Ganley Museum trustees. Persis and Henry Wald were fixtures, like Millicent Revere McKinley. Henry, a retired lawyer, had been the moderator at Town Meeting for more than thirty years, a position of enormous power that he wielded with great fairness and dignity, rarely cutting off discussion even as shadows lengthened. He had either served or was serving on every town board. Aleford was run by volunteers and proud of it. A Personnel Advisory Board hired the police chief, the school superintendent, the library director, and other positions. The Walds were the town's institutional memory, and Henry had saved Aleford from countless lawsuits from developers by recalling and citing zoning articles passed. He was at ease taking on the state. Persis kept sheep and trained sheepdogs, traveling during the summer months to sheepdog trials at agricultural fairs all over New England. Faith had seen her compete, and win, at the Blue Hill Fair. The way Persis kept the sheep and dogs in line with a few whistles and words was much the way she kept the town in line. Henry was born and grew up in Aleford; Persis came by way of Chestnut Street on Beacon Hill. She had the Brahmin voice and straight posture to match. Both husband and wife were much beloved by the town.

"Faith, it's Persis, and you know what I'm calling about."

"Yes, I do, and no one could be sorrier than I am about having to cancel Henry's eightieth." She would be sure to mention the possibility of vaccination appointments for them both before she hung up.

"I'm not criticizing, dear, but I do think you could be a bit more creative about alternatives. A large tent with heat lamps. Finger sandwiches, cake, and champagne. Very little work for you. I'm making favors."

Persis sheared her sheep, spun the wool, and dyed it with natural plants. The results were much sought-after by knitters as well as weavers. The favors would undoubtedly be wooly. Faith took a breath.

"It will be lovely when we can legally have a gathering of that size. Even under a tent—and think of the time of year, we could have twelve inches of snow—the number of people you want to invite, almost the whole town, would violate the law. Henry would not be very happy about that. I know you want it to be a surprise, but would want a good one."

"You put on that excellent thinking cap of yours and have another think. By the end of February—as you know, his birthday is the twenty-seventh—I'm sure all this Covid will be gone."

Despite her occupation, Persis's own thinking cap was not wooly and just maybe she would be right. One of the most disquieting things about the pandemic was the ebb and flow.

"I could certainly pull together his party quickly once it's safe."

"You do that. I'll keep working on the favors."

Faith told her about getting appointments through Zach and Ben. She told Faith to sign them up.

"And how is that lovely Samantha doing? I understand the baby is due at the end of the summer."

"How did—" Faith started the sentence, then stopped. This was Persis. Her next call was going to be to Pix anyway, about the vaccine appointments, although she probably knew, and she'd better tell her the cat, or ewe, was out of the bag before Ursula heard, upset at not having been told first.

Claudia was nervous. She wished she had told the superintendent no, but at the time she'd looked forward to showing what her students had done during such a difficult time. She reminded herself that most of her presentation would be screen sharing their art while she spoke about her goals—getting the kids outdoors as much as possible, observing their own backyards in effect, and when indoors, learning what could be done with limited materials, the paper structures particularly. She'd post the link to the animated short the older students had made using Legos. Above all, she planned to stress that she wanted her students to have fun, feel connected even though remote, and for a while push other thoughts away.

Henry Wald was moderating the State of the Town and was moving through the agenda, starting promptly at nine Saturday morning the thirtieth with "You will all be happy to hear that despite a time that has tested us to the core, a time no one could have predicted, the state of the town is strong, Aleford Strong. We will now hear the particulars and what we must aim to do going forward."

Claudia had worn what she thought of as a grown-up outfit: white silk turtleneck under a black Eileen Fisher bias-cut cardigan, with a simple silver necklace and matching earrings she'd bought at the Ganley Museum gift shop.

At last she was next, and Henry's generous praise for her efforts banished her nervousness. She started by saying that her work was only possible because of the support of other teachers, particularly Brian Kimball, her high school equivalent; the school administration and other staff; parents; and most of all her wonderful students.

"A shout-out to all, and everyone feel free to clap from wherever you are watching." She did so herself.

The clap turned into an ear-splitting roar, and Claudia looked very puzzled at the sound.

The end of Ben's quarantine and Tom's second shot had been on Thursday, so all four Fairchilds were at the church watching on the big screen, which Faith had to admit was fun, compared with the size of the set at the parsonage.

"What's that noise? Feedback from her mic? Or Henry's?" Tom asked.

The roar became shouted words—despicable words—and then Claudia disappeared from the screen, replaced by rows of photos. Shocking ones of nudes in poses ranging from mildly titillating to filthy pornography. The shouts amped up to unprintable slurs, and one voice louder than the rest kept repeating the singsong refrain from "The Lady Is a Tramp."

Ben immediately jumped up and was yelling at the screen. "It's a Zoom bombing! Shut the meeting down, Mr. Wald!! It's not rocket science. Shut it!"

What was only several minutes seemed like an hour before the screen went black and all the voices were muted, but it had been long enough for everyone watching to identify the face on every figure. There was no doubt.

It was Claudia Richards.

Chapter Six

Everyone started talking at once. "What idiot set this up?" Ben was apoplectic. "Screen sharing should have been turned off except for Ms. Richards and the host. And everyone should have been muted from the start. Plus no one admitted from the waiting room!"

Faith had no idea what most of what he said meant and would ask him sometime, but at the moment she was frantically trying to call Claudia on her cell and the landline, getting, as she expected, a constant busy signal. "Damn!" she said. "The whole town must be calling."

Amy had covered her eyes, and now she uncovered them. "That was Ms. Richards? Are we sure?"

Tom was heading for the door, saying, "I'm going over there. Thank God I got my second shot. She shouldn't be alone, not just given how she must feel, but because whoever did this has targeted her. She's not safe. Faith, call Chief Franklin. Since he's new to town, he may not know how isolated the house is. Zach and Samantha aren't staying there any longer, right?"

Faith nodded. "I'll call right away."

Chief Mooney had retired just as the pandemic was ramping up, and Faith hadn't developed the close ties with Chief Franklin that she'd had with former chiefs. She did know the longtime dispatcher, though, and was put through right away.

"Ms. Richards rents the carriage house from Patricia and Edward Sinclair, who live in the main house but have been gone since last March. Both dwellings are at the end of a long drive, and whoever planned what happened today obviously wished to harm her virtually but may want to harm her physically as well. Tom is on his way there now."

"I've sent a patrol car, and they'll stay there for the rest of the day and tonight if she wishes. We're taking this Zoom bombing very seriously, Mrs. Fairchild. There haven't been any incidents in Aleford, but there's been a huge increase in them elsewhere. Open public meetings like today's are popular targets."

"But why would the person, or it could be more than one, a group getting their kicks this way, choose Claudia?"

"I'm sure it was random, as these usually are. It looks like her photo from the school website was photoshopped. When the media gets wind of it, we will only confirm that a Zoom bombing incident disrupted the meeting and that it will be rescheduled. We will not provide any other details. If you can reach your husband, will you ask him to assure Ms. Richards of this? Her name will not get out."

Faith said she would, thanked him, and hung up. She liked him, and he'd been doing an excellent job under Covid-19 conditions, especially as his small staff kept testing positive and the department was under extreme stress. But if he believed Claudia's name would not get out, Faith had a bridge in Brooklyn he might want to buy.

Tom texted, "C. distraught. Will be staying awhile. Trying to get her to eat instead of drink. What did Chief Pat say?" As a member of Aleford's standing clergy, a term that caused Faith to picture the group as a collective like an "exultation of larks" or a "murder of crows," Tom had had close contact with the new chief—especially since the start of the pandemic—to the point where he called him Chief Pat. She texted back.

"Chief P. has sent patrol car. Will stay as long as C. wishes. Switch the glass for a mug. Favorite Yorkshire tea bags and Lorna Doone cookies are there. Put plenty of sugar in the tea."

There was nothing more she could think of to do, so she called Pix, who was incensed, and they agreed to meet at the hedge opening later in the afternoon. "Zach watched with us, but fortunately Samantha was napping. Her hormones definitely kicked in while they were in quarantine. She weeps at anything remotely upsetting."

Ben had planned the dinner-box deliveries for later this afternoon after the meeting. They were ready, but she could go to the Have Faith kitchen and help him load the van. He'd streaked home, leaping over the stones in the burial ground that separated the parsonage from the church, and now she could hear him upstairs tapping away at his computer. Amy was at hers as well, and Faith decided to go ask her what was showing up on social media. She was sure Amy was checking out posts. What Ben was doing was something she was sure she would have no way of understanding, but before she went into her daughter's room, she knocked at her son's door.

"Hi, Mom. I know I have to start delivering soon, but Zach and I are trying to trace the troll or trolls that did this to Claudia. I got a screenshot, but Zach got a better one. We're pretty sure that this is going to be a low priority for the police, if it's even on their radar now, with Covid hitting the department hard, and even without that they don't have anyone with the skill set needed." Ben was crowing a bit, but Faith knew he was right. It's not that Aleford's finest were still using spiral notepads and pencils, but there was not much IT above that. "Mom, what's weird is that the really gross ones have obviously been photoshopped—not hard to tell—but a lot of them haven't been. They *are* of Ms. Richards. She looks a little younger and her hair is long, but they're real, Zach says. I mean maybe she was like a Playmate, you know, in *Playboy,* and these were outtakes? She had the bod."

This reminded Faith of what Pix did when years ago she found a centerfold in her oldest son Mark's underwear drawer when she was putting away laundry. (Every mother's excuse.) She hung it on the wall next to his dresser, and when he came home from school and saw it, she told him that a woman's body was beautiful and he shouldn't be ashamed of admiring one. Mortified in case one of his friends saw what his "insane" mother had done, he removed it and found better hiding places—he admitted as an adult much later.

Faith would be surprised if Ben hadn't known that there was another meaning for "playmate" as in "friend." Images like this and much worse bombarded kids from an early age. Still, she would be surprised, and very upset, if he was familiar with the other poses that had been on the screen.

"I don't think that's likely. And what do you mean? That they were 'trolls'?"

"Not those dolls Amy had or the ones in fairy tales. People who get off by interrupting stuff online. At the least harmful, they just post stupid jokes off topic in forums or chats. At most, what you saw today."

Faith picked up some dirty laundry that had inexplicably not made it into his laundry basket and left. She dumped the clothes down the laundry chute into the basement, which a very tired former minister's wife must have demanded be installed in the linen closet, and tapped on Amy's door.

"Come look at this, Mom. Sometime Ms. Richards should see what people are saying. All my Facebook friends, especially those who had her as a teacher, are furious. Zoom bombing like this is illegal, by the way. I hope Zach and Ben find out who did it and they go to prison. The problem, Ben told me, is that you could do it from anywhere. I mean the person or persons responsible—

according to what Zach saw on the FBI website—could be in another state or country."

Or right here in Aleford, Faith thought.

"Are the posts mentioning her name? We really hope it doesn't become public."

Amy shook her head. "No way it wouldn't have, and that was the point. Disrupt the meeting but use her in particular. That's what the guys are investigating. Did she piss some student or a parent off with a low grade? The bombing didn't take much skill. 'Amateur,' Ben says. Most of the posts are just saying 'Ms. R,' but some are using her whole name and demanding the police investigate."

"Let's hope the *Globe* and the *Herald* don't print it."

"Zach thinks that everyone is so worried about the pandemic and getting vaccinated plus the wicked big storm coming that there won't be much, if anything, in the papers."

"I hope he's right."

"He usually is." Zach was a favorite with Amy.

"I'm going to go over to the kitchen and help Ben load the van. You hold down the fort here."

"No worries."

If only.

The landline rang as Faith was leaving. She was tempted to ignore it and let the machine pick up, but too much was going on. She was glad she did when she saw it was the Walds' number.

"Henry is devastated! He thinks it was all his fault! You have to ask Tom to call and talk some sense into him. He keeps saying that he should have done something sooner and not allowed this, I don't know what it's called, bomb the Zoom? But, Faith, anyone would have reacted the same way. Aghast. We all were, as was he. Just froze looking at the screen. He snapped out of it faster than I did. I couldn't even move for a while until he started trying to call Ms. Richards and then the superintendent."

"Tom isn't here now." Faith didn't think it was necessary to broadcast anything at the moment. Tom's was a private visit, and Persis was like an old party line. "I'll have him get in touch, but I can't imagine anyone is blaming Henry." She crossed her fingers, thinking of Ben's immediate reaction. "He couldn't have predicted that this would happen."

"That's what the superintendent said, but she hasn't been reading the *Aleford Crier.*"

Faith hadn't thought to ask Amy to check the local online media site, especially the comment section, and would do so right away.

"What are people saying?"

"Most are outraged at the disruption of our time-honored State of the Town Meeting and express sympathy for the poor teacher. But others are saying the moderator—they don't call him by his name!—should have learned how to cope with the possibility of something like this. It happened twice last year in Sudbury during open meetings. If it did, and I'm skeptical, no one mentioned it to Henry or me. And as to training how to use this horrid Zoom thing, Henry had been trained very well before last year's virtual Town Meeting by the Town Hall's IT person. He never mentioned anything about Zoom bombing. That's what it's called. Zoom bombing. Whoever makes these things up? Hooligans! A few bad apples who need to be in school in person to keep them out of trouble. Yes, definitely hooligans."

Ah, Faith thought, *the good old vagrant-passing-by solution.*

"I'm sure this will all die down very soon. My concern is for my friend Claudia." Persis could see to Henry, and in any case, although he was feeling responsible now, "devastated," the town would sooner change its name than its venerated moderator.

"Yes, the poor thing. I'm afraid there were a few comments that were *not* in her favor."

"What!" Faith exclaimed.

"You know the kind. 'Where there's smoke there's fire' and insinuating things about what she might have done in her past."

"I must go now, Persis. You two take a nice long walk to get his mind off all this, or make him your herbal tea and put on a movie." The Walds had not seen any reason to replace VHS for DVDs and now streaming on demand. "*Our Town* is his favorite, right?" Faith wanted to get off the phone, and throwing out ways to nurture the equivalent of her own personal ram would get Persis moving. It did.

"We'll do both. Good-bye, dear."

Faith raced to her laptop, which was on the kitchen table, and quickly saw that Persis was all too correct about the negative comments. You didn't have to post your name in the comment section unless you chose to. Most who were frequent contributors used a pseudonym that became familiar to readers and gave strong hints as to positions and party. The editor kept a list of the real names associated with these and would not post anonymous comments.

There were too many to read, and they kept popping up. True, the vast majority were indignant over the event, did not blame Henry—rather praised him for his swift action—and expressed great compassion for the teacher—only a few named her—as the victim of the assault. There were, however, more than Faith would have expected that hinted there must have been a reason for the use of the photos of Claudia.

Disgusted, she closed the laptop and went off to help Ben with the deliveries.

When the State of the Town screen went black, Brian and Margaret Kimball sat mute. Then Margaret turned toward her husband and said, enunciating each word clearly, "Don't you say a goddamn word."

He didn't.

"I'm going to work." She took the remote from the glass-topped Noguchi table and turned off the TV screen they'd connected to a laptop.

Brian exploded. "Work. Sure. You do that. Go to work. That's what you do, isn't it? All. The. Time."

"Somebody has to if you want all this." She waved her arm around the room, pointing at the end to the soaring windows beneath the tented ceiling. Just before the pandemic they had added a narrow catwalk. Ceramics and other items they had collected were displayed on shelving set into the wall, creating a gallery.

"I'm going for a drive," he said. "I'll be back when I'm back."

"You do that. Hope she's feeling terrible."

Margaret went into her office and watched her husband speed down the driveway in the Tesla she'd given him for his birthday last month—no more Mr. Bean car. Had he been in the room he might not have been able to figure out the look on her face. It was blank. Yet her eyes weren't. Anger—or fear?

After helping Ben load up, Faith took Claudia's dinner over to the carriage house. Tom's Subaru was there, also an Aleford patrol car very evident at the start of the drive. This horrendous day was waning, and it would be dark soon. She hated the way this time of year always made her feel. How did Scandinavians live with it? In pre-pandemic times, all the ones she knew headed for the Canaries.

The shutters that protected the carriage house's large first-floor front windows were closed. Probably in anticipation of the storm expected to arrive late that night. She knocked at the front door, a whimsical knocker shaped like an artist's palette, and texted Claudia, "It's Faith. I'm leaving dinner. Love you very much. Call me when you want. Any hour, day or night." Wishing she was vaccinated and could go in to be with Claudia, comfort her in person, she also texted Tom. Claudia would not be looking at her phone now.

Driving out, she hoped the police would stay put, although if the storm was as bad as predicted, all hands would be needed.

Pix must have been watching for her. As soon as Faith closed the garage door, she saw her friend silhouetted in the opening and went over.

"Oh, Faith, if ever we needed hugs, it's now. Tell me what's going on. Have you spoken with Claudia?"

"Not directly, but Tom has been there all day, and Chief Franklin sent a patrol car that's been there, too, at the driveway entrance."

"That's a relief. Zach has been at the computer since it happened, and he's concerned that attacking her online might translate to a physical attack. Apparently some of the photos *are* of Claudia. Taken a while ago, but not all that long, he thinks. There has to be a rational explanation, but the attack is irrational and worse. He would move back into the big house to keep an eye on her alone in the carriage house, but that would upset Samantha. She might get nervous about something happening."

Pix continued: "We just decided that Sam should call the Sinclairs—I'd be very surprised if they haven't heard about it—and Zoom bombing is against the law, by the way—suggesting that Claudia move out into the main house. The carriage house *does* have an alarm, but it doesn't have a generator. No one was living in the carriage house. Edward used it as his studio, so they didn't bother when they updated the one in the big house. It comes on automatically and powers everything, not like ours where we have to choose fridge or furnace, going back and forth. We're bound to lose power in this storm, and Claudia will be there cold and I'm sure frightened. Oh, I hate that we can't just take her in here with us!"

"Exactly what I've been thinking all day. Getting her to move into the other house is an excellent idea. When you go in, urge Sam to call. They would certainly not object. You know how close they are to her." As she contemplated the approaching storm and the one that was following on its heels, Faith tried to think of arguments to make to the Vestry for them to buy the kind of generator the Sinclairs had. The parsonage's qualified as a collectible.

"I can see from here your lips are turning blue, Faith. Go inside. Even after all these years, you haven't adapted to Aleford winters. I'll let you know what the Sinclairs say."

Besides the winters, there were a bunch of other Aleford, New England, things, to which Faith had not adapted. To start, she had never been able to find a real bagel, and Boston's songs—"Where Everybody Knows Your Name" and "Sweet Caroline"—didn't hold candles to "New York, New York," which still on occasion brought a lump to her throat as it always had those first years in Beantown. And beans! *Don't get me started,* Faith would say. Beans and boiled dinners as a cuisine?

"Pix," she called out to her friend. "Could you ask Zach to get in touch? I thought of a question about all this that I'm sure he can answer. Ben could, too, I'll bet, but he'll be gone a while and it's nagging at me. Like one of those sores in your mouth you keep poking your tongue into to see if it still hurts, knowing of course it will. Something doesn't make sense."

The storm hit at 3:24 A.M. and by sunrise had dumped twelve inches of snow on Aleford, more as it moved north and west. They did lose power. Sunday morning Tom lit a fire in the living room fireplace—a pyromaniac at heart, he loved the task, assembling the kindling and logs with precision. They shut the doors and the room was very cozy. With a gas stove top, Faith heated French onion soup she'd made Friday, ladling it into large bowls on top of baguette slices, topped with plenty of melted Gruyère cheese, browned with her culinary butane torch. Church had been canceled. The reverend would have made his way to the sanctuary in an ecclesiastical version of Neither Sleet nor Snow, but few had power to watch or listen.

Ben finished two bowls of soup and headed upstairs. "Power

bank," he said over his shoulder as he left the room. During storm outages, his power banks were his lifelines.

"Bundle up," Faith called. She knew he and Zach were spending a great deal of time organizing their vaccine appointment service as soon as CVS and Walgreens started administering the shots. The magic number was the eleventh, they'd discovered. February 11. "It's kind of like the search for the Holy Grail or the Maltese falcon," Ben told her. "Once they roll them out, it's going to be crazy." But today she didn't think he was working on shots or even the Zoom bombing. She was almost certain he was Skyping with Catherine. She was still not a topic of conversation, and there were no more emotional outbursts, but every once in a while he'd mention her. "Catherine is deathly allergic to beestings. She carries an EpiPen. Even honey makes her break out in hives. Just the thought. The hive thing is a family joke. She doesn't really. But if she sees a bee, she runs." And then, "Catherine's family wanted to give her a car for high school graduation, but she believes in taking a bus or train instead. Maybe an electric one when there are more charging stations." Faith knew he wouldn't take off again, but she also knew how hard it was for him not to be with her—and she sensed vice versa. Catherine wasn't on Facebook, but Faith had shamelessly googled her and found an article in a local Long Island paper about the girl's effort to organize better recycling in the town and an annual roadside litter cleanup day several times a year. There was a photo, but she was in overalls with her hair tucked under a Yankees cap. That would have to go. Ben lived for the Sox. Not much to see of her, but Amy said she was beautiful.

Courting during the pandemic. Having a baby during the pandemic. Trying to get married *and* have a baby during the pandemic. She had taken so much of her life for granted, Faith realized over and over again—courtship, marriage, having the kids.

Sam had spoken to the Sinclairs, and they had already heard about the Zoom bombing. They were appalled and had been trying to reach Claudia to offer sympathy and support. They'd also heard about the storm and wanted her to move into the other house. But her phone had been busy, and when they tried to leave a message, her mailbox was full. Sam told them Tom was with her, and they called him.

"She didn't see any reason to move," Tom said, repeating some of what he'd said the night before when he'd returned from her house. "She had plenty of flashlights and candles, has been through power outages before, but I convinced her by asking her to do it so I wouldn't worry. She said she'd move over, but just for the storm and then wanted to be in her own 'little nest.'" He looked tired as he put more wood on the fire. "I know it's not five o'clock. Not even noon, but would you like a little cognac?"

"Think of it as medicinal. I'll get it. Amy, do you want some cocoa?" Her phone was plugged into a power bank, too, and she was rapidly texting someone, or a group.

"Not right now, thanks, Mom. A bunch of people are writing a letter to the *Crier* about what a terrific teacher Ms. Richards is and the coward responsible should come forward and take the blame."

"People as in students?"

"Yes, and parents, too. When it's done, I'll show you and Dad so you can sign. We're saying 'coward' because that's who it was. If somebody had a problem with her, they should have told her, or even the superintendent."

Ignoring the grammar, Faith asked, "You think the person responsible is a former student who had a problem with her? Or a current one?"

"We can't think of any other reason, but what we don't get is why not pick another teacher? Just saying. There are a bunch of other candidates. It's actually been pretty funny listing them. Although," she added hastily, "there's nothing funny about all this."

Hours later, Faith was trying to fall asleep under as many duvets and blankets as she could find, listening as the town plows came and went. It wasn't that she was cold. It was that her mind was racing. Why Claudia?

She went back over the conversation she'd had late yesterday with Zach. The question that had nagged at her from the start was how someone could have obtained the Zoom link to the meeting. It was simple to sign up for it, but you had to sign up. You emailed your name to the town clerk's office and got the link the day before. Zach's answer had shocked her. She hadn't realized, stupidly, she thought now, how vulnerable they all were. She knew not to open mail from a source she didn't know or answer spam phone calls, even ones claiming to be her nephew in sudden need of bail money. What she didn't know was that you could assume *any* name in Zoom. Once on, you don't have to have a photo; you can use one of those black squares. The list was computerized, so if there were two Faith Fairchilds on it with two different email addresses, both would get the link. "There are other ways to hack into a meeting, but one as large and public as this one would use something like this. Easy-to-find lists of names of town residents," Zach had said. "Remember I told you years ago that saying—I think it was from a *New Yorker* cartoon—'On the Internet nobody knows you're a dog'? It was when I was still at Mansfield and we were trying to uncover a student's identity. I also told you never write anything in an email or elsewhere that you didn't want the whole world to see."

"It still doesn't mean that the Zoom bomber or bombers live in Aleford, right?"

"Right. The attack could have been launched from anywhere."

Faith was drifting off to sleep now, her last thought *Anywhere, but that still includes Aleford.*

After a brilliantly sunny Monday with temperatures that verged on balmy teased everyone, the storm returned, maliciously dropping nine inches more. Temperatures all over the Boston area plummeted. One good thing was that Zach had been right. The Zoom bombing and Ms. Richards were old news, and when people did have power to go online it was to post photos of yardsticks in backyards—another thing Faith had never understood. The competition for which town had the most snow and lowest temperature, i.e., the worst weather. Very weird bragging rights. Ben had shown her a clip from the local news station where the intrepid weather reporter, sole person, is out in the gale, darkened skies, snow coming down sideways with drifts fast mounting up when two guys appear out for a walk and he lurches forward to interview them. The first question concerned their take on Tom Brady's Tampa Bay Super Bowl win. Priorities. Weather—what weather? After exploring his abandonment of the Patriots in depth, the reporter finally asked, "So what brings you out in this blizzard?" Even Ben said that he'd expected something like "I have to get medicine for a family member who will die if I don't." Instead, one said, "Trying to find an open Dunkin'." "Yeah," his friend said. "No luck yet."

"Massachusetts is a different country," Faith told Ben as she laughed.

When Amy had gone into the kitchen the day before to make spaghetti sauce for dinner, Faith asked Tom to tell her more about his conversation with Claudia the night before.

"As I told you, she'd been drinking. I don't know how full the decanter had been, but it was more than half empty." Faith knew that Claudia hated the aesthetic of even the Swedish Absolut vodka bottle and poured the liquor into a simple glass decanter. "As you suggested, I made up the mug of tea and switched it for the glass. She didn't object. Not sure at that moment she even noticed. She'd been crying since I got there and obviously had been ever since the photos appeared. The landline was ringing constantly, and I took it off the hook. She'd turned her cell off. After a while she calmed down and ate a few cookies. She said she didn't want to talk about what happened, and I started asking her about her recent work, which seemed to help. I told her I knew nothing about printmaking techniques other than woodblock, and she walked me through the etching process."

"She's very talented," Faith said. "Remember the reviews when she had the show at the Clark Gallery?"

"And she loves to work, the whole process from an image in her mind to a finished print. That was how she put it. Loves her teaching, too. I do still think she's alone too much, and you know pre-pandemic she reached out to me once to talk about belief, but usually when people do that it's for the contact—or they're those MIT science guys trying to fit God into their universe."

One of Faith's own beliefs was that it is a truth universally acknowledged that a woman in possession of a good marriage/relationship must want the same for a single friend. After she had known Claudia for a while and ascertained her preferences, she began to invite her for dinners or other gatherings with what Faith considered likely single male prospects. Claudia finally told her that much as she appreciated the thought behind the matchmaking, she was happy as she was, but "do please keep inviting me for your yummy dinners."

The rest of the time until Tom left, making sure she set the alarm, they had talked about favorite books and films. "It seemed the best course. Normalcy. The last thing she needs is to relive the experience."

Amy had come in to say the sauce would be better the next day but would still be good tonight, and Faith thought what a wise husband she had, as well as a daughter who cooked like a pro already. Maybe she should let her choose her own path when it was such an obvious one. Claudia's talent must have emerged early, too, and Faith wondered about her family. Had they encouraged it or urged a different direction as she may wrong-footedly be doing with Amy?

February had a slow start as it dug out from the storms and waited anxiously for the Commonwealth and CDC's march to what surely would be an end to it all. Moving through the various phases like lightning. Or not.

Zach and Ben had called for a meeting after prioritizing those eligible under the Commonwealth's phase two eligibility list that started with seventy-five and older, followed by sixty-five and older with a preexisting medical condition. Spread out, the Fairchilds and Millers plus Zach met in the parsonage backyard.

Zach started. "There's been a lot of chatter online that appointments may open up before the eleventh, so we're going to start staying up tonight. We figure Ben's grandparents, Ursula, and Miss McKinley need to get the first shots. Dora has been eligible as a health care worker, and she can get hers at Emerson Hospital. Caregivers who need to accompany someone are also eligible, so we think we can pretty much get everyone safe at once."

"What do you mean?" Sam asked. "How would that be possible?"

"Kind of like a buddy system," Zach said, smiling. "Tom, your sister and brother-in-law would be the caregivers, accompanying your parents, and Ben is taking care of that scheduling. They qualify, since Mr. and Mrs. Fairchild are living with them. Sam, your heart condition makes you good to go, but no way can we finagle a caregiver for you. You don't need or have one."

"Well, I like that!" Pix said. "What am I? Chopped liver?"

"I've never been sure what that means," Zach answered, "but don't worry. You are very legitimately your mother's and will be her plus-one. This all sounds like we're arranging some kind of social event. Too bad my mother isn't here. She's a genius at this sort of mix-and-match thing."

"Which leaves you, Mom, going with Miss McKinley," Ben said with more than a note of triumph. "We're going to try to get everyone the same day, same location, and roughly the same time."

"They're taking it as a challenge," Amy said. "My job is to keep Ben awake and supplied with food in the wee hours. Plus, monitor stuff people post on Facebook and other sites. Where shots are available. The problem will be that as soon as you go to one that's publicized so widely, it will be gone."

"This is amazing!" Faith said. "But I'm not Millicent's caregiver. It doesn't seem right. What do the British say? 'Jumping the queue'?"

"Not Miss McKinley's caregiver?" Amy was indignant. "She'd be dead if you hadn't taken care of her that day, and you've been bringing her food through the entire pandemic."

"Besides," Zach said. "Under phase two at some point, food-industry workers are eligible. Samantha's—or I should say our—ob-gyn thinks she will have some doses by next week. I may be able to get a shot then, I'm hoping, but the main thing is that Samantha gets one to keep the baby and herself safe. Ben and Amy will be eligible in April, so we just have to stay cautious around them, and everyone else in general."

Tom clapped his gloved hands together. "I suggest a round of applause. I've been feeling guilty about being the only one protected. Thank you."

Ben and Zach each took a bow. Pix had switched into organizational mode, one of her strengths. "As soon as we have the appointments, we can figure out the driving, and I do hope it's same day, same place, and if anyone can do it, you both can. We'll make a caravan. Let's pray the weather doesn't mess everything up. That can be your job, Tom."

Everyone laughed, and soon drifted reluctantly back to their separate houses.

As the days passed and the search for slots continued, Faith was busy with the regular food boxes and the occasional more elaborate ones, which filled the catering company's coffers the most. She had stopped taking her salary right away, and Niki had pushed to do so as well, but Faith had shown her the numbers these dinners brought in, Niki's desserts an incentive, and finally got her to agree to one, lowered. "But only if the special orders keep up," Niki stubbornly insisted.

Faith had had a call from Ellie, who first of all wanted to know how Claudia was doing, and after talking about the horror of having something like that happen to you, she unveiled her latest plan. "I don't know why I didn't think of it before! Eggs! I'll freeze my eggs."

"Have you researched this and talked to Adam?"

"What's to research? I'm healthy, and this way as soon as we have the wedding Adam can add his swimmers, the egg gets implanted, and we're all set."

"Do some googling, sweetie. First of all, even for one egg the cost is something like fifteen thousand dollars plus storage fees."

"Storage fees? That's ridiculous. I'm not paying that. I can make room in the freezer and be sure Adam doesn't mistake it for something else."

Faith suppressed a giggle at the thought of Adam with a sudden Cherry Garcia craving mistaking the container. "You also have to inject yourself with fertility drugs and other preparations. Like for in vitro, and you didn't like the sound of that—how the drugs might make you look."

"Eeeuw. You know I hate needles. When everybody was getting little butterflies on an ankle in high school, I said no way."

"And you do know the egg is removed surgically. Also, it may not work the first time."

"Well, I guess we'll cross this off the list. I'm expecting you to come up with something better. Time is running out."

"Have you talked to your parents about it recently?"

"Yes, that's why I came up with the frozen Easter egg idea. Although, I think my mother is starting to come over to my side even more. She was much younger than I am when she had her babies. And she's dying to become a grandmother again. She's very jealous of Pix Miller. And I'm even more jealous of Samantha. Why didn't I get married sooner? Well, I hadn't met Adam and would have married the wrong person. It's all up to you, Faith. Bye!"

"Thanks a lot," Faith said to her phone.

A few days later Persis called. Faith had been surprised at the silence. Henry's birthday was fast approaching.

"Faith, it's Persis." There was a long pause. Persis didn't do pauses. Faith stepped in to nudge her along.

"How are you?"

"Fine. Henry's received so many kind calls about, you know. What happened at the State of the Town. The bombing. Anyway, he's put it all behind him, as have I."

Faith was tempted to say she doubted Claudia had, but waited to hear the reason for the call. Persis always had a reason.

"I've decided this is not the best time to celebrate Henry's milestone. The weather alone is a drawback. I'm postponing the party."

"I think that's wise, and it will be all the more celebratory when you do have it."

"Since it was going to be a surprise, Henry won't be disappointed. We'll have a nice quiet dinner, just the two of us."

"Which I will cater as my gift," Faith said. "And Niki will bake that chocolate cake with raspberry mousse filling he likes so much."

"That will be lovely, dear. I'm knitting him an argyll vest."

Persis's knitting ability was legendary.

"I'll say good-bye for now." There was another pause, and she said wistfully, "Maybe further on we could think of something special to do . . ."

"Of course we can. I'm putting my thinking cap on this very moment," Faith said, touched by Persis's devotion to her husband.

Astonishing as it seemed, Zach and Ben pulled off the group's appointments as planned. Tom's parents, Betsey, and Dennis got appointments and shots first on the Cape at a CVS in South Yarmouth on the twelfth. Five days later everyone else, safely loaded into two cars, drove to Chicopee, eighty-eight miles and an hour and a half away, for theirs. Both Samantha and Zach had been able to get vaccinated by the obstetrician.

The first thing Faith did when they got home was call her sister. "After the second dose, I can come down." She knew she'd have to be very careful and there might still be a restriction on travel out of state, but she desperately needed to be with her family in person. She was tempted to pull a Ben. But mothers were supposed to set examples. *Damn.*

Next, she called Claudia. "You'll be getting your jab soon, but I'm safe to come for a real visit."

"That's wonderful! You and Pix must be so relieved about your parents."

"We are, and Millicent, too. Since they have continued to be isolated, there was very little chance of their being exposed to the virus, but it's a sneaky devil." Faith had been euphoric on the way back from the CVS. "Ben and Zach were hoping for Valentine's Day appointments, but we can make this date a new family holiday. Tom only had a sore arm, so I am hoping the same for everyone. I'll give myself a day, and then why don't I bring lunch and see you Friday?"

"I would love that, but ask Tom if he thinks it's safe."

"I already have, and he gave me all these statistics. I've completely forgotten about how protected you are just after one. But how are you? We haven't talked in a few days. I hope you saw the letter in the *Crier* that your students wrote and their parents signed, too. There were too many names to publish, I understand, and they'll do them in groups."

"I did, and it was a big boost. It will be heaven to go back in person even if we have to be masked. I miss the kids so much. And people have been dropping off casseroles and other food, almost as if I had a death in my family. I mean, you know what I mean."

"I do, and people just want you to know they care, and the shock of it was kind of like what a loss produces."

Claudia decided not to tell Faith about the hang-up calls she'd been receiving at odd hours of the day and night, or the tire tracks in the snow she saw one morning. There wasn't an Amazon van or other delivery to explain them. But she was safely guarded by the alarm system. She'd let Faith know sometime maybe. As for a death in the family, she'd had two, two she still thought about almost every day. On the tenth anniversary of her mother's death, she'd sent a note to her father at the New York address after she'd had too much to drink. Drunk writing, the equivalent of drunk dialing. It was a brief one, saying how much she missed both women and hoped he was well. There had never been a response. He'd meant what he'd said. She wasn't his daughter.

She pulled her thoughts away from the past to the present. "And poor Henry. He and Persis left a box outside with the most gorgeous scarf Persis knitted from her wool and a book of reproductions of Dürer etchings from Henry's own library. When I called to thank them—and the book was really too much, quite a rare one—I had to get all teachery and tell Henry to stop apologizing or I'd make him clean the blackboards."

"Until Friday, then."

"Yes."

Faith was about to hang up, but there was an odd note in Claudia's voice, almost as if she was choking back a cough—or a sob.

"Claudia?"

"Oh, Faith! Who hates me this much?"

Chapter Seven

"I'm coming over. Be there in a few minutes," Faith said.

"No," Claudia protested. "I'm fine, really. It's just that every once in a while, the *who* in all of it gets to me. I'm about to ink a plate I just took out of the acid and run it through the press to see what more I want to do. And then I need to prepare for teaching tomorrow. The weather is supposed to be sunny, and I want to get the kids outdoors. See what they can find in or on all this melting snow to make into a collage."

Her voice sounded all right now, although Faith wasn't convinced. Even if Claudia didn't want to speculate about the who, she needed company. "I could watch. I haven't seen your latest work."

"You will. And, Faith, it's very sweet of you, but don't worry. We can talk about everything Friday. By the way, I would love one of your egg salad sandwiches. Yours with the chives and something else—maybe mustard?—are sublime."

They were quite sublime, Faith agreed, having created the recipe when she was starting out in Manhattan and discovered that often her high-flying clients wanted this sort of homey sandwich filling instead of foie gras. She'd also been one of the first caterers to offer old-fashioned cookies like snickerdoodles and chocolate milk in little glass bottles with straws for dessert. And yes, besides the chives, there was a touch of mustard—plain old yellow Heinz mustard, and the mayo had to be Hellmann's.

Yet, she still wanted to drop by now. "Are you sure? I have to go out to deliver the food boxes. I can bring yours early."

"Faith Sibley Fairchild!" Claudia used Faith's full name emphatically. "And you a sky pilot's wife! You told me that Ben and Amy were doing the deliveries today since you were going to get your shot. It's H–E–double hockey sticks, as one of my PE teachers used to say, for you."

Claudia was laughing and Faith was reassured. Maybe the best thing to take her mind off this was working, which always totally absorbed her. As for the lie, Faith had forgotten she had mentioned the delivery arrangement to Claudia earlier in the week, and she'd also ignored her cardinal rule about fibbing. Don't give a reason, don't embroider. She should have stopped after just saying she had to go out.

"And besides," Claudia added. "You must at least have a very sore arm and need to lie down."

Faith gave in reluctantly. "Yes, Ms. Richards. I will. I don't want to clean the blackboard." She was glad to hear the amusement in Claudia's good-bye.

Faith's arm did hurt, but so far she didn't have any other side effects. She thought she'd call next door and check on the Millers. Pix answered. "I sent Sam to bed with a Tylenol. Why do men think they have to be such stoics when they're obviously in pain? It's not as if they've been through childbirth. Oh, don't say anything about that to Samantha! Pain, I mean."

"I'm sure she has a pretty good idea that it won't be as much fun as it was getting the baby there in the first place. She isn't opting for anything like having the baby in one of those birthing pools or something other than push like crazy, which is what I remember. I think. It's a little hazy."

"It was still hazy for me when I found myself home in my own bed with a very small, very hungry person in my arms. No, I don't think so. They are very happy with the arrangements at Emerson's birthing center. They couldn't tour in person because of Covid, but they watched a video before their appointment and the doctor suggested they fill out a birthing plan, either one she had or one they found online."

"A birthing plan? I am definitely behind the times. And isn't one already in place? She's pregnant!"

"When they told me about it—essentially best-case scenario, like who you want with you, Zach, in this case, pain management, and even details like music, no music, lighting, and yes, a tub or what looks like a kiddie pool during labor or birth—I couldn't help but compare it to what Sam and I have filled out. The Five Wishes. You did it, too."

They had, and regularly revisited the document that specified aging and end-of-life requests. It sounded as if some of the options overlapped, although not the pool.

"Tom would say something if not profound at least apt at this point. The Circle of Life, maybe. I'll stick to 'Let's just talk about Samantha and Zach' right now."

Never had death seemed as inevitable as it had these past months, but Faith still clung to the notion of a day far in the future when she and Tom would go quickly and at the same moment.

"You haven't had any severe reactions, or have Millicent and Ursula? Have you spoken with Dora?"

"We're fine, and yes, I spoke to her," Pix said, "and she's got them both in bed, drinking mint teas with honey spiked with liquid Tylenol. So far nothing untoward, but she did say my mother is 'full of beans as usual,' asking Dora to write down a dinner party plan for when all seven of us are fully vaccinated. She told her she hasn't given a party since Christmas 2019 and it's past time for one."

"Ursula's absolutely right. Inviting just us, almost her total pod, will be safe. And she's given me an idea about what to do for Henry Wald's postponed eightieth birthday."

"That would mean way more than seven people. I thought you had convinced Persis to cancel."

"I have, and what I'm thinking of wouldn't be a party, wouldn't be a gathering as such. Let me mull it over a while. I'll need your help. In any case, it can't be until we're sure about the weather."

"So, July?"

"Very funny, but think July and you're on the right track."

Faith had spent Friday morning at the catering kitchen baking beer bread (see recipe, page 254). At the start of the pandemic, finding yeast was impossible. Even her suppliers couldn't get it. Her friend Patsy Avery's mother in New Orleans had a source and periodically sent a package to her daughter, who shared with Faith—"I feel like I'm dealing an illegal substance every time I call you and tell you a new shipment has arrived," she'd said to Faith. It was Niki who remembered beer bread, the carbonation acting as yeast, and the result was delicious. Faith had played around with adding shredded cheese and spices, but her simple original recipe was the best, and she'd stuck to it. Today she'd made large and small loaves, the large ones for a few family-size dinners that had been ordered for tomorrow, the small for the single dinners. She was bringing a large loaf to Claudia as well as the sandwiches, fruit salad, and mint chocolate chip cookies.

"It may not look like picnic weather, but this feels like a picnic," Claudia said after Faith spread the food out on the big table and they sat at either end.

"Only ten more days and it will be March, which I count as the beginning of spring even if it doesn't officially arrive until the twentieth."

"I'm with you. I guess other people would call us cockeyed optimists," Claudia said as she took a big bite of the sandwich.

Faith poured herself a glass of cold water from the pitcher she knew was kept in the fridge and wondered how to introduce the subject uppermost in her mind—and she was sure Claudia's as well. Best to go slow.

"Ben needs to concentrate on his courses, which he's let slide, and Zach is handling most of the late nights for a while. He told his work what he was doing, and they were not only all for it but gave him a list of names. Told him he was providing a public service, which he is."

Claudia swallowed and nodded. "He called and thinks he'll have a time and place for me soon. That teachers and day care workers are next."

They sat in companionable silence for a minute, then spoke at once. "That's . . ." and "So . . ."

"You go," Faith said, having intended to say that getting the shot scheduled would be wonderful.

"I don't know how long those terrible photos were up on people's screens. It seemed like forever on mine. It was long enough for me to see that some of the nude ones *were* of me and that I would be recognized."

"You had long hair, but it was your face. The porn ones were photoshopped, Zach says, using your face from the portrait shots taken from the school website's individual faculty photos."

Claudia frowned. "They were taken with the student ones, I think, three years ago. Before the pandemic. That's how we date everything now, I keep realizing. Anyway, it wasn't a good one, but I didn't— don't care. Brian told me I should ask for a retake or at least have a new one the next year."

Claudia remembered how she'd been flattered by his remark.

That the photo didn't do her justice. It must have been three years ago, soon after he was hired and they were getting to know each other. She started to tell Faith that ever since the Zoom bombing she hadn't heard from him except for a brief answer to a text she'd sent saying that she was all right. She'd had so many from her colleagues expressing horror and indignation that she'd assumed he felt the same way. He'd written, "Good. TTYL." Except he hadn't. That was almost three weeks ago.

"The other photos?"

"I meant to tell Tom—he was such a comfort that night, saying and not saying exactly the right things—but it truly slipped my mind. I came to Boston to take the coursework I needed to get certified to teach right after I graduated undergrad." This was true. She had just graduated. "With tuition and rent plus the occasional meal I was pretty strapped. Posing for life drawing classes paid well, and I was good at holding a pose. I liked it much better than the waitressing jobs I'd picked up. You have no idea how rude customers can be. And worse. The photos that were of me are from one or more of those classes. I couldn't tell you where specifically. Mass College of Art, the Museum School, smaller places. The instructor at the Ganley Museum School got in touch, but I didn't have a car and it was too complicated to get here by public transportation. That would have made this simpler."

Faith got it immediately. "Because then we would know how the photos were taken and it would narrow down who took—and posted—them."

"Exactly." Claudia nodded. "As it is, I can't think how. I need to talk to Zach. The taking part isn't hard to figure out. I always zoned out when posing, thinking about my own work, but I was aware that people sometimes had phones out to record what they had drawn and maybe to take a photo of the model to compare later, or work on a new rendering."

"And one of those students may have decided to post that or

more photos of you and other models, which means they would be accessible to anyone."

"I know it's the World Wide Web. So, it's back to the question 'Who is the spider?'"

Faith took out the small notebook she carried in her voluminous pocketbook. She'd gone from a sleek clutch to a diaper bag that held most of life's necessities besides baby Ben's needs—her trusty Swiss Army knife in particular had gotten her out of a perilous situation in those early days—and ever since she'd opted for a big handbag. Juice boxes, Goldfish crackers, and small toys were no longer staples, replaced these last months by small bottles and wipes of hand sanitizer, N95 masks, and a copy of her vaccination card. Among other essentials like phone, wallet, keys, tissues, lip gloss—not used lately—blush, and a folding comb and brush, she had the notebook, a pen, and a pencil.

"You used the word 'hate' the other day. I can't imagine anyone hating you, but can you think of anyone who might have wanted to humiliate you? Get back at you for some reason?"

Yes, I can, but it was years ago now, and how would they have been able to pull this off? They don't even know where I am.

"I've been going over this, and not that I haven't ever pissed anyone off, but I can't think of someone who has been pissed off to this extent."

Thinking about what Amy had said, Faith asked, "How about starting with something school-related? Aleford is no different from any other town, here in Massachusetts or the whole country. Schools, and teachers, are a flashpoint. Think before the pandemic. Did any parents object to what you were teaching? Accuse you of some kind of hidden agenda?"

"Like worshipping Bob Ross instead of Rembrandt?" Claudia joked. "No, although wait, I did have one mother who complained at a parent night that I wasn't teaching enough about perspective and the golden mean. That I was emphasizing creativity over learning the basics. Fortunately, I was able to give a quick demonstration that I *was* doing it, using the artwork I had displayed on the walls. I pointed out things like a series where the kids placed the same objects in various positions on the paper to show how they looked different in relation to the horizon line. I threw in a few vanishing points, and although she wasn't satisfied, she let it drop."

She really was an amazing teacher, Faith thought. Dealing with some parents she'd observed at school meetings was like walking through a minefield. "How about grades? A parent upset that little Ignatz didn't get an A?"

"Middle and elementary art are pass/fail, and if a student is particularly outstanding, I can add a plus to the P. It's very hard to fail. You would have to not complete anything. I pass students who show they've tried."

"How about a student? Your middle school, or these days even the elementary school ones are beyond tech savvy." Faith was recalling the cyberbullying when Ben was in seventh grade, participating in it to avoid being a target. Adolescence was characterized by impulsive action, and even something this extreme could have been the work of one or more tweens or teens.

"I've had kids who aren't all that interested and some who need to be the center of attention with what they think are witty observations about some of the art I show them, but never any remarks directed at me. Art is not the kind of class where it's hard to control your students, although I've had to intervene between kids who are bringing problems with each other into my room. Separation, or as we now call it 'social distancing,' works well."

Faith had been jotting things down. "Safe to say not a parent or student. How about colleague or administrator?"

"Let me think. The egg salad helps."

"Thank the Ogden Farm hens. I get as many eggs as I can from the farm." Ogden Farm was the largest in Aleford, a nonprofit community one run by a farm manager and his wife. By the end of March 2020, recognizing the desperate need, the farm store that sold eggs, milk, their own chicken, pork, and beef plus veggies in season went to seven days a week, twenty-four hours a day. Over time Farmer Pete expanded offerings, an outlet for other area farms, an artisanal bread bakery in Waltham, and, much to Faith's delight, two fish trucks that came down from Gloucester on Wednesdays and Saturdays. It was within walking distance of the parsonage, and while she couldn't get bulk orders, it had kept the Fairchilds extremely well fed.

"Because of my subject area, I don't get involved in department clashes, and I've always gotten along with both my colleagues and administrators, particularly the superintendent, who has been very supportive of what we're trying to achieve in all the arts curricula. The only exception might be the teacher I replaced. He was not ready to retire and made a point of stopping by after school when I first started to tell me I'd 'stolen' his job."

"How so?"

"He claimed the superintendent 'had it in for him,' preferring female teachers over males. It wasn't true. She hired a male, Brian, when the high school position became vacant. Mr. Childs, that was his name, was eased into retirement because he basically didn't do anything. He'd put a bowl of fruit or a vase of flowers on a stand in the front of the room, tell the kids to draw, and go to the lounge for coffee and to sneak a smoke."

"Is he still in the area?"

"I have no idea," Claudia said.

But then again, Faith said to herself, *he wouldn't have to be,* and started her list of names with his.

"Were there other teachers who were his friends? Who resented you?"

"I don't think so, or if they were, they kept it hidden. Everyone was very welcoming when I was hired, and a large number came to the opening of the show at the Clark, not just the art teachers."

"And all those parents as well as other Alefordians. By the end of the evening there were red dots on almost every print."

Claudia smiled. "I *was* pretty surprised, and they want another show next fall. They're looking forward to opening up in person. I've sent them photos of the arachnids, and they want the whole show devoted to them. They are playing around with titles incorporating the fact that spider silk is the strongest fiber in nature and five times as strong as steel. I gave them the Ethiopian saying 'When spiderwebs unite, they can tie up a lion.' I'm thinking it would make a good poster."

"Can't wait, and so good to have something to look forward to instead of always looking back," Faith said. "Okay, now let's broaden our scope. Other people who might have a grudge? Or just plain don't like you, hard as I find that to believe?"

"It helps that I don't know many people, Faith, so the field isn't broad." Yet as soon as Faith asked the question, Christopher Sinclair popped into Claudia's mind. He had certainly disliked her, but this much? She told Faith about the encounter, and Faith wrote it down.

"Just because someone has great parents doesn't mean he's great. Could be what Persis calls a bad apple," she said.

"He didn't *imply* I had ulterior motives. He was blunt about it. That I was abusing his parents' trust and friendship to get them to keep him from doing what he wanted with the property."

"And make a pile of money. Zach is eager to look into the Zoom bombing as a break from scheduling appointments. He can find out how Mr. Childs is doing and look into just how successful this Christopher is. He is the prospective heir and may be doing deals based on what he'll get."

"Patricia and Edward aren't that old. Early seventies! They have years left!"

"I agree, but he's the only one so far that we've come up with who has been overtly hostile to you."

"Can we eat cookies now?" Claudia said faintly.

February did go by fast, as Faith had predicted, clouded by the news of Covid's Delta variant and more bad weather. Vaccination appointments got canceled, and Zach and Ben, when he could take the time, scurried to find new ones. They were able to schedule a group of Aleford's teachers, including Claudia, for March 6 at Foxborough.

The idea she'd had for Henry Wald's belated eightieth had percolated to the point where Faith thought she'd run it by Pix. It had been a welcome break to think of a celebration. She called, and a few minutes later, dressed for the cold and clutching travel mugs of coffee, they met at the hedge.

"I can't claim that it's completely original—I saw something on the news about another town doing it. Think Fourth of July parade, which we didn't have last summer and probably won't this one."

The Aleford parade was an old-fashioned one, complete with the group of kids riding bikes decorated down to the spokes.

"I think it was on the North Shore, but instead of a parade, they had cars decorated for the Fourth drive all over the town in a cavalcade, as a loudspeaker on one played Sousa marches. People sat on their porches or lawns to watch. I thought we could have a birthday parade drive past the Walds' house, doubling back to make it longer, like the Fourth parade on Sanpere."

"That's a terrific idea! We could make 'Happy Birthday, Henry' signs for the cars, and the speaker could play something like the Beatles' 'Birthday.'"

"Yes! Or Zach and Ben can download Marilyn Monroe singing 'Happy Birthday' to JFK, substituting 'Mr. Moderator' for 'Mr. President.' I'm sure the Fire Department will bring up the rear with the vintage truck as they always do on the Fourth. Henry was a volunteer back in the day when it was a volunteer department."

"How will we keep it a surprise? We'll need to tell Persis so they'll be outside. She'll keep mum, but how to get the word out without Henry picking up on it?"

"Getting the word out isn't a problem, and we'd be sure to say it was a surprise. This is Aleford! All we have to do is tell several people and it will be like the old telephone game. Plus, we can put it in the *Crier* and tell Persis to keep Henry from reading it."

"You're right. When were you thinking of doing it? Before or after Town Meeting? It's virtual again."

"Why not make it after? I know it's April but can't remember the date."

"The third." Faith relied on Pix for keeping track of all town events.

"Things will be in bloom—at least some things. I thought the kids and I could hand a little box with cupcakes to each car. Niki is a whiz at decorating them. Maybe a gavel with 'Happy Henry Day.'"

"We need this. The town needs it. Tell me when you're putting it in the *Crier,* and I'll get the word out. My mother will be pleased. She's very fond of Henry—and Persis."

"Persis was making wooly favors for the party. We can hand those out, too, whatever they might be!" Faith had run through possibilities and, not being crafty herself, drew blanks.

They chatted a while longer. "Samantha told you about what Alexandra sent, right? She went online for the layette, all French from a fancy Manhattan store. It came in two huge boxes."

"She not only told me but sent a video of all of it. Gorgeous. Must have cost a fortune, and assumes a nanny in residence. Samantha said every piece of clothing said 'Hand Wash Only.'"

"The sweet wicker Moses basket will come in handy, and the lining comes out. I've made a couple more."

"I remember them from that summer we lived in France. And the Bonpoint shops. Ben was a toddler, and his little OshKosh B'gosh overalls turned out to be what was the mode, but with very expensive dressy little shirts. No tees."

"It did make me wonder whether Alexandra remembered anything about what babies need, how fast they go through outfits. But then I'm sure she never changed even a diaper for Zach."

"Well, it was good of her, and shows she's acknowledging being a grandmother."

"We'll see." Pix laughed.

The plans for Henry's parade fell into place with remarkable smoothness. "He doesn't read the *Crier,*" Persis said. "I tell him anything he needs to know. The same with gossip. Always the lawyer. Very discreet, besides not listening in the first place."

As Faith worked on the parade, she hit on a plan for Ellie, who was calling only twice a week now. Faith waited to act on it, though, hoping time would convince Nathan Porter, since his daughter had failed in her attempts. Maybe Persis was right and Faith *did* have a little thinking cap!

The number was unfamiliar, but it was Aleford's area code, although scammers had tricked her that way before. Faith answered.

"Hello, Mrs. Fairchild, Faith? It's Ruth Collins."

Ruth was the superintendent of schools, and Faith had gotten to know her as a friend after the two worked out a problem in town some years earlier.

"Hi, how are you? All well? Such a difficult time for you. Surely by next fall there won't be any need for remote learning."

"That's what we are planning, and now that our teachers are getting vaccinated, we may be able to move it up. But I'm calling to ask a favor."

Knowing the woman, Faith was sure of her answer. "Anything I can do to help you."

The deep breath Ruth took was audible over the phone. "Claudia Richards dropped off a letter of resignation effective the end of the school year. I called her immediately, and we spoke for a long time, but I couldn't get her to change her mind. I thought of asking Brian Kimball, her high school counterpart, but then I thought of you and decided it made more sense. I know she's been working with you at various times, and I've heard about the illustrated instructions she does for your food boxes. Also, you know her as a parent. The Zoom bombing was devastating, but no one thinks it had anything to do with her personally. Just a sick person or persons launching a random attack, as is all too common these days. She is such a gifted teacher, and it would be a tremendous loss were she to leave."

While not believing that Claudia had put that day behind her yet—and wouldn't for a very long time, she was sure—Faith was surprised that she was resigning over it. Claudia loved her job, her carriage-house rental, the town, and the whole area. Where was she thinking of going? Quitting teaching altogether? She'd been so excited about the fall show at the Clark. Faith also felt a little hurt that Claudia hadn't told her, or Tom. Then she immediately realized that Claudia would think that Faith would do exactly what the superintendent was asking her to do—talk her out of it.

"I'll speak to her, but how will I tell her I know?"

"You can say I spilled the beans. That I was upset, which I am. Nothing I've told you falls into a confidentiality category."

Faith hung up. It wasn't simply a loss to the school system; it was a personal loss. Their plans for the cookbook! A friendship that she had come to treasure even more over the last year. Claudia couldn't leave Aleford!

"How about I come over for another picnic to celebrate your first jab, and I want you to help with Henry's parade," Faith said. "I also want to see how the new print came out. The one using the Scottish spider."

"I'd love to get together, and I'm very pleased with my Robert the Bruce. Maybe a little too whimsical. I know you'll give me an honest opinion."

They settled on the following Monday. Claudia didn't say anything about her resignation, and Faith decided this was definitely a topic for an in-person conversation. "I'll bring my Piggy Goes to Market sandwiches, the ones with fig jam, cheddar, apple slices, and smoked ham."

"Oink, oink," Claudia said, and hung up.

Faith had asked Pix about Mr. Childs, Claudia's predecessor. "Oh, he was dreadful. Ben must have had him. All three of mine did. The most creative thing any of them learned was how to make terrific paper airplanes. He didn't spend much time in the room. Parents complained, but it wasn't until Ruth came as superintendent that anything was done about him. She made sure it was all by the book—no possible lawsuit. I heard about it from the president of the PTO after it was over. She'd been keeping an eye on it as requested by Ruth. Mr. Childs had to do what he'd never had to do previously. His job. He had to turn his weekly lesson plans in, and Ruth dropped by his classroom at odd times almost every day, telling him she was particularly interested in student art. He had never included his students' work in any of the art shows both the elementary and high school teachers mounted. After some months of this, he resigned. He was extremely lazy, and the job suddenly became too much for him."

Pix had no idea where he was now and told Faith she sincerely hoped he wasn't teaching. However, she thought it was unlikely that he was the bombing perpetrator. "He used to ask Dan to enter information for the front office on the laptop in the room—attendance, the pass/fail grades. Not at all computer literate."

"With you fully vaccinated and me halfway there, this is heaven," Claudia said as they sat only slightly distanced and unmasked eating lunch. She had opened the outdoor shutters on one of the large windows, and a burst of welcome March sun shone in.

"A taste of things to come: meals together, all kinds of gatherings," Faith said. She put her sandwich down and stood up, leaning over the table to look more closely at the row of prints Claudia had pinned to the large section of thin plasterboard. She spotted the Bruce-inspired ones immediately. The spider wasn't wearing a kilt, but instead of occupying the center, it hung suspended from its intricate web. The Scottish touch was the way she had shaped the top of the head. It looked like a tam.

"Too corny?"

"No, authentic. Surely all the spiders in Scotland have heads like these. I love it. Save me one?"

Claudia gave Faith a big smile, obviously pleased. "I'll make a note to include this, and any others, for you in my will when I get around to it."

"You don't have a will?" Faith was always surprised at the number of people, all ages, who didn't. Although Claudia was young and had plenty of time.

"Nope. I don't have anyone to leave to, but I promise you can have any of my artwork you want. Except the signed Edward Gorey print from *The Doubtful Guest* I found on eBay. The seller had no idea what it was and spelled his name wrong. *That* I am taking with me. I lit the fire in the Franklin stove and made coffee. Grab a mug and let's sit over there. First, you can tell me what you want me to do for Henry's parade. I have the feeling it could become a yearly event. It just sounds right. 'Henry's Parade.' Second, you can try to change my mind about leaving, but you won't. It isn't a decision I've made lightly."

Faith was chagrined. "How did you know?"

"You have a face like an open book, Faith, despite what you may think as a sleuth. Also, I called Ruth about trying to get more supplies, and I could tell from her voice she was hiding something. More telling was the fact that she didn't ask me to reconsider and stay. The time we spoke after she read the letter, she said she wouldn't accept it and wouldn't give up trying to get me to rip it up."

"I'll probably say everything she said—about no one thinking this horrific act reflects on who you are as a person, and a teacher, and that in fact everyone has rallied against it, concerned about your feelings."

"I'll never figure out how to return all the Pyrex casserole dishes, especially the ones without cards." Claudia drank some coffee. "I know this, and I'm both touched and grateful for the good wishes. It isn't changing my mind. I need to move on."

"I started with that, but what about the friends here, and yes, I mean me especially? But others, too, and all your students."

"My students change every year, and *they* move on. They may think of me fondly looking back at their school days, but no, my students are not a factor. You are, Faith, and Tom, too, and it was the hardest part of my decision. Leaving you. I love the town as well. I've applied for jobs in Maine and Vermont. I'm hoping for Maine because it will keep me close to you here and on that island of yours. Ours is a friendship that will never die. As for the cookbook or any other projects we dream up, thanks to technology, we'll accomplish them. If the show at the Clark comes off, I won't be that far away." She put her mug down and reached for Faith's hand. "Don't worry. You'll no doubt be seeing more of me than you ever have, since the pandemic has kept us isolated. I haven't seen the Sinclairs for longer, and they have been so good to me. Almost like family. One of the school systems I've applied to is in Bangor. Close to all of you."

Faith felt herself tear up and said, "I know, I know. But it won't be the same as having you here." She realized she was placing a burden on Claudia, who had clearly made up her mind. She joked, "There's a mall in Bangor. We can meet there. Hang out. Also, Bangor has a good Mexican restaurant."

"Thank you," Claudia said. "You do see. If I stay here, despite all the outpouring of support, I'll always be that teacher in the Zoom bombing. The nude one. Even now, I'm sure in some quarters the incident has been embroidered, and yes, I saw the comments—not many, thank goodness—in the *Crier* about no smoke without fire. I am sure, as most people believe, it was a random attack and somehow someone, or a group of sick people, found the life-drawing ones online and thought they'd have their twisted idea of fun." Claudia told Faith it wasn't a decision she had made lightly, and it wasn't. It was a heavy one, but it *was* a decision she had made right away. As soon as she'd seen what was on the screen, she knew she'd have to leave.

"Okay, enough. What do you want me to do for Henry's parade?"

"You are staying until the end of the school year?"

"I am, so we have plenty of time to do things around here together. Maybe even without masks! One last thing, for now would you keep my news to yourself? Of course, tell Tom, but not even Pix. I'd like to enjoy the rest of my life here without people trying to get me to stay and/or looking sadly at me when we are able to go freely."

Faith nodded—she understood completely—and took out her notebook, turning to the page where she'd jotted down some notes for the parade. "Most people will make signs to hang on their cars and decorate them in other ways, but I thought it would be nice to have two big banners, one at the start covering the whole side of the Have Faith Delivered van and maybe an even larger one for the fire engine at the rear."

"This will be fun. I have exactly the right paper, rolls of it that I had planned to have my students use to make murals for the hallways. And how about something like a big two-sided lawn sign that both the participants and the Walds can see. You can stick it in at the beginning. Are you having music of any kind? Too bad it can't be the high school marching band."

"Ben and Zach are arranging that. A mixtape of a wide variety of birthday songs that will play as Amy and I hand out cupcakes and some sort of favors Persis is making from her wool."

"I'm sure they'll be baad, as in good."

The two dissolved in laughter, and when Faith left, she could almost believe she was okay with Claudia's decision. And when she told Tom, he was firm. That it was the right choice, and a healthy one. "Despite knowing we'll all, especially you, miss her like hell."

It had been hard to resist Faith, as Claudia had known it would be, but she knew she had made the right decision and was now looking forward to a new place, a fresh start. She put the mugs away and reached for a glass and her old friend, the cold decanter of vodka in the fridge.

Sunday night Faith's cell rang at nine o'clock. It was an unwritten law in New England that you never called anyone after eight unless it was extremely good news, bad news, or an emergency. She saw it was Pix, and they had talked outdoors earlier that day. The caravan had gone to Chicopee for the second shots, so it was unlikely Covid-19 related unless the Delta variant had made its way past one of the group's protection. Or something else had happened. A fall? Both Ursula and Millicent had bird bones and were careful, but tripping on a rug or some other minor accident meant a major problem for them. As of this afternoon, Samantha was that rare pregnant lady avoiding morning, or any time of day, sickness and was blooming at the end of her first trimester. Pix had brought the list of names the couple had made so far, which included Timothy, Tim, Zach's first choice, as homage to Tim Berners-Lee, the inventor of the World Wide Web; if a girl, Ada, after Ada Lovelace, Lord Byron's wife, who was the first computer programmer back in the mid-1800s. "The grandmother of tech," Zach said. Faith had been happy the two were enjoying this time, especially as they weren't able to go anywhere except to walk. When she'd been pregnant, she'd been advised to see movies, go out to dinner before Ben's arrival. That wasn't an option these Covid days. She mentioned the impromptu concert Yo-Yo Ma had given those waiting at his vaccination site in the Berkshires and wished he had turned up at Chicopee!

"Pix? Hi. Is everything okay?"

"I hope so, but I'm worried. Claudia and I had arranged to Skype at six. I think I told you she'd been drawing a family tree, which I'll get framed, for Ursula's birthday. I've seen some of the sketches she scanned and sent. Tonight she was going to show me the final draft. Not the typical kind you see on those ancestry sites, but I gave her a lot of information about each person, and she's doing portraits hanging from the branches attached to a twisted tree like the one by the library, the catalpa, with roots above- and belowground. It's going to be quite large, and she'll hand color it. She told me she's working on a self-portrait as the last in her spiderweb series, so she's into portraits now."

"You mentioned it, but not in such detail. It sounds incredible, and Ursula will be over the moon."

"But, Faith, she didn't get on Skype at six or after. I thought I was doing something wrong, but Zach said it was on her end. She wasn't connecting. I've called repeatedly. Both her cell and the landline. She hasn't answered. I just get a message, not a busy signal. Were it anyone else, I would assume they'd forgotten or got involved doing something. But this is Claudia. You know how conscientious she is. Besides, we spoke at four and she said she'd 'see' me at six."

"You're right. This isn't Claudia. I can go over. I know where the key is. She showed me once when I had to pick up some menus for a dinner in a hurry and she was teaching. The in-person days."

"I'll come with you."

"No, you stay put in case she does start Skyping. I'm sure everything is all right. Tom is still Zooming with the Vestry, and I'm not doing anything, so I'll run over and will give you a call."

"I'm sure it's nothing. But call as soon as you see her."

Claudia's car was outside the carriage house in its usual space. The shutters were closed, but there was a small streak of light seeping out from the bottom of the front door and more light from the two-side clerestory windows that had illuminated the ground floor for the chauffeur staff when it was used as a garage. Claudia was certainly home.

Faith knocked on the door several times, but there was no answer. She found the key buried in the soil of one of the bronze urns on either side of the door that were filled with seasonal flowers but now sported bunches of red dogwood sticks. If the alarm was set, she also knew the code, which Claudia had given her at the same time as the key location. It was ETCH 3824.

She didn't need either. Before she tried the key, she turned the doorknob. The door wasn't locked. And when she stepped into the room, there was no sound. Looking at the keypad, she saw that it wasn't armed.

Yet, Claudia was home. Sprawled over the table. There was a terrible odor in the room, and as Faith quickly ran to her friend, she saw the cause. She was facedown in a pool of bloody vomit. She'd been drinking. A glass was overturned. But it wasn't vodka that had caused her tongue to swell hideously, yellow, and there were blue marks on her hands, which looked like they'd been burned by something. She knew there wasn't going to be a pulse.

Claudia Richards was dead.

Chapter Eight

Time stopped. Faith couldn't move. She knew what she had to do, but she was unable to open her bag and take out her phone. The figure in front of her that had been Claudia had erased every thought from her mind save one.

How could this have happened?

The thought pushed her into action, and she called 911. She gave her name, the address, and said that she'd found the occupant of the house, Claudia Richards, dead. The dispatcher asked whether Faith had tried resuscitation.

"No," she said, her voice beginning to break. "There is clearly no hope."

"The police are on the way. Are you able to let them in and answer some questions? This must be a terrible shock. She was someone you knew, I'm assuming?" The dispatcher's calm, kindly voice was helping Faith focus.

"Yes, she was a friend. A good friend. I'll be able to help them in any way I can."

"Why don't you stay on the line with me until they arrive," the woman said. "You can go to a window and look out for them."

She was obviously trying to move Faith away from the sight of the body.

Faith didn't tell her there weren't any windows she could stand by without a ladder, but she went to the door and opened it. The cold night air was like a slap on the face.

The police chief's car was first, followed closely by the ambulance and fire truck. Standard procedure, Faith knew, even when a fire had not been reported. The sirens and flashing lights made the scene look like a film or TV set. But this was real.

Chief Franklin and his deputy ran toward her. "Are you all right? Sorry, of course you're not," he said, adding, "I was afraid something like this would happen," as he stepped past Faith.

"Something like what?" She was puzzled.

"Suicide. After what she's been through—and I know she's resigned from her job—the motivation is all too clear."

"Claudia would never kill herself. She was excited about going to a new job, and we had plans together for all sorts of things." The nightmare was getting worse.

"It could have been accidental. We'll let the medical examiner tell us what happened."

Faith felt herself get angry. "I know what happened!"

Chief Pat cut her off.

"I'm sorry. Forgive me. This has been an enormous shock. I called Tom on the way, and he should be here soon. Why don't you go sit on that couch and we'll get on with what we have to do? You have identified the deceased as Claudia Richards, yes? I need this for the record. And could you tell me what time you arrived?"

She took a deep breath. "It is Claudia Richards, and I arrived about nine this evening, March twenty-first." She took a breath. She heard herself talking as if on a news interview. "The door was open and the alarm wasn't set. I was able to walk right in. I didn't touch her, or anything else." She pointed to the wall where Claudia hung finished work and work in progress. It had shocked Faith in some ways as much as the corpse. Thick black ink was slashed over every piece. It was a desecration. "Claudia would never have done this to her work. Destroyed it."

Faith went over to where they had sat together so happily only last week. There was no fire in the Franklin stove and no mug of coffee. Claudia's phone was on the table, a glass-topped steamer trunk, probably Patricia Sinclair's grandmother's or grandfather's. Without thinking why, Faith put the cell in her coat pocket. She closed her eyes and thought about exactly what she had seen.

Once Tom came, the police—by then joined by the State Police Crime Scene Squad to photograph and dust for prints in hazmat suits before removing the body and sealing the house with that yellow tape—would usher her out. She wished she could go back for a closer look but realized it wasn't necessary. It was as if she had one of Claudia's etchings of what it looked like in her head.

On Claudia's right, next to her hand, was an overturned glass, a highball one, and beyond that were two glass decanters. Faith recognized the one Claudia used for her vodka. The other was like those that the artist had for various supplies. Turpentine, the acid for the acid bath after she had finished her design, other liquids. She kept everything on a wall shelf on the far left above the end of the long table. This glass container next to the vodka was similar in size and shape.

To Claudia's immediate left sat an inked plate. As well as Faith could recall, this meant the zinc plate had already been submerged in the acid and now, after covering it with the black ink, Claudia would remove the excess and run it through the press. Tom had told her about his conversation with Claudia the day of the Zoom bombing. That she had explained the process in detail and he had found it fascinating. He could remind her about the details.

There was a dish on the table near the decanters with a few crackers and the remnants of some cheese. No other food. Ben had left last night's dinner box after knocking on the door. She'd have to ask him whether Claudia had opened the door and called out her thanks as usual. Either she'd finished the meal or what was left over was in the fridge.

She was wearing her work clothes. Jeans, a long-sleeved black tee—"The ink marks don't show and I can get away with not having to do a lot of wash," she'd told Faith. The Sinclairs had installed a stackable washer and dryer unit in a closet years ago for Edward's studio use. "I'm both criminally messy and equally lazy," Claudia had said, laughing. "The closet also makes a good dirty laundry basket until I run out of clean clothes."

The mess was obvious on the table. Faith tried to block the image of the central figure in it from her mind, concentrating instead on what else was there. Sheets of paper with drawings were strewn about, some crunched up. Brushes, pencils, tubes of ink, used and unused, as well as the canopy of spiderwebs she'd suspended from the ceiling, some of which hung low. Her body lay partially on top of her laptop.

She let her inward gaze wander to the small stove and sink. A few clean dishes were in the dish drainer; a plate, cup, and saucer in the sink. Not a mug. Claudia had a collection made by friends who were potters. Faith had never seen this cup and saucer before, but she recognized it as a Russel Wright, a pale orange color. It struck a midcentury modern solo chord.

The area where Faith was sitting was much tidier than the work/kitchen space. Sections of today's *New York Times* were the only signs of disarray. The framed Edward Gorey hung on the wall in a prominent spot, and Faith realized with a start that the conversation they'd had about making wills was also just last week.

She felt tears well up. She wished Tom would hurry so she could go home to shed them in private. She knew if she started here now, she wouldn't be able to stop.

The house was filling with people. Faith stood up. "Unless you need me for anything," she said, trying to control her quavering voice, "I'll go wait for my husband outside."

The chief glided toward her. She hadn't realized he was wearing those booties, too. "Of course. I'll need some information like next of kin, her doctor's name. But it can wait."

"She doesn't have any family, she told me, and if she has a doctor, it would be ours, Dr. Kane. She asked me once who we used. But isn't it a little late for that?" Faith felt she was bordering on hysteria.

"It would be to check whether she was on any kind of medication. For depression. Something that would not mix with alcohol."

"I don't think she was on anything . . . Are you suggesting she took pills with her vodka?!"

He shook his head. "She might have, but I don't think that's what she used. This death is more than likely acid-related."

Tom came through the door and Faith rushed into his arms.

The chief walked them out to the car. Faith had used the van. "We'll have someone drive it over to the parsonage later," he said. "Take care, Faith. I'm so sorry for your loss."

Empty words. Empty words made almost comic by what he said next. "We won't need your fingerprints. They're on file from those other times."

And that made her cry.

When they pulled into the driveway, Ben and Amy came running from the kitchen doorway and the Millers were all standing at the opening of the hedge. Everyone was in tears. Pix broke away and hugged Faith hard, whispering in her ear, "We'll talk tomorrow. I love you." Faith nodded as her children hugged her as well. "Come inside, Mom," Ben said. "It's cold." He and Amy steered her across the lawn and up the steps. Inside she collapsed on the window seat in the kitchen. She couldn't go any further. The horror and the grief poured out of her, and she sobbed, a keening noise coming from her mouth that she knew she had never made before and did not recognize as her own voice at first. Tom had pulled her almost onto his lap, and her children had draped themselves across them both.

She had lost friends and close family, most recently Aunt Chat, but this was so different. Not simply the death of a dear friend, but the discovery and the manner of the death. No one had said anything, just murmured words of love, and she could feel their pain. Amy got up and came back with a warm cup of tea. Faith took a sip. It was very sweet, and for a moment she stopped crying and drank it down. The panacea in British novels, novels for which she and Claudia shared a fondness, passing books back and forth. Amy took the empty cup and returned with more. Faith grasped it, feeling the heat spread from her hands to the rest of her body.

"The chief thinks she killed herself. I *know* she didn't!" Faith said.

There wasn't anything to say in response. None of them had seen what she saw, and she could never describe it to anyone. The face, that tongue, her hands. She closed her eyes. They were swollen. Her whole face felt swollen. Amy was handing her a dampened hand towel. She held it over her eyes, nose, and mouth. How long had they been sitting like this? Five minutes? An hour? For the second time that night, time had stopped.

"Faith, darling, tell us what you need now," Tom said. "Do you want to lie down? Or try to sleep soon? It's late."

She was exhausted, but she knew sleep wouldn't come. She wanted to be together with them.

"We'll move to the couch. You can make a fire."

So, that's what the Fairchilds did, sitting together, keeping a vigil, praying and mourning for their friend lost forever as they watched the flames become embers in the early dawn.

Tom was shaking her. She was in their bed. She didn't remember coming upstairs. "Faith, wake up! You're having a nightmare."

Someone was screaming, and opening her eyes, she realized it was herself. The screams became sobs.

"Oh, Tom, she looked so horrible! Who could have done this to her? After the Zoom bombing she asked me who hated her so much. Who took that hate to this level?"

Tom pulled her close. "We don't know what happened. I can't erase it from your mind. So wish I could. Right now we need to take care of you. And each other."

Faith stopped crying. Tom wasn't getting it.

"You think she killed herself."

"It may have been an accident, not intentional, although we have known she was deeply depressed."

Faith sat up, swung her legs over the side of the bed, and stood up, facing her husband.

"It wasn't suicide or an accident. It was murder."

The next days passed in a blur. Faith knew her phone was filling up with messages, and Tom had been answering the landline, making a list of calls. The news had obviously spread, although when she asked him, Tom said there was nothing in the *Globe* or the *Herald*. She was relieved. She didn't want Claudia's death to become an object of public speculation outside of Aleford. That was bad enough. For once she was glad there was too much else going on—Covid-related news, especially the hunt for vaccination appointments, and as always world and national events.

Pix had met her late Monday afternoon for a long walk on one of the conservation land trails. It was just what Faith needed. They reminisced a bit about Claudia, and Faith told Pix about her resignation. Pix had been predictably upset, but she said she would most likely have done the same. "It would never be the same for her here, much as we all would have supported her." Faith also told her about the show at the Clark Gallery scheduled for the fall, and they decided to call the owner to urge that it go on. Thinking of the prints that had been defaced, Faith hoped Claudia had put other finished ones in the studio's large flat cabinet where she stored her artwork. She wondered what that last print looked like. The one Claudia called a self-portrait. The plate was inked. Had she made an impression? Was it one of the ones besmirched?

Pix excitedly spotted a Carolina wren. She'd already pointed out a cedar waxwing and a tufted titmouse, and made the chickadee call every time she saw one of the little birds. Faith found it oddly soothing. A reminder that life, with Pix toting binoculars and her Life List Bird Notebook just in case she spotted something rare, was still continuing on its path. Faith began to hope they would spot a cardinal or blue jay, the two birds she was sure of until robins made an appearance. She was good with seagulls, too, after many years able to distinguish a laughing gull from a herring gull (the cry was the giveaway).

While they were walking, Faith had suddenly remembered it was a Monday and she had prepped boxes yesterday afternoon but not assembled them for delivery today. "I have to get to the catering kitchen and get the deliveries ready!"

"Done and dusted. Ben and Amy are taking care of it. We told them not to bother with ours, so that leaves two less. I'm making dinner."

Since Pix's culinary skills were limited to preparing dinner from boxes that had "Helper" on them, Faith was touched and also felt bad.

"Don't look like that. I'm roasting a chicken the way you taught me, and I can make rice. The peas are frozen, but at least they're a veggie. And Samantha will help. She's hungry all the time. I think she's baking an apple pie for dessert."

They had turned their steps back the way they'd come.

"I'll get the Wednesday deliveries ready, and you'll be on the list," Faith said.

But Claudia wouldn't.

By Thursday Faith had expected the police chief would have been in touch, but Tom said he anticipated the investigation would take longer because of the pressures of the pandemic. She had been avoiding the subject with him for the most part. She knew from the expression on his face when she'd said Claudia had been murdered that he didn't agree. It had been a combination of skepticism and empathy.

When she did get a call about Claudia's death it was from the superintendent. After asking how she was, Ruth said, "Faith, Chief Franklin has been in touch with me for information we might have about Claudia. I pulled up her job application. She listed her current address as 54 Delle Avenue in Boston, no permanent address. I recall from her interview that she said she had grown up in Connecticut and New York but had been planning to live in the Boston area since college. She went to the University of Connecticut and then Mass College of Art. She said she'd move within the area depending on whether she got the job. She listed Miss Kingman, a high school teacher, and Dr. Schwartz, a professor at UConn, as references. After she was hired here, she filled out a personal information form, which she updated after a year. You and Tom were her emergency contacts in the most recent one. The Sinclairs had been before that, and she continued to list them after you. Her rental here was her permanent address. Dr. Kane was her doctor."

"She was a very private person," Faith said, thinking this didn't give her much to go on, either. She didn't intend to bring it up with Tom, or anyone else at the moment, but she needed to vindicate her friend. Which meant finding out who did it and why she was killed. Was it the same person as the Zoom bomber? The superintendent was still speaking, and Faith brought her attention back to what Ruth was saying.

"I thought her references might know about Claudia's family.

Next of kin. The professor, sadly, was an early casualty of the pandemic, and I haven't been able to trace the art teacher through Google. Claudia didn't list the school, just an address for the woman, and she apparently doesn't live there anymore. There is a dearth of information, and I thought since you were such close friends, you might know more. I asked Brian Kimball as well, but he wasn't able to help."

"I'm afraid I may not know much more than you've mentioned, except she told me when we first became friends that she didn't have any family. Her mother died when she was fifteen, as well as a grandmother she was very close to, and she had no contact with her father. She was an only child."

Faith *did* know where Claudia had gone to high school, Miss Porter's in Farmington, Connecticut. The Kennedys had come up in a conversation they were having, and Claudia had smiled and said, "Jackie and I went to the same school, of course not at the same time, but Miss Porter's was very proud of her and a whole bunch of other A-list people!" She'd told Faith that she was happy to be teaching public school and didn't believe in private education, but she had received a good education with small classes and some caring teachers at Miss Porter's.

Claudia hadn't mentioned Miss Kingman, but Faith wrote her name down in the notebook where she'd made the list of possible Zoom bombers with Claudia not long ago.

"Knowing that the news would spread, we sent a letter to parents telling them of her sudden death with information about reaching our counselors to help students deal with it, and parents, too. She had so many supporters. I dreaded announcing the news that she was leaving."

Sudden death.

It was, Faith thought. *That and more.* "She was sorry to leave Aleford but excited about going to a new place. She was hoping for a job on the Maine coast."

"It's always a tragedy when someone so young is a suicide, or the chief thinks it may be termed an accidental death. She had her whole life in front of her. And so much talent as an artist as well as being a gifted teacher. You know it was her birthday. She was twenty-nine."

Faith hadn't known. Claudia had always been firm about no birthday celebration. Faith knew it was in March but not the date. She herself had come to a point where she didn't enjoy marking her birthdays as much as in the past—and poor Tom always agonized over what to get her until Amy was old enough to give him hints. But Claudia was young.

"They've been through the house but haven't found any personal papers."

This did surprise Faith. "She must have had a file with her birth certificate, passport, things like that. She had a two-drawer wooden unit under her worktable where I know she kept school-related papers and artwork."

"I'll remind the chief, but I'm sure they must have gone through it. He did say that the place was a mess but that she was very organized in some ways."

Faith felt depression settle over her, an unwelcome garment, molded closely to her body. She needed to shrug it off, get air. Needed to hang up.

"She was. It was when she was inspired and working that she may have not been tidy. If I think of anything else to tell you, I'll let you know." Faith chose her words carefully.

"Thank you, Faith. I hated to bother you when I know what a hard time this is for you."

"Yes, it is. And thank you for understanding."

"We will be thinking of some sort of memorial for her. Not being able to gather makes me want to wait. Good-bye."

"Good-bye."

The superintendent had called Brian Kimball early Monday morning after she'd been informed of Claudia's death. "I know you were friends and most of your students would have had her in middle school, so I wanted you to be prepared to deal with what they will feel when the news gets out." He'd said all the right things, he thought, and went to tell Margaret, waiting until she finished a call to London.

Since then, the atmosphere in the house had changed. He was still sleeping in the guest room, but the blatant hostility between them had altered into a kind of truce. "What would you like for dinner?" "Let me know if you want me to pick up some things at the farm." "If you want to take a break, we could walk someplace." "I'm doing a wash. Do you have anything to go in it?" They were tiptoeing around. A wary tiptoeing. They didn't meet each other's eyes.

She didn't need to prep dinners until Friday, but Faith headed over to the catering kitchen. Cooking was always a sure cure for a mood like this, although she had never had one this severe before. Part of her wanted to shake herself and throw it off, but part felt it was appropriate.

When she pulled in, she saw Niki's car, and that immediately made her feel a little better. She knew Tom had called her. Niki had grown close to Claudia over the years, and pre-pandemic Claudia had painted a frieze of whimsical animals in the nursery awaiting Sofia's arrival and created a book of them for Alexander, since she couldn't add to the decoration for his.

As soon as she entered, Niki ran to her, tears starting, and hugged her hard. No need to distance. She'd gone as her mother's caregiver to get both shots at Fenway Park, and telling Faith about the experience after the first one, they had laughed over Eleni's amazement at the place. "It's like a Greek amphitheater," she'd said. "And they use this just to hit a ball?"

Still clinging to each other, they moved toward the work

space. Niki was making cheesecakes. Some were in the oven, and the smell, along with the aroma of the coffee she had made, was comforting. Faith poured herself a cup, and they sat side by side on the high kitchen stools. She pointed to a mound of silver Philadelphia cream cheese cartons. "Did you hijack a delivery?" She knew Niki bought the cheese in bulk from a supplier.

"Close, but as you might imagine, it was my mother. By the way, I have a tray of her secret-recipe baklava I was planning to drop off for you—her panacea for all ills, mind and body" (see recipe, page 256). "About the cream cheese. After the second shot she headed straight for Market Basket and just happened to be in the aisle when one of the workers was filling a refrigerator unit with a delivery and asked her if she could take more than one. 'Take as many as you like. It's not toilet paper or anything else on the list.' Mom loaded what had been taken out of the carton and then the remaining full cartons. When she got home, she spread the word that I was back in business for a little while!"

Eleni Constantine was a small but ample woman—her usual stance hands on hips or arms crossed in front of her chest. She brooked no opposition. Niki had kept Faith entertained over the years with countless examples, most involving Niki herself. Faith could picture Eleni in the store loading her cart and scooping up a bagger to help her unload the booty into the trunk.

"Why don't I make small ones, however many you need, for the Saturday deliveries? And a regular-size one for you and one for the Millers. Tell me what flavors."

It was a welcome diversion, and the prospect of presenting both the baklava and cheesecake—she knew that when Niki said a tray, it was an amount that could have fed most of Alexander the Great's forces—to her family and Pix's brought a momentary glow.

She drank her coffee while Niki worked. They talked about the convenience of having a built-in grandmother babysitter. Niki had been able to see more of Philip than she had in months. Eleni had arranged for him to drive and accompany a very elderly friend of hers to Fenway as well, so he'd been fully vaccinated.

Finally, Faith began to tell Niki everything. What she'd seen when she walked into the carriage house and everything since. She hadn't told anyone else. Not Tom, not Pix. She knew that Niki was the person who wouldn't try to change her mind, wouldn't tell her the police, the medical examiner, and the machinery set in motion would find out the truth. Niki had been her confidante other times, although none of those occasions came close to this. She listened and said, "Okay, what do we do first?"

"You do just what you did. Be my sounding board. I read somewhere that murder in the present is always in the past. It's not something to needlepoint on a cushion, but the idea has always stuck with me. It's obvious, yet not immediately. Murder can be a sudden act, spontaneous. The present. I'm sure this one wasn't. It was very carefully planned, maybe over years, to appear as what everyone except the two of us thinks. A suicide or an accident. I don't have the police or medical examiner's report, but I'm betting they don't find any fingerprints except Claudia's, and maybe mine from last week."

Niki nodded. When she heard the news, like Faith, she had thought that Claudia would never have killed herself. And an accident? How would you do that? From Faith's description and what the police chief had said, it looked like acid. You wouldn't be that careless. Claudia used chemicals in her printmaking. She knew the danger.

"I thought I should work backward, starting with a call to the Sinclairs. They might know more about Claudia's past. She was close to them. Then I have the address of where she lived in Boston before coming to Aleford. It's a long shot. She would have been a student at MassArt then, and she told me she'd been short of money. That was why she did the modeling. So she would have had roommates. Mission Hill, the area, is very popular. One or more of them may have stayed. And since I know the name of the teacher she gave as a reference when she applied for the job here and that it was at Miss Porter's, I can find her through the school. Claudia would have been there when her mother and grandmother died. I'm betting this teacher was close to her and not just someone she used as a reference."

Niki was taking the golden cheesecakes from the ovens. "Let me know what I can do. We can meet here to go over any information you've collected. And I have my laptop at my mother's. My fingers can do the walking, too."

"Yes to meeting, but I plan to enlist Zach not for surfing the web but diving deep. If he can't uncover information about Claudia before we knew her, no one can. And he'll keep what we're doing to himself."

"I'm going to do one more batch and pack up the ones that are cool. I'll deliver most of them today. Why don't you go into the office and get started? Call the Sinclairs? It will make you feel better to do something."

"Better" was a subjective term, but action of any kind would help.

She went into the office, a small space she had carved out some years ago. The Sinclairs were the logical place to begin. Faith would also have thought Brian Kimball, but from what Ruth had said, he didn't know anything. This was a bit surprising. Claudia had been close to him, Faith thought maybe even too close at times, from the way Claudia spoke about him.

Patricia answered the phone. "Oh, Faith, I still can't take it in! Chief Franklin said suicide or an accidental death. It's such a huge shock. We have wanted to call you but didn't want to intrude. We'd come down to be with you if it weren't for the virus. Even vaccinated it's a risk for Edward."

She was crying. Faith could hear soft sobs. "I can't take it in, either." This was true, despite having seen Claudia very much dead. "We'll be able to be together in Maine. I know how much she loved you both."

"And we her. We became even closer four years ago when she came to go to the Haystack Mountain School for a graphics course and stayed with us for the session. It was a bit of a drive to Deer Isle, but she wasn't keen on boarding there. She was a very private person in many ways."

Faith began to think she would hear this phrase a great deal in her search for information.

"Did she ever talk about her family to you?"

"No, we understood that there really wasn't any. A father with whom she didn't have contact—I never heard where he lived—and her mother died when Claudia was in her teens. A terrible time to lose a parent, not that any time is a good one."

She needed to call Hope, Faith thought. All this had created an ardent desire to see her own immediate family—in person.

"Claudia answered an ad for a summer house sitter we had posted on a bulletin board. She was the first applicant, and we recognized her name as the artist of a print we had purchased from a student show the previous fall. The three of us took an instant liking to each other. She said so later and we certainly agreed. When we decided to spend more months in Maine, we didn't hesitate to offer the carriage house as a rental. She was a perfect tenant."

"Did she have many visitors? Friends not just from Aleford?"

"No, again, she treasured her privacy. Told us she had the ideal situation for her art. No interruptions. Other than you and several colleagues, I never noticed any cars. Of course we haven't been there for a long time."

And don't know about your son's unwelcome visit.

Faith hung up with Patricia; Edward had gone to get birdseed at the feed-and-grain store in Ellsworth. Claudia had taken on their Aleford feeders as a solemn trust, like the alarm system. Faith would enlist Pix to help her keep them filled. The thoughts, Claudia's conscientious care of the feeders *and* the alarm, reminded Faith that it had not been set, nor was the door locked. This suggested that she was either expecting someone or was killed earlier, before she closed up for the night. Faith hadn't noticed any tire tracks in the snow when she drove in. She was concentrating on the house. And afterward, when she left, the police and fire vehicles would have obliterated them.

She opened her laptop and went to the staff directory at Miss Porter's. No Miss or Ms. Kingman was listed in the Art Department, which had extensive offerings. She wrote down the name and phone number given for the department chair. He had a pleasant face. The pandemic was making her investigation more than difficult. In the past she would have driven down to Connecticut and talked to him, the same with the address on Mission Hill. She'd have to call or email, preferably speak on the phone.

Going to White Pages online did not give her a phone number for the name, Ati Patel, listed as currently living at 54 Delle Avenue, and these days she couldn't go knock on the door. Frustrated, she tried other sites, with no luck.

Niki stuck her head in. "I'm leaving, but tell me what you've found out."

"Not much, but it's a start. I have the contact information for the Art Department head at Miss Porter's. The teacher is not listed as being there now. And Patricia didn't know any more than we do about Claudia's family, or anything else before she answered their ad for a house sitter. I have the name of a woman living at the Mission Hill address, but no phone number, and I can't go there in person."

"Try Facebook. If she has a page, you can direct message her, you know, DM."

"Of course! You're brilliant. I'll do it before I leave." It wasn't that she planned to keep everything a secret from Tom, but it was going to be on a need-to-know basis only—for a while at least. Until she had concrete evidence.

"Please thank your mother," Faith said, giving Niki a hug. It felt so good to be able to have this kind of contact with near and dear at last.

"Ati Patel Boston" yielded several hits, but as she went through the profiles, only one listed Mass College of Art as an alma mater. Now, how to phrase the message? Eventually she wrote:

"Hello, I am a close friend of Claudia Richards, whom I am very sorry to tell you has died recently. She may have been a roommate of yours on Delle Avenue, or you may be able to give me the name of someone who was. You may get in touch here, by email: Faith@Havefaith.com, or phone: 781-742-8991. Faith Fairchild."

She pushed the chair away from the desk and leaned back. The question that dominated her thoughts was whether the Zoom bomber and the murderer were one and the same. That old trope "There are no coincidences" applied, she had come to believe. The Zoom bombing was to plant the seed of deep depression, and it *had* caused Claudia much anguish. It was necessary in order to give credence to the suicide. Faith was sure the medical examiner would come to that conclusion, or accidental death, as the cause of her demise. Either would tie in with the bombing event. She needed to know the results of the autopsy, the investigation at the scene. And waiting was unbearable.

She drove home slowly. Her thoughts kept skipping around from one possibility to another, and always, despite best attempts, to the scene on Sunday. The scene on Sunday . . . She pulled the car over. She was sitting on the couch looking at the cold Franklin stove. Claudia's phone was on the coffee table, and Faith had put it in her pocket! She had grabbed the first coat she'd touched in the closet, a dress coat, not her warm everyday one. The one she was wearing now. How could she have forgotten this? She turned back onto the road and drove faster. Pulling into the driveway, she sprinted to the front door, not the back, and opened the closet. Of course the coat was still there, hanging where she'd left it. And of course the phone was there, too. Identical to Faith's own iPhone.

The kids were in their rooms and Tom in his office at the church. Still, she went into the bathroom off their bedroom, closed and locked the door. She turned the phone on, but it had run out of power. After locating her charger, she plugged it in, then decided to change the sheets on their bed and keep looking until there was enough charge to check contacts, recent calls, texts. You could bounce a coin off the bed linen, but the phone was still a dark screen.

Claudia's case was Van Gogh's *Starry Night.* Faith took it off and switched it with her own cover, then headed into the kitchen, where she plugged it in. She pulled a whole chicken from the fridge and spatchcocked it, removing the backbone and cutting the sternum so it lay flat. She'd rub it with oil and spices, put it on a sheet pan to roast at high heat. By the time she put the chicken back into the fridge to wait until dinner, the phone had enough charge for her to open it.

It was password protected, yet Faith was sure it was the same as the alarm code, ETCH, and it was. She went to Contacts first. There were very few, and Faith was almost positive the few names she didn't recognize were colleagues, area codes the same as Aleford's and Boston's. She'd try them, though. Maybe she did have a friend closer than Faith. The call she made immediately was to Ms. Anna Kingman, hopes high only to be dashed by a recording declaring it was not a working number and to check the listing. She did, and there was no Anna Kingman or even plain A. Kingman listed anywhere in Connecticut. She'd search further later. Next, she checked Recents and Missed. They were from Faith, Pix, and the Sinclairs. Claudia had deleted any prior to two weeks ago. Untidy in some ways, she kept her phone neat. It was the same with texts. Faith and Pix. The superintendent. Frustrated at trying to get into the history, Faith opened Photos. Beautiful shots of the Sinclairs' property and surrounding conservation land. No people. These, too, were recent. She must have deleted older ones, transferring those she wanted to keep to her computer.

It was getting late. Shadows crept across the yard, and Faith closed the phone, plugging it in to keep charging while she took the flattened chicken and tried to think what to make to go with the unusual presentation. Smashed potatoes?

When Faith returned from packing up the Have Faith Delivered boxes for delivery on Monday, Tom was sitting at the kitchen table.

"I thought you had one of those Zoom meetings with your God Posse," she said. This was the name a group of interdenominational clergy had come up with for themselves as a support group for one another at the start of the pandemic.

"I'll go next time. Chief Franklin called me with the results from the medical examiner and the State Police investigation."

Faith pulled out a chair and sat down quickly. She was annoyed that the chief hadn't called her. She'd found the body. Past chiefs and her friend State Police Detective Lieutenant John Dunne, now retired, would have let her know. Her annoyance wasn't important, though. What was important was the information. Tom took out a sheet of paper.

"The cause of death was nitric acid, ingested by mouth. Faith, it would have been quick. The acid caused vomiting, but essentially it suffocated her immediately as it traveled down the throat. Some spilled, burning her hands and wrists, causing discoloration. Nitric acid is what's most often used in an acid attack, thrown at someone's face, the chief mentioned. There's much more technical stuff that I didn't get to write down, but we can request a copy as her emergency contacts and so far the only contacts they've been able to find."

"But this doesn't make sense. Why would Claudia drink the acid? She knew its effects."

Tom reached for Faith's hand. "They have come to two very

probable conclusions. She'd been drinking heavily. Her blood alcohol level was close to .20 percent, the amount where someone, particularly as thin as she was, would not be aware of their actions, would soon black out. You know she kept her vodka in a decanter that was similar enough to the glass one in which the acid was stored. She didn't label them. Nitric acid is clear and odorless. She must have poured the acid into the glass instead of the vodka and was so impaired that the pain didn't register until it was too late. A horrendous accident."

She was hearing his voice, but the voice inside her head was saying something very different. Someone had lined the decanters up or even poured the acid into the glass after Claudia was inebriated to the point where she had passed out. Waking, she reached for the glass.

It was as if Tom was hearing the voice, too. "Only Claudia's fingerprints were on the decanters and the glass. Clear prints."

"Wiped clean and then her hand was wrapped around all three," Faith blurted out. "You know it could have happened that way."

"Oh, Faith, I wish I could believe it, but everything points to suicide, the second probable conclusion according to the investigation. Maybe not intentional at the end, but at the start. All the signs were there. The heavy drinking on her birthday. She left the house open so she would be found, although I'm sure she never thought it would be by you. We don't have any information about her life before she came here except that she lost her mother in her teens. Her mother may have been a suicide. Children, especially female children, of mothers who have killed themselves are significantly more likely to commit suicide themselves. Dr. Kane said Claudia was not on any medication, so no access to pills. The acid was close at hand. Her last physical pre-pandemic as required for her job showed excellent health. He was not aware she had a drinking problem. The medical examiner spoke to the chief about cabin fever as a possible factor. Claudia was very isolated, and the pandemic has seen a rise in incidents like hers due to the lack of contact with others. Addiction—"

"Stop!" Faith had heard enough. "What happens now?"

"It's likely the death certificate will list accidental death as the cause, and her body will be released to next of kin, and failure to identify any within two weeks of the discovery means that we can file to take charge as her listed emergency contacts. I will need to ask Sam how to go about it if it comes to this."

"Two weeks! In a morgue! It's horrible, Tom. Indecent. You have to talk to your buddy Chief Pat!"

"I intend to, and meanwhile they are looking into any possible relatives she may have had. Unfortunately Richards is a very common name. And as important as this is to us, it's far down on the list of what's important to all the law enforcement involved during this time."

Faith hated it when her husband was logical. She'd taken in everything he'd said, but her way was still crystal clear. She hadn't heard back from Ati Patel, the possible roommate, and the phone of the department head at Miss Porter's went straight to message. She hadn't wanted to leave one and would keep trying to get an answer. Claudia's phone had stubbornly revealed nothing except what Faith had initially found.

It was time to call Zach in.

Chapter Nine

Fatherhood was a whole new world for Zach, and he was more than eager to explore it. Given his history, he should be approaching the territory with some trepidation. He could count the number of times he had seen his own father in person on one hand and other contacts on both plus a few toes. Sid Cohen divorced Alexandra and his son, too. Afterward, as soon as Zach was old enough, outgrowing a nanny, Alexandra found boarding schools and summer camps for her only child while she satisfied a wanderlust that took her from the Hotel George V in Paris to tribal yurts in Mongolia. Essentially Zach brought himself up. That he didn't end up disaffected or even in jail he credits to his good fortune in finding people like Patsy and Will Avery, Dan Miller, Faith, and a few others who came to his aid especially when he attended Mansfield Academy in Aleford for high school. It marked the start of his close collaboration with Faith in several joint searches for the truth and justice.

The computer had been his closest friend since childhood and could have so easily been his sole one. He learned from his mentors to be brave enough to let them become close, breaking out of his shell and even altering his uniform of black shirts and black jeans. Marrying Samantha was the happiest day of his life, except perhaps for the day he met her, adding now the day she told him she was pregnant. There would be the birth and raising the child, or children, together surrounded by those most important to them both. He had already run out of fingers and toes for counting, run out of his beloved algorithms to calculate the joyful moments. Having the baby during the time of Covid made him cautious but not fearful. He would keep Samantha and the miracle growing in her womb safe.

When Faith called and asked whether he could take some time and meet with her to talk about Claudia's death, he had not hesitated and told her to name the time and place.

"The catering kitchen? Thursday afternoon?" With no food to prepare until Friday for the Saturday deliveries, Faith had picked Thursday so they would have uninterrupted time. After the live stream Maundy Thursday service, it was also Tom's day at the VA hospital, in person now.

"See you at one? And I'll keep it to myself unless you want me to share it with Samantha and my parents-in-law."

"I would like you to keep it to yourself, although it's a rule that spouses are not supposed to keep anything from each other." A rule, she reflected, she'd broken on more than one occasion. But always for a good reason. Like now. Tom had been giving her sad puppy-dog looks ever since he'd reported the police findings. A look that said how sorry he was and that he was there for her. The undercurrent was that the matter was supposed to be closed. Grieve, yes; investigate, no.

"Samantha and Pix are happily producing enough teeny little garments for quintuplets, God forbid, and there's no need to upset the baby cart. I have a feeling we may want to bring Sam into this at some point in the future, but not yet." Both Pix and Sam had opted for first names instead of Mother and Father

Miller—"Sounds like patent medicine, Lydia Pinkham type," Pix had said.

"See you Thursday, and thank you," Faith said.

"Glad to be of help, ma'am," he teased. "Ma'am" was for a very different kind of woman.

"Faith, dear, it's Persis. Henry and I want to convey our condolences to you and Claudia's family, if you're in touch with them. It is heartbreaking."

What Persis did not say, but Faith knew from Tom, was that Henry felt responsible for the Zoom bombing, which all Aleford had decided was the trigger for the suicide, not that they were calling it that. They were calling it an "accidental death." It also had not taken long for the news of Claudia's resignation to get out, and everyone believed that was an additional factor for the depression leading to the tragedy. No one believed Henry was culpable, save Henry himself. He had reached out to Tom, his pastor, and Faith knew that it would take a while for Henry to get over the connection between the two events; maybe he never would. Tom had talked him out of resigning as town moderator—Town Meeting was once again to be on Zoom, as it had been in 2020—convincing him that people would be extremely upset and it would get in the way of essential business that had to be accomplished to keep Aleford on course. It was a covert "Think of the town and its inhabitants, not you" message.

"Thank you. No family has been identified yet. She was an only child, and her mother died when she was young. It seems she was estranged from her father."

There was another reason for Persis's call, and Faith knew it would come out eventually. After some more comments about how terrible it all was and at this wretched Covid time, it did.

"I know we spoke of having the little celebration for Henry

just after Town Meeting, which is this Saturday, but we didn't set a date and we haven't publicized it, have we?"

All this must have rattled Persis more than Faith had realized. Persis rattled was akin to an asteroid hitting Aleford's Town Hall.

"No, we haven't. Did you want to set one now?" Maybe the town needed a celebration.

"I think I'd rather wait a bit. What with the weather—you do know we're supposed to get a storm on Sunday, a white Easter—and, well, just the state of things in general. Let's wait until late April or May. Henry won't know the difference since it's a surprise."

And Henry wouldn't want this surprise now in his current state, Faith thought.

"I think that makes sense, and by then more people, especially younger ones, will have been vaccinated."

Persis's sigh traveled over the wires. "It's hard to think of pleasant occasions at the present."

"But we will, and soon." Faith found herself comforting the comforter, and they soon hung up.

After talking to Persis, she felt in need of real comfort and called Hope. Tom had called her, speaking also to Faith's parents. Faith had spoken to all three on Monday and then several times over the last week, mostly to Hope. Hope had known of Faith's friendship with the art teacher and had encouraged her sister to do the graphic-format cookbook. Hope answered immediately.

"Hi, sweetie, how are you doing? That's a stupid question, but you know what I mean."

"I do." Her sister would worry if Faith told her that she was sure Claudia was murdered and intended to investigate. Ever since Hope had had to rescue Faith from a madwoman intent on adding Faith to her list of victims, Hope had taken a dim view of Fay's sleuthing activities. "I keep thinking this can't all be real. That she is dead. She was so young, vibrant, so alive. The last time I saw her, less than a week before, she was filled with plans for her future."

"This kind of death is the hardest to accept. So many questions that will never be answered. I know you, and it will always be with you in some way, large now, but smaller with the passage of time. I wish I could be with you. Or even better, have you here with all of us."

"I'll come as soon as Ben and Amy get a first shot, and it may be sooner than projected. Early April."

"What Ben—and Zach—are doing for people is a boon. I've been telling everyone about it, and it's encouraged a few of their kids to do the same for their parents and others. Goodness knows spending hours facing a screen constantly refreshing it is a way of life for that generation. And there are so many scams out there. People, especially seniors, paying for appointments that don't exist."

They hung up, and Faith thought she'd round things out with a call to her sister-in-law. Her mother-in-law, Marian, answered.

"How lovely to hear your voice," she said. "We're hoping you might be able to come down after church on Easter this Sunday now that we are all vaccinated, but it seems a major storm is on the way."

"I know," Faith said. "This may be as strange a Holy Week as last year's. Tom had so hoped to have Easter outdoors, masked and spread out. Now he and Ben are planning to tape it in case we lose power, which would make live stream or Zoom impossible. They're live streaming the other days."

"Dick is getting cabin fever and wants to go back to the house. He plans to fix the canoe so he can fish on the North River as soon as the snow melts. Betsey doesn't want us to leave until the weather is more like spring. It's true that we lose power even in a high wind in Norwell. The town keeps talking about replacing the wires, but that means cutting down more than branches. Whole trees."

Another puzzling New England trait. Tree worship, even at the cost of massive power failures that are not merely inconvenient but dangerous, especially for elderly people. When a storm took down the huge rotten oak, its branches almost draped across the parsonage roof, Faith gave a silent cheer.

Cabin fever. That phrase again. A common condition since the start of the pandemic, and she had expected that her father-in-law would have a problem with not being able to go out and about as he pleased. But not Claudia. She had often told Faith that the carriage house was the perfect location for her as an artist and also as a person who liked being alone. And she wasn't a prisoner within the four walls but often took walks and drives. Human contact was satisfied by phone. Her phone . . . Faith had it in her purse and would give it to Zach to unlock its secrets.

"I doubt we'll see you Sunday by any method, but Tom and I will come sometime next week. Who knows? We might be able to have a picnic." Marian was, like all the Fairchilds, an outdoors person, preferring a meal sitting on a blanket under the sky even with ants to one indoors anywhere.

Zach arrived promptly at one o'clock, blew Faith a kiss, took his laptop out of its case, and set up at the end of one of the tables.

"Okay, start from the beginning. I'm sorry to make you go through it, but I need to hear what you saw and what you thought from the time you arrived at Claudia's."

Faith nodded. "Thank you for doing this. I'll start from the beginning, but first I want you to understand one thing. I am sure Claudia was murdered. I can start by telling you why."

"I figured that out right away, and you don't have to convince me. I trust your intuition or whatever you want to call it. I'm assuming you knew her better than anyone else. I'm also assuming that you think the killer was also the Zoom bomber."

"Yes. He or she had to lay the groundwork, create a motive, for why she would take her own life, push her to resign, all of it."

Zach started typing rapidly. "Walk me through that night, starting with getting out of the car."

Faith thought it would be hard, reliving it, but with this all-important goal, she found it rewarding to relate every single detail she could remember, from how Claudia had looked to the desecration of her artwork. She handed him the phone.

"This is good. I'm assuming the police took her computer."

"I'm sure they did, although it may not have been possible to get anything from it. It was open, and she had vomited directly on the keyboard from what I saw."

"No problem for me, but we can't get at it. When Tom spoke to Chief Franklin, did the chief mention any information they'd found on it?"

"No. He did say they had been unable to find next of kin, so they must have been looking for that." Faith was sure the police must have looked for a phone, in the house and Claudia's car, but no mention had been made. Not that they were conveying any information to her, but it might have been mentioned to Tom. No, to them it was a suicide, and the case was quickly closed.

She relayed all the findings from the medical examiner and the chief that Tom had passed on. Also her conversation with the superintendent.

"At some point, we'll need the full ME/autopsy report, but no need to ruffle feathers yet," Zach said. "With no next of kin, you and Tom qualify as nearest." Faith had told him about the information Claudia had entered on her school forms. No family emergency contact. The Fairchilds were it.

And Faith knew exactly what he was implying when he mentioned feathers. Their investigation would be viewed as a nuisance or worse.

"Make me a strong cup of coffee, please," he said. "I want to get all this organized. I'm creating a file to send to your computer labeled Artwork, so we can both have access to the contents and add as we go along."

Faith appreciated the subtlety.

She made herself a cup, too, and Zach stopped typing while he took a sip.

"We have more information than you might think. We know the means—and I'm already pondering the how—approximately the time, you have some names to follow up on, which may produce more. What we don't have is a motive. How about the good old cui bono?"

"I don't think it applies in the usual sense here." She realized she had forgotten to tell Zach about the conversation she'd had with Claudia about a will. "She hadn't made a will, she told me not long ago, because she didn't have anyone to leave to." She related the rest—the Edward Gorey that Claudia was taking with her and the prints Faith would have. "She didn't say she didn't have anything to leave, but she couldn't have had much. I know she modeled for the art classes because she needed the money. After that, she had her teacher's salary and benefits, plus a small amount from sales of her artwork. She drove a used car she found on Craigslist, and her clothes were not big-ticket items. The Sinclairs wanted her in the carriage house because they liked her very much, but also to keep an eye on their house and the rest of the property. She told me that as time went on, she had to push them to accept more rent money. Which reminds me. Their son dropped by last August, and it wasn't a pleasant encounter." She related what Claudia had said.

"I'll check him out. If he's on the skids out in California or elsewhere, he may have wanted to get rid of an obstacle he believed might be influencing his parents in their estate planning. Especially if he was borrowing with an inheritance as collateral."

He'd been taking notes while they talked for almost two hours. "I shouldn't keep you any longer, and I should be getting home, too," Faith said.

"It's a fine start, Faith. I hope it helps, in a number of ways."

He was such a good person. And he was right. That they were doing something about the death was one. That it was making her feel less depressed another.

"I'll get to work on my end. I have a few tricks up my sleeve. All legal, no problem. You concentrate on the art teacher, the roommate, and anyone else that talking with them turns up. Covid is making this harder but not impossible."

He removed the flash drive he'd attached to the laptop. "Let's keep this and the others I'll create here. What's the best place? And no, not in the bottom of your flour bin."

"The drawer in my desk with hanging files. We can tuck it in one, maybe in one I already have, Things I Don't Know Where Else to Put."

Zach laughed. "Perfect. And keep thinking back over any conversations you had with Claudia, even years ago, and jot down anything that comes to mind."

Faith gave him two large loaves of the cardamom raisin bread glazed with egg, vanilla, and sugar she'd baked especially for Easter, a tradition started in the Fairchild household when Ben was born. She drove home feeling better than she had in almost two weeks. It would be exactly two weeks this Sunday, and the significance of the day had been in her thoughts constantly. If no next of kin had been located, the decision about Claudia's body would revert to the Fairchilds. Tom had talked to Sam Miller soon after speaking to the chief, and in Sam's frequent role as estate lawyer, he knew what to do to ensure that Claudia would get a decent burial, decided by Tom and Faith. They had discussed it late one night, and they were in agreement that Claudia should rest in the plot the Fairchilds had purchased years ago on Sanpere not far from Pix's ancestral one. With an eye to the future, Tom had insisted at the time they get a double one. He liked the idea of having plenty of company, Faith had said, kidding him. There was room for Claudia, and Faith reflected ruefully that Claudia had wanted to be on the Maine coast. Driving home, she thought it was unlikely that a relative would spring up suddenly. Prayed one wouldn't. Whoever might appear wouldn't be someone Claudia considered close.

Saturday's Town Meeting went off without a hitch, and the school building project, expected to be a contentious vote, passed almost unanimously. Whether it was the season of the year with observances marked by a number of religions or whether it was weather—voters anxious to turn off their computers and prepare for Sunday's storm—it turned out to be one of the shortest on record. And uneventful. Zach had offered Henry his services and Zoom-bomb-proofed the meeting: no screen sharing, questions only in the chat, registered participants admitted from the waiting room one at a time, no dropping in, and other safeguards. Henry began the meeting with a moment of silence for all those lost since the last meeting, Claudia's name included.

Faith represented the household, since Tom and Ben were at the church taping the Easter Sunday service, anticipating that the Zoom service would most likely be canceled due to power outages from the nor'easter. Tom was also getting ready for the Holy Saturday vigil at seven o'clock, which would be live streamed.

Amy had gone for a masked, socially distanced walk with a small group of friends. It was a beautiful, bright day, only a bit chilly. As well as feeling the continuing emotional strain of being separated from Catherine, Ben had been spot-on about his sister in his outburst. Amy and all the seniors were being deprived of what should have been a significant year in their young lives. One filled with conflicting emotions of not wanting to leave and looking forward to doing so. Friendship ties had intensified for her daughter during the pandemic, and Faith hoped Covid, which she had long ago begun to personify as a deadly villain, would give the kids a break so they could have some kind of nonvirtual graduation ceremony and maybe a prom. Like postponed weddings, she'd heard of school systems that had already invited their seniors to come back for the Class of 2022's proms.

She had made Moroccan lamb stew the day before for a hearty

early dinner for the family. They would all go over to the church for the vigil. Now she put the stew on simmer to heat up. Soon the kitchen was filled with the tantalizing aroma of cinnamon, cumin, ginger, cloves, nutmeg, and turmeric. She got out the ingredients for the couscous that would go with it and was just measuring the grain when her phone rang. The ID was Zachmantha. Zach had given her the number of the cell he used for work, a private number. Still, Faith was surprised to hear Samantha's voice.

"Is this a bad time? I know Town Meeting is over. I watched for a while, but you may be busy cooking."

The couscous could wait. "No, it's fine. What's up? If you and your mother have run out of yarn or thread, I'm afraid you've come to the wrong person."

"Highly unlikely. Mom cornered the market on thread as soon as there were supplies again, and I have the feeling she's been stockpiling yarn for booties and sweaters since she was making them for us. No, I'm actually calling for Ellie. She doesn't want to bother you now, and we've been talking. We're Wellesley sibs, you may remember, and the pandemic has made us even closer."

"She wrote a beautiful note. She and Claudia became close planning the wedding—invitations, and other things. I should have called her."

"No worries. It's just that my being pregnant has made her even more broody than before, and I wanted to run a solution by you that we've come up with that we think will satisfy her parents, particularly her father."

"Miracles do happen. Tell me!" Faith said. It would be a welcome relief.

"I know it would have been a dream wedding. She told me all about it, and I was looking forward to it almost as much as she was, but during these past months the wedding is not what's on her mind. Getting married, yes, but marriage *and* starting a family are what's most important to her, Adam, too. She knows how much the wedding itself means to her father for all sorts of complicated reasons. The wedding he and her mother didn't have, no money in either family for such a blowout, and then her sister and brothers didn't have the kind her parents hoped for, where they could invite all their friends and family to witness."

Faith knew this and hadn't been able to come up with a solution except to postpone, maybe subtly encouraging Ellie to forget to take a pill. Scheduling it for June 2022 might mean a very tiny infant if they got pregnant right away.

"What's the plan?"

"A nuptial intervention with you as facilitator."

"Oh, great," Faith said.

"No, wait a minute, let me finish. Claudia had completed the Save the Dates and all that's needed is to change the year, the zero to a two. She'd made some sample invitations, and my clever husband can duplicate the one they choose and print it out on paper similar to the parchment Claudia selected. The big change is the numbers. Everything else the same. Venue, menu. She has the dress, person of honor, bridesmaid ones, too. But it will be a much smaller wedding. She and Adam were never comfortable with invitations going to people Ellie's parents knew whom they didn't. You can think of a nice way to say that. The basic point, and Adam is going to make it plus his parents, who will be in on the FaceTime, too, and agree, is that what's happened since June 2020, not just with Covid, has brought a new perspective for them. Their hope is that having a definite wedding date to look forward to, talk about, will overshadow the whole baby question. If it happens, it happens and will mean altering the dress, or I'll dress up as a medieval nanny, taking charge of the wee one with mine."

"Why can't you be the facilitator? You've worked it all out with Ellie." Faith thought the idea was the solution, but she'd just as soon stay on the sidelines.

"Duh, Faith, you're the expert and have to be there to deal with any questions not just about the food, but seating, the Ganley location, et cetera. Besides, you're a real grown-up. Ellie and I aren't there yet."

"Wait until the stork lands in August," Faith countered, and then yielded. "Okay. Let me know the time, and Ellie should call me to run through it all."

"She's going to be ecstatic! If it's a girl, she's naming her after you, by the way. I'm not because it would be too confusing since we're family. By choice."

They chatted a bit more. Samantha wanted to hear all about Ben's Catherine.

"She's down on Long Island with her family for Easter, and since in New York State sixteen and older are eligible for a vaccination starting next Tuesday, she's staying to get her first shot. Ben already scored an appointment for her and a brother who is eighteen. He has to wait until the nineteenth but thinks he may be able to get it sooner. In any case, the two of them figure they can both be together in Providence by sometime in May. And once she has her second shot, I would not be surprised to see her on our doorstep."

"It's the real thing, isn't it? That's what Ben has been telling Zach."

"If that's what he's saying, that's what it is."

"Be happy, Faith. You should know. When it's the one, it's the one. I've heard about you and Tom. And look at my parents. Public displays of affection, at least in the house, even at their age!"

Pix and Sam were not that much older than Faith and Tom. She was tempted to say something but told her she *was* happy, and hung up.

Except she wasn't. Couldn't be now.

As expected, Easter Sunday's storm dumped ten inches of snow on Aleford, and most of the town, including the parsonage, lost power. Faith once again made a mental note to try to get Tom to push the Vestry into allocating funds to rewire what had no doubt been installed shortly after the advent of Mr. Edison's ingenuity, and since it still worked—somewhat—Yankee thrift had seen no need to change. She made eggy French toast with the cardamom raisin bread, and they ate it in front of the fire with jelly beans. Ben showed her a photo Catherine had texted of her grandmother's Easter bread, baked with dyed whole eggs on top of the braided dough circle that hardened as the bread baked. It was beautiful. "Next year we can make both," he said.

Everyone went to bed early, the sound of the town plows lulling them to sleep.

As was typical of the time of year, the next day dawned sunny and warm. The snow had been deep but light and began to melt. Faith had waited until today to mention that two weeks had passed, asking Tom to get in touch with the police chief or to ask Sam to do it. It might be better for the lawyer to request possession of the deceased on their behalf.

"I'll call Sam and see what he advises," Tom said, and pulled his wife close. "I know how hard this is for you. Me, too."

"But you do think there won't be any problem?"

"I *hope* there won't," he said, and Faith had to be satisfied with that. Or dissatisfied.

Ati Patel, the person currently listed as residing at 54 Delle Avenue, called Tuesday afternoon.

"I received your message about Claudia," she said. "I'm sorry I didn't call right away, but I've been out of town. I can't believe Claudia is dead! We were roommates for a year. What happened?"

Ati's words ran into one another in a pleasant, somewhat singsong way. Faith wasn't sure how to answer her reasonable question.

"It was an accident with some acid that was spilled and ingested. Acid used in her printmaking. Is this your area, or were you familiar with the techniques and materials she used?"

"I was starting my master's in drawing and painting, not printmaking, but I know a lot about it. And I know for certain that Claudia was always very careful in the studio. She mentioned it often."

Faith wanted to keep Ati talking in the hope that she might know about not just Claudia's work habit but also the rest of her life. "How have you been dealing with the pandemic? Have you been able to do your artwork?"

"The pandemic has put my career on hold, but I've been able to work in the apartment. My parents didn't want me to have any roommates during Covid and have helped with the rent. I've been able to sell some of my drawings through a gallery's website, and they're interested in representing my paintings, too. If we can finally be in person, they'll hire me as staff to gallery sit, although I'll still have to waitress at night. I don't mind it, just shut my ears. Claudia hated it. That's why she modeled for life drawing classes. And if my parents ever found out I was posing nude, I would be back in Philadelphia and locked in my room for a very long time!"

This was the opening Faith wanted. "If Claudia's family had known, would they have been upset, too?"

"Claudia didn't really talk about her family. She was a very private person. I was closer to her than our other roommate, who was a pain. One of those 'Who ate my Brown Cow yogurt' people, which no one had, since she labeled everything. And she was a neat freak. Claudia was not messy, but not tidy. She'd leave a mug in the sink, and Cassandra—that was her name, really—would go off on her. Claudia ignored it all. The two of us were kind of tight. She told me her mother had died when she was a teenager. Cancer. She'd been sick for a long time. That was as open about personal stuff as she ever was. I had the feeling that besides her mother's death she'd had some kind of very negative experience, but that could just be me. My friends keep telling me I should have been a shrink, not an artist."

"Besides you, did Claudia have friends at the school? Did she go on dates?"

"She knew people and was friendly, but not exactly friends with people. Very intent on getting her credentials and a teaching job so she could support herself while still devoting herself to her printmaking. You must have seen her work. She was more than talented. I tried to get her to go out when a bunch of us would, and I know there were guys who tried to date her, but she kept to herself. She said she was saving her pennies. She was focused on her work. We didn't talk about it after she'd made it clear she wasn't interested in a social life. In a way, although she was the same age as the rest of us, she seemed older. More mature."

"So no guys who might have kept pursuing her? Didn't take no for an answer?"

"You mean like stalkers? I'd have known. And the school is a close, and good, community. Word would have gotten around and something done."

"How about the neat freak? Would she have held a grudge of some sort against her?"

"She would have been more likely to have one against me—she wasn't into ethnic, to put it mildly—and moved out at the end of the semester. We decided we could swing the rent without a third person."

"We've been trying to find Claudia's next of kin, without any luck. Did she mention any?"

"I'm sure her father was alive. The only time parents came up, that's when she said her mother had died, she added she didn't have any contact at all with her father. I have a gazillion aunts, uncles, and cousins. She never spoke of any. And she was an only child. I joked that she was lucky not to be the youngest of the smartest, most successful siblings on the planet. She never got any snail mail; I wouldn't have known about her email or texts. She knew a lot about New York City. The museums and galleries, so I assumed she lived there or visited often."

"Did she mention Connecticut? Maybe growing up there?"

"She did go to UConn. She may have grown up there. She just never said."

"Was she close to any of her professors? Anyone else at Mass-Art you can think of?"

Faith could picture Ati—she'd seen her FB page—shaking her head, thinking. After a pause she said, "No, nobody. But I don't want to give you the wrong idea. She was a happy person. Very funny, and she loved what she was doing, loved the teaching when she started practice teaching. That's what I can't understand. How can she be dead? She was so alive."

As soon as she hung up, Faith called Zach. Samantha was napping, so he had time to talk. Even though she hadn't gotten much concrete information from Claudia's roommate, Faith felt the image of who Claudia was before she came to Aleford was less fuzzy. Maybe knowing all this—how someone had lived—would lead to how she died. Go backward and forward in turn.

"After I spoke to Ati and thought about who Claudia had been, I had a strong feeling that if the Zoom bombing had never happened and obviously her death, she would have continued to blossom here. She had friends, students who loved her, and until the pandemic shut everything down, she was active in the community. Not just Aleford, but in Boston, too, at Rosie's Place, the shelter for women, and the Boston Food Pantry. I think she started there in college."

"I agree, and I also have news. I've entered it into the file. First, I've gone back through her call history for the last three years. That's when she must have bought this phone. She never made a call outside Massachusetts except one early on to the number you had for her teacher, Anna Kingman, and to the Sinclairs in Maine. No texts to them. Her Massachusetts calls were all to people I've identified in town or to businesses, inquiries I'm assuming about whether they had something she needed—quite a few to Pearl Art in Cambridge. Some galleries, the Clark in Lincoln. A couple to the landscaper/plow service the Sinclairs used."

"Texts? She used to text me."

"Found them, and again, the rest were to people she occasionally phoned, like Ellie Porter and her parents, the Millers. But, Faith, her texts to her colleague Brian Kimball got pretty suggestive at times, especially on his part. I've checked, and they started right after he was hired. The early ones have to do with their teaching. Trading ideas. And about their art. He's a painter, also a photographer."

"Photographer! Could he have been at MassArt and in one of the classes where she posed?"

"Could have been but wasn't. NYU and the Art Students League. The texts got to be flirty, and then they started to meet up for walks, bringing sketch pads. During the lockdown, his became more than that. Texts about how beautiful she looked the last time they were together. 'A unique face, tall lithe body like no other woman,' and so forth. Close to, but not actual sexting. I've sent you them. Her responses were guarded at first, although you could tell she was flattered. After a while she began to respond. I'd say she was falling in love with him. Then he pulled a full stop after the Zoom bombing. He didn't reply most times she'd text and finally didn't answer at all. She stopped, too. But her last one said, 'I hope I haven't offended you in some way.' I would have expected him to be very sympathetic about what she'd experienced. Angry even."

"Oh, poor Claudia. I wish I had known. Tom and I went to the Kimballs' house once. It was some kind of gathering sponsored by the MetroWest Friends of Modern Architecture to interest people in joining. I always like to see people's houses, so I dragged Tom along, and the place was amazing. Someone has money."

"That would be the wife. Major job. Commodities trader, a big-time international firm."

"There was a Russel Wright cup and saucer in the dish drainer by Claudia's sink. She wasn't a fan of midcentury modern, and I'd never seen it there before. A gift from Brian, or he left it there? A calling card? Or someone else wanted it to be one?" Faith was sure the pale orange pottery must be connected to the murder. It was a glaring wrong note. "We need to add his name to the Zoom bombing/murderer list."

"*And* his wife's," Zach said.

If Faith had seen texts like the ones Zach described on Tom's phone, she'd have gone crazy. Maybe Margaret Kimball had.

"How about Christopher Sinclair?" Faith asked. "Any luck?"

"That was a breeze—I added it to the file—and I'll tell you quickly before the real pay dirt. He is a property developer, primarily golf courses, but even before the pandemic he was in trouble. Was living the high life in Montecito, multimillion-dollar house went into foreclosure, his company, Sinclair Greens, went bust. He's working for another outfit and living in a studio apartment in Santa Monica, not exactly slumming, and word has it that he's trying to get investors for a new project, what would be a world-class course. Dropping major names, but my source—this time not just the web—says there's a lot of skepticism."

"So if things don't go his way in California, he may pressure his parents into letting him develop in Aleford. They were spending more and more time in Maine even before Covid, and if anything the winters there are milder than here, since they're on the water, or they could always head south. Be snowbirds. But Claudia couldn't stay in the carriage house, be around to influence Patricia and Edward. Edward made it clear he doesn't approve of Christopher being so far away. His mother defended him, as mothers do."

"That's Christopher for now. Stays on the list. Here's the big news. I've started delving deep into the web, and today I got lucky. I used a search engine that's light-years beyond Google and entered 'Claudia Richards' and 'Connecticut' in various ways. She came up in the graduating classes of Greenwich Academy,

Miss Porter's, and the University of Connecticut. She was also listed as participating in various tennis and golf tournaments at the Greenwich Country Club—membership by invitation only. Go to the website. Pretty luxe."

"So we know she grew up in Greenwich or nearby. That's money."

"Indeed. But we also now know her father's name, and I can get going on finding him."

"And you know his name how?"

"Two ways. They won mixed doubles several times, but the clincher was this brief announcement in the local paper, *Greenwich Time.* The headline reads 'Miss Claudia Richards to Marry Charles Hamilton Junior,' and goes on, 'Mr. James Richards is pleased to announce the engagement of his and the late Eleanor Schuyler Richards's daughter, Claudia, to Charles Hamilton Junior, son of Elizabeth "Bitsy" and the late Charles Hamilton. Miss Richards is currently a student at the University of Connecticut Storrs. Mr. Hamilton, a graduate of Yale, is studying law at the City University of New York. A June wedding at Saint Thomas Fifth Avenue is planned, and the couple will reside in Greenwich.'"

"Claudia was married!"

Chapter Ten

"Engaged, anyway," Zach said. "If she got married at Saint Thomas Fifth Avenue, she would have needed a New York license, and it will be easy to check the certificate of registration filed after the I do's."

"Before my own marriage, when Have Faith was in Manhattan, we did a number of receptions following Saint Thomas nuptials. Putting her Greenwich and private school upbringing plus the legendary church together must mean Claudia was not poor, but maybe a poor little rich girl. Ati said she had the feeling there was some other negative experience aside from her mother's death affecting Claudia, and I'm sure of it. She had a kind of underlying sadness. Tom thought so, too. Could it be because of her marriage?"

"Or being jilted? I have to do some work work, but I should finish by tomorrow and can resume the digging."

Faith felt slightly guilty at taking Zach away from his job, and his wife, but only slightly. Now that information was pouring in, she felt closer than ever to finding out who killed Claudia and told Zach so.

"I do, too. How did Sherlock ever manage without the web, relying on cigar ash and clay caked on a boot? I wouldn't mind channeling those powers of deduction, though. I keep coming up against a sticking point—the how."

"You mean how did the murderer know she was so totally impaired? The containers looked almost the same, and I've double-checked on the acid, no odor and clear. It had to have been that she was so drunk she mistook the acid for vodka. Is that what you're picturing?"

"Yes," Zach said, "unless the person was actually there watching and waiting. And had been for a long time before that night. The alarm system didn't have CCTV, did it?"

"I don't know, but that reminds me of something we should check. In January the alarm company got in touch because they were getting a low-battery signal and they had to replace it. She described how strange it felt to watch a technician enter the house in full hazmat while she waited in her car. What if . . ."

"It was to plant a device? How soon do you think we can get into the house?"

"I drove over a few days ago, and it doesn't have that yellow tape up anymore. So not sealed. And I know where the key is, and the code. Same as her phone."

"It's time to do a thorough search. I'm sure the police went over the place, but they weren't looking for what we are."

"No. They found the acid, the vodka, what they wanted to find for suicide, and stopped."

Faith was feeling very, very tired. The how was all very well, but she wanted to find the why.

Niki had called and offered to help Faith do the prep work for tomorrow's dinner-box deliveries. The numbers were decreasing a little as people felt more comfortable getting their own supplies, and throughout the pandemic home cooking had developed a cachet equaled only by the craze for French cooking in home kitchens with pioneer Julia Child. Niki's car was already parked outside when Faith pulled in, and she felt her spirits rise. Philip and she were still in the two houses, but Niki had told Faith that her mother's frequent babysitting had added a new kind of spice to married life with child-free conjugal visits.

A familiar aroma greeted her. "Banana bread?"

"Yup. The cream cheese gravy train is over, and I think the initial banana bread oversaturation has waned, and it's such comfort food. I've made mini loaves, some with walnuts, some not."

Isolated at home with towers of toilet paper, heaps of hand sanitizers, and shelves of canned beans, people turned to baking quantities of banana bread—no yeast, an ingredient even if a bit old readily available, posting photos of finished loaves instead of pets and selfies.

"Another time we can do a date-and-nut bread, making little sandwiches if we can get cream cheese. Hope and I used to stop at Chock full o' Nuts on our way home for school for them. I've never been able to duplicate those."

"I think you'd have to add an ingredient equivalent of freedom to them, as in 'school's over,'" Niki said, laughing.

Faith started to prepare a much larger amount of the Moroccan stew she'd made Saturday, one batch spicier than the other, for tomorrow's entrée.

"Bring me up to date," Niki said.

"There's a lot." She saved the engagement announcement for last. Niki said what Zach had.

"Many a slip. Doesn't mean she made it to the altar. She didn't wear any rings, but many artists don't. They get in the way."

"Zach said it was easy to find out. What I'd like to do now is get into the house and look through everything. And before that I want to take down the prints that were mutilated and destroy them."

"I know you think the murderer and the Zoom bomber are

the same person," Niki said. "I agree, and defacing Claudia's prints was the same kind of attack on her."

Faith hadn't linked the two acts. Had Claudia seen the damage? Did that drive her to the heavy drinking, feeling attacked?

"Why can't you go into the house now?" Niki suggested. "You could call the Sinclairs, so it would be aboveboard. As in lieu of next of kin, you have to pack up her belongings. They'll say there's no rush, wanting to spare you, but you could tell them it would make you feel better. Which it would."

"It would. I can't do what Zach is doing, but there must be information about her past the police missed. Once they filed the autopsy report, notes, photos from the scene, it wasn't on a back burner, it was shut off. At some point, when and if Covid is over, some eager new hire might come across it and try to find next of kin, but I doubt it." Nothing the police had done had made her feel good. Going into the house, any action on her part, was what she needed. "I also want to ask the Clark Gallery if they would run the last plate she made and never printed. She said it was a self-portrait."

She thought again about the prints on the wall. Tom had intimated, gently but firmly, that Claudia might have done it herself, an indication of her frame of mind. Faith knew he'd picked up the idea from Chief Pat, even mentioning that there was ink on Claudia's hands. There was *always* ink on her hands. Claudia would never have slashed her work. Faith wouldn't destroy them after all. She'd keep them in a separate folder. Evidence. But not of frame of mind.

Niki took several batches of the breads out of the oven to cool. "So, what's new at the parsonage? The kids, Tom?"

"You don't fool me for a minute, Ms. Theodopoulos. You want to know what Tom thinks about what Zach and I have been doing. But before we talk about that, I can quickly tell you Ben is still head over heels in love and Catherine is down on Long Island with her family getting her first shot. Amy and her friends are trying to plan an outdoor gathering next month. Someone saw one online where a group made a huge socially distanced circle heart on a football field and held cardboard hearts overhead while a drone photographed it. They had music playing. Amy thought they could hold their mortarboards decorated with whatever they wanted with a banner on the grass in the center, 'Congratulations Aleford High Class of 2021.' It all involves much texting and even actual phoning back and forth, so she's not as depressed as she was. I've been enlisted to help her bake and package cookies with the congratulations to place at each spot where a senior will stand."

"And back to Tom?"

"Well, he's very busy, more than ever now that he can have in-person interactions," Faith said, hedging.

"Faith!" Niki's tone was unmistakable. She knew her friend was avoiding the question.

"Okay, so maybe he doesn't know what Zach and I are doing."

"Maybe?"

"No maybe. He doesn't. I'll let him know at some point, but I don't want to hear what I know he'll say now. That I should accept the medical examiner's finding and let it all go. Concentrate on remembering Claudia as she was, mourning for her, but not playing sleuth. Period."

Niki handed Faith a slice of warm banana bread. "Eat. I'll bet you haven't been much. Not a diet I'd recommend."

Faith gave her a wan smile and took the bread. It was delicious.

"I seem to recall," Niki continued, "that you are the woman who told me that marriage vows implicitly included 'talk to each other.' It was when Philip and I were having that rough patch when he lost his job the day I found out I was pregnant with Sofia. Remember? I kept the news from him for a week, and it was hell. I'm not saying you have to share every little detail with Tom, but start with going into the house. That you need to do it."

It's never nice to have someone quote your own advice back, but Niki was right. She'd start with telling Tom that she wanted to ask the Sinclairs if she could get in to pack Claudia's possessions. As for the rest, she'd wait until she had something major. Although, Claudia's engagement announcement was no small thing.

"I'll come with you," Tom said that evening when Faith told him she wanted to ask the Sinclairs about emptying Claudia's belongings from the carriage house.

She was ready for him. "It's going to take a long time. I want to make separate packages of all her unused art supplies, any clothing for Rosie's Place that they could distribute. The Sinclairs own the press, so finding a home for that is not a problem. I'll donate the supplies, unused plates to an artist the Clark or MassArt suggests." She could ask Ati, too, and the name almost slipped out. "I want to do this as soon as possible and get it out of the way. Not keep thinking about the job." This was true.

Tom pulled her close. "I don't have any time to spare these days it seems, but how about asking Pix, or Niki, to go with you?"

"They're both involved with their families. Niki can't leave the kids with her mother too often, much as Eleni would like it, and Pix has been going off with Samantha so she gets some exercise and fresh air. Zach is working." He was. A lot.

"Call me if you want company, and if it starts to feel too hard, stop. I know you want to do this. You'll never get over her death, but this can be the start of some closure."

"I'll call the Sinclairs tomorrow. And what has Sam said about the release of her body?"

Besides determining where Claudia should be buried, Tom and Faith had discussed cremation with interment when they went to Sanpere in June, a graveside memorial service with the Millers and the Sinclairs.

"Things are chaotic now with Covid deaths, but he is in touch with a funeral home in Concord and they are dealing with the

State Police morgue. It won't be long, since the two weeks are up with no next of kin located."

Faith gave a sigh of relief. She could stop thinking of her friend with a toe tag, in a very cold place.

The engagement announcement from December 2011 listed her father's name, but it was ten years ago. Zach was tracking James Richards down, but given that Claudia, and Ati, too, had said they were estranged, Faith wanted to keep control of what would happen to her friend's remains. She was sure it was what Claudia would have wanted.

The Sinclairs had been worried about what to do with the contents of the carriage house and readily gave Faith permission for access. "She volunteered at the shelter for women, Rosie's Place, so that is a fine idea," Patricia said. "She was such a good person. I still can't believe we won't sit down and talk about her work, all sorts of things, over tea."

"She gave me the alarm code and told me where the key was. When I'm finished, I'll let you know. I think you should change the code, and I'll keep the key until I can hand it to you."

She didn't say why.

Thursdays were always the easiest day of the week, with Saturday's Have Faith Delivered preparation on Fridays and only an occasional special order to do on a Thursday. Like the thrifty New Englander he was, Tom had saved a flattened stack of mover's boxes that, given how long ago they'd moved into the parsonage, almost qualified as antique, vintage definitely. She loaded a number into the van and several garment bags, although she didn't think Claudia had much in her wardrobe that would need to hang.

As she was backing out of the driveway, her phone rang. The caller ID was Zach's number. She stopped and answered.

He sounded ecstatic. "I've found out how the bomber got the

photos! Unfortunately, they're accessible to a large group. People surfing porn sites, and that's billions. I can narrow it down somewhat. More once we figure out if there was a surveillance device monitored by an individual. You're going into the house soon, right? Let me know immediately, and I'll come with you."

"Whoa! How did you find the photos? And I'm on my way there now."

"Sorry. I wasn't sure it would work, but when it did just now, I got pretty carried away. I'd isolated all the nude photos from her life drawing modeling and run each separately for a match anywhere on the web, eventually places you really don't want to go. It's taken time, and I didn't get any hits until this morning. And only on a single pose. The most sexually provocative. I found one site, then several more began pouring in either as original posts of the photo or shares. The sites have all the usual names: 'Hot Nude College Girls.' 'Pussy Galore.' Those are the tamest."

"This is terrible! To exploit her this way. Someone must have taken photos during the class and loaded them to these sites!"

"Or just posted them and they got copied. In any case, I can track down the shares that lead to names to see if any we know pop up, but the next step is for me to get into the carriage house and look at the alarm system, or the person posing as the technician could have planted one or more surveillance devices. I can't go today, though. We have an appointment at Emerson with the midwife who works with the obstetrician. Our baby is halfway to the finish line!"

"Oh, Zach, that's wonderful. I won't keep you. Give Samantha my love."

"We don't have to leave yet. Anything else you can think of about the photo?"

"Not the photo. I've been thinking of that repair call. The battery replacement. Assuming the alarm company is legitimate, and I'm certain it is—the church uses them—how would an individual get a truck with their logo or even know that the Sinclairs had an account?"

"Oh, Faith, the world is a much more evil place than you imagine. Technology has meant practices Tim Berners-Lee never intended and has spoken out against. Google Maps can enlarge the Sinclairs' home and grounds, giving a nice clear image of the sign proclaiming 'Protected by' and the company's name. Go to the company headquarters, take a photo of the van, and print up what's on the service vehicles using your handy-dandy laser printer and clear plastic easily attached to the side of an unpainted one. Or they may even have been able to find a used one online. Companies sell the old ones when they upgrade. And most of all, Claudia was expecting to see a truck with their logo, so even if it wasn't a perfect job, she wouldn't have noticed. And just like all cats are gray in the dark, so is everyone in a hazmat suit."

Before she unlocked the door, Faith opened the heavy wooden shutters that covered the large windows. It was cool out, but sunny. Inside, the house would be cool, too, although the heat would have been left on by the police. She'd dressed warmly.

Walking into the empty open space was so depressing, she almost panicked, turning back to call Pix to be with her, but after a few moments her heartbeat slowed and she stepped forward, shutting the door behind her.

She had to do this alone.

The team from the State Police had cleared the table Claudia used for most of the activities of her life from printmaking to teaching to eating. It was eerily tidy and had been scrubbed down. The defaced prints and all the arachnid photos and sketches were still pinned on the wall. The webs she'd woven for inspiration remained in place, hanging from the ceiling. At the far end of the table the shelves held some art supplies and the plate she had etched and inked lay below, the only item on the table. Her last creation.

She decided to start with the mundane and made up one of the boxes to hold the galley kitchen's contents. It didn't take long to wrap the plates, mugs, and glassware in newspaper, adding the single frying pan and a few saucepans. She kept the Russel Wright cup and saucer out. It was a discordant accent and she intended to hold on to any that were.

The rugs and furniture, except the worktable Claudia had purchased, all belonged to the Sinclairs. Faith thought they would probably want to take down the wallboard Claudia had placed behind it to tack up finished and in-progress work. They would probably want the table moved out, too, opening up the ground-floor space as it had been before Claudia occupied it. She took out her small notebook and started a new page with the reminder to ask them.

The art cabinet with the drawers to hold her work might also belong to the Sinclairs, and Faith added it to her queries. She'd ask the Clark Gallery what to do with the finished prints. She hadn't been in touch with them about a retrospective show, not current work as planned, in the fall. She very much hoped they would still do one. If not, the Sinclairs might have an idea. Post the artwork for sale and have the proceeds go for scholarships to MassArt?

She stood facing the wall of infamy, as she was calling it, noting the anger behind the slashes of ink, none missing the images of the spiders. This wasn't arachnophobia, though. This was something deep-seated. Hatred. The images stared back at her. She'd preserve them. They were evidence.

What had happened that night? Or had it been earlier? She wanted to sit down with Zach and try to sketch out a scenario. If there was some kind of surveillance that was able to detect when Claudia was incapable of logical thought, the two glass vessels would have had to be placed close together. There *had* to have been someone there. She sat down on Claudia's work stool imagining possibilities. At some point, the decanters are switched. Or the vodka one, which was slightly different, is filled with the acid. No. That wouldn't work. It had to be plain vodka, or the police would suspect foul play, not just Faith. So, Claudia is drinking heavily. She's being watched. Goes to the bathroom or upstairs. The container of acid is placed where the vodka had been, within easy reach. On her return, she wouldn't notice. Both bottles would have only her prints on them. Someone could have easily moved them by touching only the tops with gloved hands, two fingers, or even a long-handled stainless tong, like what Faith used for pasta and salads.

She wanted Zach to see the prints, so she left them in place and wearily got up, moving toward the stairs to the bedroom and bath. Seeing the book about Dürer that Henry had given Claudia on the coffee table, Faith picked it up. Nothing had been slipped between the pages. She'd return it to Henry. Persis's gift, a scarf, would keep someone on the streets in Boston warm.

Upstairs the bed had been stripped and the linens folded. The spread was a modern patchwork crazy quilt, brilliant colors with lightning-bolt fabric shapes. Faith put everything in a Hefty bag she'd brought. She'd wash them and whatever clothes before donating. She lifted the mattress up on all sides. Nothing underneath. She got down on the floor to peer under the bed. Again nothing save dust bunnies.

A small chest of drawers was testament to Claudia's lack of wardrobe interest. Aside from necessary underwear, socks, and the oversize tees that seemed to have served as nightwear, there was a pile of bright scarves, a stack of black tees, one of white, and one of mixed colors. Faith put them and the scarves in the bag. Claudia also had striped tights, a few pairs of pantyhose for the occasions when she wore the navy-blue suit hanging in the shallow closet along with the jumpers, jeans, and two denim skirts that were her usual garb. She had one dress, a black jersey knit with cap sleeves. A staple that could be dressed up or down.

A mirror in a Florentine frame hung over the chest of drawers. Faith took it down and looked at the back—"Tuscany 1983" in what was probably one of the Sinclairs' handwriting. She didn't know what she was searching for. Claudia had said she hadn't made a will, and that's where people in books hid them, and in the pages of books. On top of the chest were Claudia's hairbrush and comb, Guerlain's Mitsouko and a less expensive scent, a jasmine eau de toilette.

There was a nightstand next to the bed with a gooseneck lamp that proclaimed IKEA. The drawer held a packet of tissues, a tin of Fishermen's Friend cough drops, Nivea lip balm, and Neutrogena Norwegian Formula hand cream. Faith had a bag for trash and threw them in. Two books were stacked on top of the stand: Virginia Woolf's *A Room of One's Own* and E. B. White's *Charlotte's Web*. Both looked well read, and Faith had the feeling these were books Claudia always kept next to her, the way some people kept the Bible. She might be reading another book as well, but these old friends would always be by her side. There was nothing tucked in either of them, nor in the books in the small bookcase below one of the windows. Faith looked out over the garden and pond. The view would soon be filled with spring flowers and leaves on the trees, a green haze at first. She felt anger surge as she thought about the fact that Claudia would not be here looking out. Ever again.

The bathroom did not yield anything save VO5 shampoo and conditioner, Dove soap, and lavender body gel. Crest toothpaste and floss. Extra toilet paper, Tampax, a hair dryer, and towels in a basket below the sink. The medicine chest held Regular Strength Tylenol, Tums, Band-Aids, first aid cream, a thermometer, Q-tips, a package of disposable women's shavers, Clinique makeup, including small sizes Faith recognized as having been included in a bonus, as was the zippered bag the makeup was in. There was a bar of Lava soap, no doubt to get rid of ink on her hands.

She walked back into the bedroom and looked around once

more. Since she entered the house, she had thought she would feel Claudia's presence as she went through her things, a kind of intimacy that might also feel like an intrusion. Yet she didn't feel anything; didn't feel Claudia was with her in any way. Claudia wasn't here.

Beneath the other window there was a small window seat. The only other seating was a comfy-looking overstuffed armchair covered in William Morris chintz—the Strawberry Thief. The cushion on the window seat had the same fabric. Had Claudia selected it, or had it been here when she moved in? She was an Anglophile, and whether it was the Sinclairs' choice or hers, she would have been happy with it. Faith lifted the cushion to look underneath and turn it over. It was starting to fade on top. The seat was hinged. What had Claudia kept stored here? Her footwear had been on the closet floor, a knapsack and small suitcase plus a straw sun hat and several caps, a Yankee one and a Sox, on the shelf above. She lifted the seat, but it was stuck. No one had put anything in it for a long time. It wasn't glued shut; she could see it lifting partway. There had been a nail file in the medicine cabinet. Faith got it and slid it along the opening until the full length loosened and she was able to open the lid.

A strong scent of lavender escaped into the air. She lifted what appeared to be carefully folded fabric and shook it out. Yards of lace cascaded to the floor attached to an elegant diamond tiara.

It was a wedding veil.

Faith recognized the lace, Alençon. The elaborate pattern would have taken weeks if not months to make. It may have started out bright white but was like well-worn pearls now. The tiara was composed of small diamond-studded flowers and trailing foliage with a sunburst of larger diamonds in the center. Some of the stitching had come loose, and she could see the mark on the back: Tiffany & Co. She pictured Claudia wearing it over her long, thick, dark hair—the style she had had when young. Or maybe her hair had been pulled back into a chignon for the occasion, like Audrey Hepburn or Grace Kelly. Claudia would not have been the first bride to wear the veil. It was obviously a family heirloom. Had she worn it at all? There hadn't been any personal keepsakes save this. Her only jewelry was a few pieces made by local craftspeople.

She peered into the chest. Resting on the bottom was a framed eight-by-ten photograph, and she took it out. It was a black-and-white print of two smiling women, the younger holding an infant in a flowing christening gown. The baby was smiling, too, and the little lace cap was slightly askew. Both women were dressed in sheaths; the older wore a double strand of pearls, the younger what Faith recognized as Tiffany's Jean Schlumberger Paris Flames brooch, the diamonds in the center surrounded by spiraling gold flames. Everything in the photo said money. But also love. The three were a unit, sitting in front of a window, perhaps enjoying a moment to rest after the service. Faith opened the back and took the picture out. Claudia's birth certificate had been slipped behind. On the back of the photograph someone had written, "Mother, Claudia and me on the big day! August, 1992." They looked so happy, and Faith felt her heart tighten as she thought what the next fifteen years would bring for these women.

There was nothing else in the seat.

She took the photo, the certificate, and the veil, closed the lid, replaced the cushion, and picked up the trash bag, almost running down the stairs. She left everything as it was, pausing to add the Wright cup and saucer to the items from the window seat before setting the alarm. She locked the door, keeping the key, and got into the van. She felt tears on her face but she was silent. After a while, she drove slowly home. She had work to do.

No one was there. Ben must be at the church—he was constantly tinkering with the equipment for Zoom or live stream *and* constantly Skyping with Catherine—and Tom was at the VA. Amy had left a note saying she was meeting her friend Chloe to pace the football field and figure out where people should stand for the drone event.

Faith got out her notebook and made a new list. Things she could do without Zach.

- Call the Sinclairs re table, storage chest for artwork, Claudia's finished prints
- Locate art teacher Mr. Childs. Eliminate from suspects?
- Call art department head at Miss Porter's re Anna Kingman

She called the superintendent's office and spoke to the secretary.

"Hi, Maureen, it's Faith Fairchild. How are you?"

"As fine as anyone is my answer these days, but we've been lucky. Stayed safe, got vaccinated, and haven't lost anyone. What can I do for you? The superintendent is on a call."

"Thank you. I think you may have the information I need. I've been asked to go through Claudia Richards's personal effects, and I found a folder of lesson plans left by the teacher she replaced, a Mr. Childs. If you have an address, I'll mail them to him."

"That's very kind of you. It may take a while to reach him, though. Ralph had family in Australia, and a year after leaving his position here went to work with his brother there. The address is a few years old, but he wrote to the superintendent to tell her how extremely well he was doing. Not a very nice letter, I must say. But we saved the address."

"Kind of 'nah nah nah nah nah'?"

"Exactly." Maureen laughed. "I'll email you the address if you want."

To keep up the story, Faith said yes, hung up, and crossed Ralph Childs off the list. She tried the chair at Miss Porter's next, this time planning to leave a message.

Luck was with her and the man answered. She identified herself as a friend of a former student who was trying to reach her art teacher, Miss Anna Kingman, and only had a past address and phone. "I'm afraid she isn't well, and she has been wanting to get in touch with Miss Kingman for a long time. It's my impression that she was a teacher who made a difference in her life. I offered to try to find her. We know she is no longer at the school."

"She *did* make a difference in not just the lives of her students, but other ones and the staff as well. We overlapped by a year. She should have been the chair, but she wanted to teach, not do paperwork, she told me. And she was right. Before she left, I learned so much from her. She had that rare ability in a teacher to be close to her students, understand what they might be going through—adolescent hell—yet not intrude."

"Would you be comfortable sharing where she is living now so I can let her know about the student?"

"Yes. She specifically told me to use my discretion, of course, but give out her contact information to former students and staff. We've also stayed in touch, so it's current. She left because her father's Alzheimer's worsened and her mother couldn't cope on her own. She left that May. Must have been 2013."

"Where do her parents live?"

"California, Northern California, in Geyserville. She keeps urging me to come out, but the pandemic has put that on hold. Her father worked in the vineyards at one of the big wineries, and her mother was an artist. Anna used to say she emerged holding a crayon in her tiny fist."

Faith gave him her email and phone number. She was dreading telling Claudia's teacher the news. As a reference and one of the only contacts saved on her phone, the teacher must have been important to Claudia.

She hung up and started to dial the Sinclairs. She was feeling better than she had for a while, and certainly since leaving the carriage house. Doing something was the key. About to hit the last number, she saw a call was coming in. It was Ellie Porter. Her good mood ebbed. She wasn't looking forward to "facilitating" an intervention among Ellie, the groom, and their parents. She answered, thinking of it as she would a dental appointment. Good to get over.

"Hi, Ellie. I spoke with Samantha and have been meaning to call you." This was true. Just not the time frame, as she was intending weeks from now.

"Don't say another word! You're an angel, Faith, and did Samantha tell you that if it's a girl, whenever it is, we're naming her Faith? But that's not why I'm calling, although I did want to tell you and hope you will be pleased. Samantha is going to be one godmother, and you can be the other. Fairy godmothers with lovely wishes."

Faith interrupted. "I'm honored—"

"No, wait. I got sidetracked. I'm calling because I wanted to tell you you're off the hook. I mean we're not having that meeting with you refereeing to convince my father about the new plan Samantha told you about—a scaled-back wedding and not until June 2022. Adam and I realized that we, especially me—or is that I—were acting like children. It's our lives, our decisions. We Zoomed with both sets of parents last night—although Adam's parents are lambs and would agree to whatever we want, which is scaled back *and* June 2022. Everyone, even Daddy, is fine with the idea. We didn't come right out and say we were going to start trying for a baby right away, tick tock, and trying is such fun, but nudge, nudge, wink, wink—Adam's a huge Python fan. Let's just say no one will be surprised and I think Mom is lighting candles or whatever Congregationalists do."

Ellie was a breath of fresh air, especially today, and Faith told her so. "Everything is done. We only have to adjust the numbers. Give me a firm date, and I'll be sure the Ganley is available.

June 2022 is going to be jammed with weddings and other events postponed, but in any case, they're not going to bump such loyal supporters like your family."

"Oh, darling Faith, can you believe it? I'm going to be a bride *and* a mom sooner than later!"

Tom came through the back door into the kitchen as Faith hung up. "Someone's happy," he said, giving her a kiss. "Why the big smile?" She told him about Ellie.

"I'm very glad to hear this. She's a sweetheart, but she's also been more than annoying for you these last months. You can cross her off that to-do list I know you carry around in your head all the time."

This was true, Faith thought, but there was much more on it . . . Right now, for example.

"What do you want for dinner? A pasta dish or a stir-fry with soba noodles?"

"Surprise me," he said, little knowing how true that could be.

She got a text from Zach as she was chopping veggies for the stir-fry: "All well baby-wise. Want to hear about *your* day. Found proof. She didn't marry Hamilton. Still digging."

Friday's mail brought an invitation to Ursula's dinner party, Sunday the eighteenth, noting it was Patriots' Day Eve, which explained the statue of Paul Revere on the notecard. Millicent no doubt had reams of them. Patriots' Day, celebrated in Massachusetts and Maine, since Maine had at one time been part of the Bay State, was another eye-opener for Faith upon her move north. Since 1894, it marked that famous day and year when the shot heard 'round the world was fired, with reenactments and parades, as well as the Boston Marathon since 1897. This was the second year celebrations would be virtual and the marathon postponed.

It was a treat to get an actual snail mail letter, and Faith went to her desk to answer in the proper fashion—the Reverend Thomas and Faith Fairchild are delighted to accept the kind invitation—on her own stationery. If Ben was correct about getting shots before the announced April 19 date for those sixteen and older, he and Amy could come, too, but for now Faith accepted only for the adults. When proposing the gathering, Ursula had insisted Faith "not bring a single morsel of food" and had added that Millicent was making a special dessert. Since the only sweet Faith had ever been offered at Millicent's was a tooth-cracking oatcake, this course would be a revelation, a pleasant one Faith hoped, for Tom's sake. After the tried-and-true meat and potatoes, he didn't consider a meal over without dessert, a real one, not Jell-O or Junket.

She wasn't able to call Anna Kingman until Monday. Whenever she thought she could make the private call, taking into consideration the time difference, there were other claims. A woman answered.

"Hello, my name is Faith Fairchild. May I speak to Anna Kingman? I'm calling from Massachusetts, and it's in regard to a former student of hers, Claudia Richards. Your department chair at Miss Porter's gave me this number." She wanted to be sure not to be mistaken for spam.

"This is Anna. My goodness, I haven't heard from Claudia in a very long time and have been trying to get in touch with her. I don't think she knows I moved to California. Her wedding invitation was forwarded by the post office, but almost seven months later! I wrote to congratulate her but didn't hear back, so it may have gone astray. I wrote a letter again. Both were sent to her home in New York. No answer to that, and as you're calling from Massachusetts she must be there. Yes?"

This was going to be so much worse than Faith had thought it might be. Best to tell her right away.

"I'm afraid Claudia died recently. She'd been living in Aleford, Massachusetts, teaching middle school art for over six years and was a very dear friend."

There was a long pause and the teacher said, "How did she

die? An accident? Illness? She was young and never sick, although after her mother and grandmother both died so close to one another, she did develop ill health, well, from grief."

Faith sensed she had meant to say something else. Ill health complicated by something besides grief? "She was your student then, I believe, and she must have felt a bond with you. I know she listed you as a reference for the job here. My husband and I are in charge of her personal effects and interment plans, as no next of kin has been found. She had very few contacts on her phone, but yours was one. The number was not in service."

"Oh dear. I changed my cell service and the new carrier assigned a new number. Yes, she was my student during that time, but no next of kin? What about her father? Has he predeceased her? And where is her husband? I think the name was Charles? Isn't he in Massachusetts, too?"

"She didn't end up marrying him. And we're trying to find an address for her father. There haven't been any obituary notices for him in Connecticut where it seems Claudia grew up, or New York, which was also home in some way."

"I'm trying to take it in. That I won't ever hear from her, talk to her again. I have thought of her often over the years. I was close to a number of my students, past and present, but never like Claudia. She was so totally on her own, even before her mother's death, and grandmother's. Afterward, she often talked about the support both those women had given her since childhood, encouraging her to be the artist she was meant to be. You must know how talented she was."

"Yes, and besides one successful show here, she was about to have another in the fall. We were very dear friends, and she had others, including my husband, who is a minister. But she only discussed her family once in the years I knew her. That her mother died when she was fifteen and she was not in contact with her father."

"I am not surprised. He wasn't at all supportive of her artistic endeavors, and he had mapped out the life he expected her to live even before her mother died. Her mother had cancer, and Claudia had few memories of her before she was sick. I'm afraid there was no recognition of what the girl was going through after her death and her grandmother's following almost immediately. Her roommate here was also from Greenwich—that's where Claudia grew up. The New York address was her grandparents' East Side townhouse on Seventieth Street. The roommate, Suzie, wasn't the kindest. I didn't teach her, but it was a small school and I'd hear about her. Like Claudia, she was from a wealthy family, although few families were in the stratum Claudia's was, and had been for generations. I encouraged her to work through her grief by spending extra time in the art studio, and we'd have tea there often. She got very thin, and she was thin to start—her height was an embarrassment to her. She couldn't be convinced how lovely she was. I'd bring high teas to put some pounds on her. I know she had become involved with a boy in Greenwich the summer between her junior and senior years. He was a little older and at Yale. I worried that she might become overly attached, swept off her feet by the attention. When the wedding invitation came, I was dismayed. She was too young. Was she happy in, what was the name of the town?"

"Aleford. And yes, she was. I think you must have been a model. Her students loved her, and she encouraged them all—even the ones who thought art was a waste of time in the march to college. And as I said, she had many friends in town and among her colleagues."

"Yes, you said that, but you haven't said how she died."

Faith paused now, and then she told her the whole thing, finding the body, the nitric acid ingestion.

"Claudia was, if anything, overly cautious when it came to handling materials, especially dangerous ones. I'm sorry, but this doesn't sound like an accident."

"It doesn't sound like an accident to me, either," Faith said.

Chapter Eleven

HEIRESS BRIDE TO GROOM "I DON'T"

Spectators Saturday afternoon outside Saint Thomas Fifth Avenue were surprised by the sight of the bride, Miss Claudia Richards, sprinting down the stairs, her family heirloom veil draped over one arm, no bouquet in hand, bolting into a cab, almost colliding with the party exiting. From the top at the church entrance, the jilted groom, Mr. Charles Hamilton, visibly angry, shouted, "Claudia, get back here!" The society nuptials have been a subject of great interest since the engagement was announced. Miss Richards inherited the Schuyler fortune upon the deaths of her mother, Eleanor Schuyler Richards, and grandmother, Rose Delavan Schuyler. As the wedding party and over 400 guests emerged from the church, the father of the bride, Mr. James Richards, refused comment. Miss Richards's current whereabouts is unknown, and she has not made a statement about her abrupt change of heart.

Zach had called and told Faith to come to the hedge immediately. When she got there, he handed her a stack of printouts, pointing to the top one. "The tabloids! Of course there wasn't anything in the *Times* or papers like that, which I'd searched. But starting with the 'Runaway Bride'—another headline—the story was a nine-day wonder for the *New York Post* and the others."

Zach and Faith sat on the large Sissinghurst garden bench, a significant birthday gift from her sister, as Faith read the articles. Early ones ran above the center fold, and all included photos, the most dramatic an enlargement of the bride halfway down the church stairs. Faith studied it carefully. Claudia had been a beautiful bride, her hair pulled back from her face coiffed apparently in some kind of chignon. The dress was deceptively simple, not off the rack, and suited Claudia's slender body and height. She didn't appear to be crying, but her expression was sad—and very determined. Faith quickly told Zach about finding the veil and tiara pictured, as well as her conversation with Anna Kingman an hour ago.

"Anna was worried that Claudia was too young, 'swept off her feet,' she said, by this Charles Hamilton. We need to find out what happened to him and locate her father."

"Done. I found several notices for the listing and sale of his Greenwich house. It was just before the wedding. A cool eleven million for the place. His law firm was in Manhattan, but he is retired. His current and past address is on the East Side, 113 Seventieth Street."

"That's the address Anna had for Claudia, the address on the wedding invitation. She said it was Claudia's grandparents' townhouse."

"Nice place, not too shabby. You can look on Google Maps."

Faith continued to leaf through the newspaper articles. Many had specific details about Claudia's worth. The Schuylers, and Delavans, were old money. Money that had continued to make money, starting with railroads and always real estate. She looked up at Zach.

"Claudia *did* have something to leave in a will. A very substantial something. Just not a someone."

"And that means we take a look at New York and Connecticut state inheritance laws. Tricky, since she was a resident here, but she was living at either or both at the time she inherited. I bet they're the same as here. If you die intestate in Massachusetts and probably New York, your property goes to your closest blood relative. If none are found, it goes to the state."

"This puts a new slant on cui bono. Claudia and her father were estranged. From what her teacher said, may never have been close. Ditching the wedding would not have made him happy. Definitely add him to the list."

"Yes. Claudia was not Bezos or Gates, but a billionaire, according to the papers, for the Manhattan real estate alone. Getting his hands on it, which may have included the house he lives in, is a powerful motive for eliminating a wayward, disliked, even, daughter."

"'Filicide.' Killing your own child. It would have been more than dislike. Hate. What kind of monster would do that? I can't think about it."

"Don't. I'll find out more about him, and you think about positive things. Get in touch with the gallery about the show, what to do with her work."

Faith nodded. "And I'll go take a look at the *Post*'s Page Six, that's where any 'source close to' would dish about the wedding and the groom. Let's find out where he's been and is now."

"Let me do it. Easier since I've gone back to the dates. Check our Artwork file. I'll forward all the columns. And soon I'd like to go into the carriage house to take a look at the alarm system. And bring a friend who knows a whole lot more than I do about surveillance devices."

"We have to find out if someone or more than one person was watching her, so yes. I didn't take everything I packed up with me. Soon is best."

"I'll call him today. What are you doing now? Maybe take a walk with my wife and mother-in-law?"

Faith smiled. It was clear Zach counted her as part of his flock, keeping watch. He was going to be a fine dad.

There wouldn't be time to take a walk today since it was a dinner-box delivery one, but Faith called Pix to suggest the idea. It was nice to talk about the blessed event and move on to town topics.

Samantha had filled her mother in on the change in the Porter wedding plans, and they talked briefly about that. "I'm so glad it worked out," Pix said. "The pandemic has taken a big toll on family relations. The Kimballs are just the latest couple I've heard that are divorcing. I suppose being in lockdown made the fissures in some marriages into valleys."

"The Kimballs are divorcing? They seemed so happy the time we went there for that meeting, so excited about their house and plans for involvement in local midcentury modern preservation efforts. I can't imagine either of them giving it up. Oh dear. At least there are no children."

"I think the house was taking the place of offspring, at least for now, and it's also the problem. Neither is moving out. They both want it and are staying put."

"Like upscale squatters! But it's not funny. Always sad when a marriage falls apart."

They arranged to take a lunchtime walk the next day with Samantha, too. Faith offered to make the sandwiches, knowing Pix's skill extended only to PB&J, using whatever jelly was in the fridge, fine once in a while but not as a staple.

Pix's news brought the Kimballs as suspects leaping to the front of Faith's thoughts. Maybe the motive had nothing to do with inheritance but with passion. Had Margaret Kimball seen the texts on her husband's phone and killed Claudia? Or had he, fearing his wife and the source of his lifestyle, far above what a teacher could afford, committed the murder to avoid discovery? Knowing he was at the house, probably not daring to step out lest the locks get changed, Faith decided to call Brian and offer him the art supplies, including the high-quality paper Claudia used, for his high school classes. Whatever kind of "friend" he was, they might have meaning for him. Offering the supplies was an excuse to hear what he might say about his colleague.

It wasn't much. After the initial exchange, Faith said, "I know Claudia's death must have been a blow for you as a close friend and colleague. She spoke of you often to me and admired what you were doing with your students. I know she would have wanted you to have her art supplies to use yourself or in your classes."

The answer was immediate and abrupt. "I'm not a printmaker and don't teach it. Yes, it was kind of a blow, but we really didn't know each other well. Most of my time here has been sequestered."

Liar, liar, pants . . . Faith said to herself.

"Your house is wonderful. Not a chore to be there, I'm sure." Pumping was a last-ditch effort.

"Yes, we are very lucky."

We?

"I'm sure you'll find someone who can use the inks and papers, any plates. Sorry, but I have another call. Good-bye."

She hung up sure he wasn't sorry and sure he didn't have another call.

He didn't. The house was completely still. She was here but silence reigned. As it had with only a few exceptions since that call from the superintendent. The call saying the body had been found.

Zach phoned while Faith was at the catering kitchen with Ben packing the orders for delivery.

"I'll take this in the office, okay?" Ben nodded, his mind obviously elsewhere. In Catherine Land, and on the appointment he had been able to make for first shots for himself, Amy, and a large group of their friends. The appointments were geographically spread out, but Amy and Ben were going to be back in Chicopee on Monday.

"Things are moving fast," Zach said. "My friend Stephen, who's had both shots, can make it Thursday. He's free all day. He's got a pickup, so we can clear everything out of the house after he's looked the place over. If there are any kind of devices, he'll find them."

"I'll call the Sinclairs right away. I don't need to say what his specialty is, just that he'll help us remove everything. The wallboard wall needs to come down, and they may want the table out, and the storage unit, if it isn't theirs."

"I have a landline number for James Richards. So far, I haven't been able to locate the groom, but his mother, Elizabeth Hamilton, transferred the title of her Greenwich house, a big one, to him in January 2013. I'm guessing wedding present. He sold it in August 2013. The mother bought a condo during the same time frame and sold it a year later. Nice investment. Almost doubled the price she paid. No current address for her."

Hanging up, Faith looked forward to the day when her ear, or eyes, wouldn't be glued to her phone and she could talk in person. With the wave of vaccinations, that day was getting closer and closer. So was finding out what happened to Claudia. She could feel it now more than ever. It was like a photograph developing—or a print lifted from the press.

After Ben left with the loaded van, she called the Sinclairs. This time Edward answered.

"How are you doing? We've been worried about you. I know Tom is there taking care of you, but I wish it were summer and you could be on Sanpere. Very healing for the soul."

"Thank you, but I'm all right. I do wish it was summer, too.

The weather has been so cold. It's hard to believe it's April. May will rush in and we'll open up Memorial Day. It will be here before we know it."

"Good. I'm glad to hear all this."

"I've packed up Claudia's things, and if it's okay, Zach and a friend of his with a pickup can help me Thursday. We can deliver the clothing to Rosie's Place and the books to the library for a future sale. I'm asking the Clark Gallery what to do about her unused art supplies. And is the storage cabinet where she kept finished work, and work she collected, yours?"

"Yes, it is, and you can leave it full for now. Patricia and I are hoping the Clark will mount the exhibit in the fall. I plan to call them. We can mention the art supplies at the same time if you like. We also have a close friend, Walter Crump, who is a printmaker."

One less call. Faith was relieved. "The table was Claudia's. What about that? We'll take down the wallboard." She hadn't mentioned the mutilated prints on it previously and didn't intend to ever.

"I'll ask the gallery about the table, and if they don't know of a home for it, Walter—he's called Rusty—will. I'll have an answer for you before Thursday. This must be so hard for you, Faith, and we appreciate your doing it."

"I want to. It's the last thing I can do for her."

Not the last yet.

Tom had come home early and declared it a family night. It was a sweet thought. More than sweet, but Faith had wanted to sit down by herself and go over some not-so-sweet ones in the Page Six file Zach sent.

"We've all been attached to screens or otherwise occupied," he said. "It's getting so I can barely remember what my own kith and kin look like. Dinner is done, right? You saved some from the delivery?"

Faith gave in.

Dinner was gnocchi with cannellini beans, chard, minced garlic, canned diced tomatoes, cubed soppressata, and a blend of Italian seasonings, her own mixture of oregano, fennel, basil, sea salt, and ground pepper—she'd used Penzeys for the boxes. They sopped up the liquid with ciabatta, eating again in front of the fire. Board games were not her thing, but surrounded by avid players from her children's first moves in Candy Land, Faith had accepted her fate. Family night during this last year had provided solace. She was now glad to gather around whatever board was out. Except Monopoly. It was Ben who came up with tonight's choice. The Game of Life. Life. And it wasn't hard to see which way his path was headed. The fire, the food, and maybe the game were soporific, and Faith was glad when Tom declared he was ready for bed, too. Tempted as she was to stay up and look at what Zach had sent, she opted to join her husband. When he'd said "bed," there had been that welcome emphasis . . .

After a long, restorative walk with Pix and Samantha on the beaver dam conservation trail, looking in vain for signs of spring, Faith went to the catering kitchen the next day. She'd read the columns in between prepping tomorrow's delivery. Niki's car was there.

"I come bearing phyllo dough," Niki said. "Thought I'd give you a hand with tomorrow's dinners. Spanakopita. We can get it all ready to pop in the oven tomorrow afternoon. Greek salad as a side and some kind of fruit with Greek yogurt dessert. Okay?"

"Better than okay," Faith said. The spinach and feta cheese pie was one of her favorites.

"You can bring me up to date while we work."

"There's a lot. Be prepared for a surprise." Faith started with finding the wedding veil and then the conversation with Anna Kingman. She got the *New York Post* printouts from her laptop case and showed Niki.

"Wow! There was no way I'd ever have guessed Claudia came from money, especially money like this. I mean she told me when she got a hole in her tights, she wore two pairs."

Faith told her about eliminating the former art teacher. "The man is in Australia, happy as a koala with a fistful of eucalyptus leaves or words to that effect, boasting in a letter he wrote to the superintendent."

"What about the other art teacher? Brian. The one she had a crush on or vice versa."

"He might have been on the brink of adultery. His texts were certainly getting steamy, before they stopped abruptly after the Zoom bombing. I'd keep him on for that and for the odd, very brief conversation I had yesterday with him about Claudia's art supplies. He claimed he did not know her well, and as he said good-bye, there was a definite 'Don't call me again' tone. Pix told me he and his wife are splitting up, but both want the house, so are rooted there, staking a claim. He used 'we' when I mentioned the house was a lovely place in which to hunker down during the pandemic. He said, 'We are very lucky.'"

"And what about the Sinclairs' son?"

"I told you Zach found out he's on the verge of bankruptcy, so he's still on the list. But I can't see him doing something so extreme after just talking to her once. I think it was more of a warning not to get any closer to his parents, or perhaps jealousy at their relationship. Maybe it's because I like Patricia and Edward so much, I don't want them to have a son who's a killer."

"And he is their only child. He'll inherit, and you've never heard them say anything about him that suggests problems?"

"The only negative thing was Edward's wish that Christopher move back east. California was too far away. That sounds like the opposite."

"Hmmm. Okay, I can make spanakopita in my sleep, so why don't you read what Zach sent, print them out for me to look at? Page Six is bound to have some spicy details."

"I'll go into the office. Zach gave me Claudia's father's land-line number, and I want to call, but not from my cell. Then I'll read the columns."

After two rings, a woman answered. "Richards residence."

"Hello. My name is Faith Fairchild. May I speak to James Richards, please?"

"Mr. Richards is not available. What does this concern?"

His secretary, or housekeeper, doing a good job protecting him from unwanted calls.

"It concerns his daughter, Claudia."

"Mr. Richards doesn't have a daughter—or any children. You must have the wrong Richards."

"I'm quite sure I don't, and he may not have heard that she—"

"Mr. James Richards has no daughter. Good-bye."

Faith went out and told Niki.

"After the non-wedding, she was dead to him is what it sounds like. I've known this to happen in some Greek families, and it would have happened in mine if I hadn't married my perfect husband. Mom would have had no problem saying, 'Daughter? I don't have a daughter.'"

"That makes sense; the woman was so emphatic."

She went back and opened the Page Six columns. Sunday's, the day after the incident, was typically loaded with gossip and included two photos, the one of Claudia fleeing and one of a short woman wearing a designer outfit, hat suitable for Ascot, and heels that added at least three inches to her height, holding her hand up stopping Fifth Avenue traffic while a crowd of New York's elite, dressed for a wedding, crossed the street. The caption read, "Elizabeth 'Bitsy' Hamilton herds wedding guests to the Saint Regis for the reception despite jilted son."

Faith enlarged the photo. Bitsy's expression was one of cool determination—staring down the traffic—and pure fury. She wondered whose idea it had been to go ahead with the reception. The bride's father not wanting to lose face *and* what would have been a substantial amount of money? For the mother of the groom it would have been saving face as well. "Bitsy is such a trouper." "How could Claudia have done this to her, and her father? Spoiled brat." And more. Page Six continued with details of the elaborate noncelebration that sounded as if it was indeed a celebration, guests staying for hours, the names mentioned including old and new New York plus some celebrities. There was mention of the humiliated groom, Charles "Chip" Hamilton, drowning his sorrow in the King Cole bar with his groomsmen and best man, "who told this reporter, 'The Chipster will be fine. She wouldn't even listen to him, or her father! Like it was not *her* fault the wedding wasn't happening? Claudia was a witch, spelled differently if you get my drift.'" The reporter did, and stated, "Wherever the bride may be, she won't be showing her face for many a moon."

It was still hot news the following week, with speculation on the cause heating up the wires. "A close source has revealed that shortly before the march down the aisle while entering the church through the basement side door, the bride-to-be discovered her betrothed in a compromising position with her maid of honor. According to our informant, Miss Richards was not willing to overlook a last fling of wild oats. And added the Chipster's partner, whose first name is spelled with a Z, is no maiden and some would say had no honor!"

Faith felt sick. She printed out what she'd read so far and decided to stop for a while. The scene was crystal clear. A very young radiant bride entering the church to avoid the front door—Faith knew Saint Thomas and this was the practice—only to come upon the man she was going to marry, the man she loved, and her best friend—obviously the Miss Porter's roommate—having sex of some sort. It was enough to send her shooting down past the saints lining the front entrance into a cab and far away from there. Why Boston? Faith had never thought to ask Claudia why she had come to MassArt, just assumed it was the reputation of the school. She would have headed to the townhouse to change, keeping the veil worn by the women she loved and their photo, before heading to Penn Station. Faith hoped she never saw the papers. From the sound of the "Chipster," Claudia had had a fortunate escape. A man who would do something like this minutes before pledging his faith was scum. About to vow "to have and to hold" just after having and holding someone else was almost beyond belief! And what about the "for richer" part? Was that the motivation? Claudia's money? So, she did the right thing and walked away from it all, including the money. Which explained why no will. Claudia had severed ties completely. She was her own woman, and she was happy. Faith felt tears start and went to talk to Niki about the disgusting new facts.

Zach was tracking down Charles Hamilton, and Faith hoped wherever he ended up it was something akin to the seventh circle of hell. James Richards had gone on with his life, without a daughter. And what about Bitsy? Zach had found that she'd transferred ownership of her house to her son, but he sold it and she'd sold her condo. Somehow Faith didn't think Mrs. Hamilton was the type to be homeless for long. And the nest would be well feathered.

Thursday was April 15, but the pandemic had altered Income Tax Day as well as everything else, with the IRS granting a new deadline. Faith had told Tom that Zach and a friend of his with a pickup were going to help her finish clearing the carriage house.

"I'm glad you'll have the help—and the company. Love you—a lot," he'd said.

The guys had stopped for extra-large coffees, and Faith brought cinnamon roll muffins, the roll batter baked in a muffin tin and dipped in sugar syrup. After eating, they got right to work.

"Faith and I will finish packing up and load the truck. You start sleuthing," Zach said to Stephen.

Stephen lived in Boston, and he'd drop the clothing off at Rosie's Place. While they worked, Faith and Zach talked about the Page Six items. He'd read them before sending them so knew the worst.

"It makes me ashamed to be a man. I hated that you'd have to read it, but it's more pieces of the puzzle. And here's another one. A year after the non-wedding, the groom's mother married the bride's father."

"Where did you find it?"

"The Greenwich paper again. Seems the 'select' ceremony and reception were at the country club. The bride's son, a Greenwich resident, gave his mother away. The venue was described as 'long favored' by the couple."

"Interesting. I'll bet Bitsy was the woman who answered the phone when I called. And I have a strong hunch the couple may have 'long favored' each other. Both widowed and moved in the same circle in Greenwich. But I thought you couldn't find an address for Chip?" Faith couldn't bring herself to say Chipster.

"I still haven't found one. He'd have friends there. Couch surfing? A little old for that. Guesthouse crashing? I did find that he must have given up on the law or gone to another state. Did not graduate from the City University of New York, which was in the engagement announcement, nor is he a member of the New York Bar. I checked Connecticut and New Jersey. Not practicing in either of those places."

"He wouldn't need to have a real job so long as Mommy can support him."

"True. That kind of guy would blame Claudia for whatever failures he had afterward, dropping out of school, lack of employment."

Faith gave a shudder. "He was using her. Counted on never having to lift a finger except to tap a credit card."

There was a shout from downstairs. "Bingo! Come here!"

Stephen had brought a stepladder, and he was on the top rung.

"I thought immediately that the alarm system must have been

tampered with but wanted to check if there were any other not-so-obvious surveillance devices, bugs, nanny cam type stuff. Nada, but both motion detectors aren't housing what would have been installed by the company. Very sophisticated spyware equipment. The links would have been deleted at the other end, or ends if going to two devices, immediately after her death, and then at some point the 'technician' would have retrieved what was installed in the motion detectors, reinstalling the original detectors. Unless you work for an alarm company, you would have assumed these were part of the equipment. That is if the police even examined them. I'm getting down and you have a look. They're tiny, about as big as my thumbnail. Not only a camera, but an additional device sending the image to a system that could be quite far away."

He came down and Zach took his place. "It looks like the mini one I have on my 3-D printer. I did it for fun. I can watch what I'm making from wherever I am. Can pan the whole room. This tells us whoever came wasn't a novice. So who had the knowledge?"

Faith went up the ladder, and whatever it was, it was indeed minuscule. "Or who knew whom to hire?"

Stephen and Zach were in deep conversation, using terminology that meant nothing to her and everything to them. "Have never seen one!" Zach exclaimed. Kids in a candy store.

But these devices in the motion detectors aimed at Claudia's worktable caused her death. Alerted the murderer to Claudia's condition. When it would be time literally to come in for the kill. She tuned in to what they were saying.

"I should still be able to trace where the signal was going within a mile or so. What I figure is that someone on that end was monitoring this place and alerted whoever was physically close to make sure she drank the acid," Stephen said. "That's why there are two devices."

Zach was nodding. "The door was open and the alarm system

off when Faith found her. She may have been too impaired to lock up and set the alarm, or it could have been a lucky chance for whoever came in and positioned the containers, and glass."

"It had to be like that. And if she had secured the house, the imposter could have figured out the code somehow?"

"Yes, the call to schedule the fake appointment would have had her set and reset the alarm to make sure it was the 'battery,' and from the sound, even I could tell the code. The key was in an obvious spot," Zach answered.

"The location receiving the video would be easier to figure out if we had her computer. Wi-Fis synched, malware installed, lots of possibilities. Do you think the police would give it to you?"

"I can try. I haven't told them, or even my husband, that we know her father's name and also that he's alive. I can request all the items they took, as we are still the closest in lieu of kin."

"Even without it, I can do it. Just will take a while."

Zach put his arm around Faith's shoulder. "So, what's next? Besides dinner at Ursula's Sunday."

He made her smile. The dinner would mark the first time they were all sitting around the same table breaking bread, and no matter what Millicent served for dessert, Faith knew it would be a very good time.

"After that I think I'll go see my family. They're all at my sister's second home on Long Island, and I've been waiting until it's relatively safe to see them. While I'm there I might go into Manhattan. Might go to the East Side . . ."

Daylight savings had started a month earlier, and light was still coming through Ursula's dining room windows. Faith had expected the damask tablecloth and napkins, Ursula's grandmother's wedding Limoges china and silver, but in addition there was a festive red, white, and blue flower arrangement with small flags. Someone, one of her children, Faith suspected, had ordered little fifes and drums as favors. The drums were filled with tricolored M&M's.

Before sitting down, they'd had cocktails in the large double parlor. "We should be drinking ale or a rum concoction for authenticity," Ursula said. "I do have rum if anyone wants it in some form. Millicent has contributed her elderberry cordial, which was a popular colonial beverage. However, I'm having my usual, Tom. Thank you for tending bar."

Ursula's usual was a very dry martini. Once everyone was settled with something to imbibe—Faith opted for the elderberry wine; she'd tasted it before, and it was surprisingly good—the celebration began.

The talk had been general—memories of past Patriots' Day celebrations, the weather, much teasing about possible names for the new baby, still known as Beanbag. "Be careful," Dora said. "You'll find yourselves still calling the baby that, and it will stick. One of my cousins is called Bunny and he's fifty-five."

Ursula announced dinner. "Millicent, Dora, and I have had great fun planning the meal. An authentic colonial one, but fortunately we had modern conveniences for the actual cooking."

Zach and Samantha had offered themselves as waitstaff, and Millicent provided a running commentary on the menu. The first course was a puréed apple butternut squash soup. "In April, they would have still had a good store of root vegetables and apples." The soup was delicious, as was the main course, cod cakes (Dora admitted the recipe was her Irish mother's, "but it traveled across some time, and cod was plentiful"), baked beans, of course, and brown bread. It may have dated back to 1776, but Faith found it very comforting in 2021, as was finally sitting down with those she loved after so long. No one mentioned the fact, but she knew they were all thinking it. When they joined hands for Tom's blessing at the start of the meal, she'd noticed everyone held on tight longer than usual after the Amen.

There was much laughter—and absolutely no mention of the

tragic losses of the last year, including the most recent one. One day last September, on the way to Crane Beach to walk, Faith had spotted a lawn sign that read, 2020: PLEASE LET IT BE OVER. She'd taken a picture of it. That year was over now, but who knew when the pandemic would finally be in the rearview mirror? She looked around the table. They were safe. And she wasn't going to think about the future or the past just now.

What was in her future was Millicent's dessert, Indian pudding. "This is my Revere family recipe handed down for many generations. I like to think my cousin Paul enjoyed it at my ancestors' table. He lived to a fine old age, eighty-three, and I'm sure this dish contributed to his health. We should be calling it Native American pudding, as that's most probably where the basic combination of molasses and cornmeal comes from. Our recipe adds eggs and maple syrup, which the colonists had at this time of year when the sap was running."

It had taken Faith a while to appreciate the New England dessert, a Fairchild favorite, especially when they were dining at Boston's Durgin Park, the iconic Faneuil Hall Marketplace restaurant now sadly closed. She had developed her own version and served it with whipped cream or vanilla ice cream. Millicent's was mercifully free of the gritty texture some dishes had, and there was a big bowl of whipped cream for those who wanted it, as all did save the maker. "I don't think households ran to such luxuries then," she proclaimed.

They went back to the parlor for coffee. Zach had darted out, returning with what appeared to be a framed piece of artwork. He held it in front of Ursula and said, "Some of us knew that Claudia was working on a family tree with portraits for Ursula. It was completed except for a few spots she hadn't finished painting by hand. I was able to match the colors from her sketches, and my clever wife took it from there."

When does he ever sleep? Faith wondered. Ursula had tears in her eyes and lifted her demitasse cup. "To Claudia, artist and friend."

They toasted, admired the one-of-a-kind piece, and suddenly it was nine o'clock. Late hours for Alefordians, and they said their good nights. Samantha had been dozing since the pudding.

Faith had no trouble falling asleep once she crawled into bed. She hadn't been so happy in a very long time.

"I think it's safe to see my family. I'll drive, not take the train, and we're all fully vaccinated," she told Tom over breakfast Monday morning. "I don't expect the kids will have any reactions except sore arms, like us, but I want to wait and see, so I'll go toward the end of the week for a few days."

"That's a great idea, honey, but if you want to go sooner, I'll hold the fort here. And stay longer. Finally have a real visit."

She didn't share that she also wanted to wait to see what Stephen deciphered from the devices in the carriage house, or that she intended to pay a call on Claudia's father and, now she knew, stepmother. She felt uneasy, more than uneasy, keeping so much from her husband, but nothing she was doing was dangerous—his past objections to her sleuthing. He might understand that she had to do everything in her power to uncover how Claudia had died, but in his mind it was suicide or an accident.

Hope, too, had urged her to come soon and stay long. "It's been so hard. I only wish Tom and the kids could, too." Hearing her sister's voice and thinking about seeing all of them propelled Faith into action. Tuesday Ben's and Amy's arms were no longer sore. No other side effects. They had assured her they could take care of Have Faith Delivered meals and deliveries. "I *am* going to be a professional, Mom," Amy had said. She had heard from all the places she'd applied to and accepted a spot in the Class of 2025 at Johnson & Wales.

Niki offered to pitch in as well, and by Wednesday morning Faith was packed and ready to go, with ferry reservations from New London, Connecticut, to Orient Point on Long Island. Before she left, she met Zach in the yard. Faith had decided not to ask the police if she could take possession of Claudia's computer. She'd have to ask Tom to do it, and she'd rather wait to see if Stephen could figure out what secrets the surveillance devices held.

"I'm glad you're finally going to be with your family," Zach said. "Mine is all right here. I'm lucky. And Stephen and I will keep going on this, don't worry."

"I keep thinking it must be at least two people. One to monitor Claudia from wherever and one to be close at hand at the time to kill her. And where would they have been? They couldn't take the chance that someone, like me, would come by for some reason and see a strange car."

"That part is easy. The Sinclairs' property is surrounded by conservation land, with plenty of places a car could park undetected at any time of day, or if detected would be assumed to belong to some hiker. The Zoom bombing could have been done by anyone with even rudimentary skills. The only clue we have to identity is that it's someone surfing those porn sites. Planting the high-tech bugs is a skill set way above."

"And since the other photo, her head shot, was from the Aleford school department page, the person knew she lived here. Again, must be the same individual."

Claudia's words "Who hates me this much?" echoed in Faith's mind. She was beginning to narrow it down. Someone right here—or in New York. She ran the "right here" by Zach. "Maybe Claudia and Brian *were* having an affair. Maybe his attraction started when he came across the photos on one of those sites. Then his wife found out or he was afraid it would get out and he'd lose his job, so he Zoom bombed her to make her a pariah, get her to resign."

"Then why kill her?" Zach asked.

"Claudia was really in love with him and wanted him to divorce his wife?"

"It's possible. I've looked at his website, and he does a lot of digital art. Could have the skill necessary." They sat in silence for a moment. "Try to put this all out of your mind and enjoy being with your family. I promise you we won't leave a stone, or byte, unturned. And if something comes up, I'll text or call. When you say New York, you mean her father. Maybe because I'm about to be one, I can't conceive of this. Great pun!"

Faith had to smile. It was. And she couldn't conceive of it, either. But it happened.

As she stood on the deck of the ferry crossing Long Island Sound under a cloudless blue sky, careening seagulls reminding her of Maine, Faith felt the cares of the last months lift. She had set in motion everything she could think of for her dear friend. Zach was right. She would enjoy every moment of her upcoming visit and let the two guys pursue the solution, however long it would take.

But she'd still go to the city. Especially since receiving a text an hour ago from Zach: "S. has discovered what Claudia probably thought were spam calls on her phone that in fact embedded the link from one of the surveillance cameras to a 646 area code, introduced to add to Manhattan's overused 212. Pinpoints location? Now, have fun."

When she pulled up to the house, everyone ran down from the front porch, and as she opened the car door, she was quickly enveloped in hugs. There were smiles—and tears. She had only seen them on a screen since Aunt Chat died. Hope and the two Quentins looked fine, but both her parents seemed to have shrunk since she saw them last, and she could feel that her father was even thinner than before. But all those strolls on the beach had given them ruddy complexions, and when they walked up to the porch, there was a definite spring in both their steps.

"Your hair is so long," Hope said. "I like it. I'll bet Tom does, too."

Faith stroked her sister's dark, silky hair. The Sibley girls looked alike except one was a brunette and one a blonde. "Tom *does.* Wanted me to keep it even longer."

"Men and the long-hair thing. Quentin is the same." The sisters linked arms and went into the house. It was big but not ostentatious. The original owners who built it were going for an oversize Cape, not Fontainebleau. Hope and Quentin had added the roomy guesthouse. The pool, tennis court, and "mature plantings" had been in place. Faith turned before going in to look out at the water. Unlike Sanpere Island with its frigid water, this was a place where she *would* swim in the ocean. At least wade.

By Friday, Faith felt as if she was at Canyon Ranch. No facials or massages, but a hot tub and a sauna. *A girl could get used to this,* she thought. The master bath at the parsonage was due for a makeover. The showerhead was more drizzle than rain forest.

She enjoyed walks on the beach with her parents and time alone with Hope. The Quentins were working remotely, Quentin III often with a grandparent by his side tutoring him with the screen off.

Hope had stocked the kitchen with easy-to-prepare or already prepared meals. It felt odd not to be in charge of cooking, but Faith soon relaxed into the rare occasion.

"Dad's with Quent and Mom's napping. Want to walk the beach in the opposite direction?" Hope asked. "See how the other half lives. Most of the houses are empty, except one or two with migrants like us."

They set off. "You haven't minded, have you? Being here? You have sounded happy, but it's such a big change," Faith said.

"I thought I would miss being at the office, miss the city, but the longer we're here, the more I've realized how we were living might not have been the best. For any of us."

"In what way?" Faith had always thought her sister's life fit her, and her husband and son, perfectly. She had her work and home life organized like the proverbial well-oiled machine. She and Quentin were successful, had many friends, squeezed in some good works, and were raising a bright, pleasant, affectionate child.

"There were no obvious cracks, but we were locked into a rigid routine, one that worked well, but being here has made us take stock. We really love all the time we've had just being us with Mom and Dad. We've realized we didn't have to work the hours we did and Quent didn't need to be programmed the way we had arranged—sports, clubs, cultural opportunities. Here he's been able to just be a kid."

"You don't miss the social life, for all three of you?"

"Not really. Having Mom and Dad has made a difference. I've learned things about them, and the family, I never knew. I won't have to say at some point that I wished I had asked them something."

Faith felt a pang of jealousy, and it must have shown. "Don't worry. I'll share," Hope assured her. "Quent FaceTimes with friends and eventually he'll be back to school in person, but no more all-summer sleepaway camps. I'd miss him too much. Fay, you may not believe it, but we're thinking of selling up in the city, just keeping a pied-à-terre, and moving here full-time. The school system is excellent, and we both figure we could commute one or maybe two days a week, working from here the rest. Most of our workday was always on the phone anyway."

This was a surprise, a big one. "And Quentin's on board with this? Both of them?"

"Yes. And so are Mom and Dad. We want them to move here, too. Mom has been thinking of retiring anyway. We're going to remodel the guesthouse once it's safe—everyone will be doing remodeling, so I already have an architect/builder lined up—to expand the ground floor into one living space. No stairs, accessible bathroom."

Her sister may be changing her address, but she still had a mind like a Rolodex.

"Most of their friends have moved away—to Florida, closer to their children, or . . ." Hope pointed heavenward. "There's a lot going on out here for people their age, and Dad was never a city boy." Lawrence's father had been the son of a minister in a rural part of New Jersey when it truly was the Garden State. It was Jane, who had grown up in Manhattan, who insisted she couldn't be a barefoot girl with cheek of tan, although it seemed she was now. She'd tapered off her work as a real estate lawyer even before the pandemic.

Faith gave her sister a hug. "I think it's terrific. We'll be empty nesters, Covid willing, when Amy starts college in late August, and I'm hoping Tom will delegate more to an assistant minister. The position hasn't been filled because of the pandemic. Maine for us is what this place is for you." Faith pictured adding a hot tub overlooking the cove. Definitely doable.

They were so busy talking, they hadn't so much as glanced at the properties beyond the dunes, and now it was time to head back. The sun was sinking, dappling the waves with streaks of gold.

The men were watching the Nets play the Celtics—Lawrence had become a sports fan by osmosis over the past year—and the women were in the kitchen drinking various kinds of tea around the rustic harvest table Hope had discovered at a house sale in Patchogue, where the potato fields had been long ago.

"Tell us how you are doing, sweetheart," her mother said. "Losing a friend, especially one so young, is very hard. And Tom said you found her."

Tom had phoned Hope, speaking to her parents as well. They had called her the next day, but there really hadn't been anything to say.

Faith found she could talk about it, wanted to talk about it. "It was hard losing Aunt Chat, and others, but this was different."

"Different how? Claudia was her name?"

"Yes, Claudia Richards. She *was* a dear friend, but very private. I've only just now found out that she grew up in Greenwich and partly in Manhattan."

Her mother and sister were staring at her wide-eyed, and she was sure they hadn't listened to anything she said after Claudia's full name.

"Claudia Richards! The Runaway Bride!" Hope gasped.

Chapter Twelve

Of course, she should have asked Hope. She should have asked her mother, too, when Faith saw the articles about Claudia in the *New York Post*. Manhattan was made up of a series of villages, and both women were very familiar with their turf—the Upper East Side, as well as others. She wouldn't be surprised if one or both had been in Saint Thomas's pews that day.

"Were you there? At the wedding? Or non-wedding?"

"No, dear, different circles. They were Greenwich people," her mother said. "I did meet her grandmother, who lived near us, on several occasions, a lovely woman, and we are distantly related. She was a Delavan and married a Schuyler."

Faith knew her maternal family tree's branches were loaded with Van Rensselaers, Stuyvesants, and other old New York varieties.

"Rose Schuyler died the day after her poor daughter, who had been battling cancer for years. Your father and I were at the funeral. I vaguely remember a tall, thin, very pale young girl with dark hair following the casket next to a man I presumed was her father. Ironic that it should be the same aisle she *didn't* go down years later. We went out to the interment at Woodlawn afterward. The soil on Rose's daughter's grave was fresh."

"You were already in Aleford," Hope said. "Otherwise, you would have heard about Claudia's sprint away from 'I do.' One of those dry news times, so everybody was talking about it. The groom's mother approached Aunt Chat about handling the spin, but Chat wasn't interested. She was closing her PR agency soon anyway but said even if she weren't, the woman was 'so loathsome,' she wouldn't have taken her as a client.

"She found someone or did it herself," Hope continued. "Word on the street soon spread that Claudia had had a nervous breakdown at the church and there had been signs of it in the weeks leading up to the ceremony. Erratic behavior. Rumors of a history of mental illness on her mother's side. Catch her father taking any blame. Or the Hamiltons. As Mom said, they were Greenwich people, plus Claudia and Charles—he is always called Chip—were younger than Quentin and I. But we knew of Claudia's father, who was a well-known and respected Manhattan attorney. The firm was started by his grandfather."

"Has he died? You said 'was,'" Faith asked.

"No, he's alive the last I heard, but he sold his partnership after he was in a bad car accident a few years ago. He was lucky to have survived, but he's paralyzed from the waist down and in a wheelchair."

Faith felt relieved, not at the thought of the injury but at the realization that he couldn't have killed his own daughter. Unless he had masterminded it to inherit, and to get back at the woman he didn't consider a daughter?

"I met Charles—no, I will not call him Chip," Jane said. "I gather he had started out following his late father's footsteps into law, but either he changed his mind or the law school did. There were rumors that he'd been booted out for hacking into CUNY's computer to change one of his grades, but in any case, he got a real estate license and I met him at a closing. I was representing the seller."

"What was he like?" Faith asked, mentally noting the detail about the computer hacking.

"One of those too-handsome-for-his-own-good charmers, but as soon as things didn't go exactly his way, he dropped the charm. Not the arrogance, though. Very stuck on himself, I thought. I had to be quite firm."

"And of course, your side was successful, as if I have to ask," Faith said, laughing. Her mother just smiled. Her well-manicured hand was the epitome of the iron fist in the velvet glove.

"I've been away from all that since the start of the pandemic, but he seemed to bounce around from firm to firm. He had and probably still has a reputation for liking the bottle too much."

"I heard one of the firms he was with was in the reality show *Million Dollar Listing* and he was on an episode, but so difficult that both his firm and Bravo axed him. Didn't think he was getting enough airtime, something like that." Hope had been following everything with interest, Faith noted. "And, Fay, to cap it all off, the groom's mother married the almost bride's father. Quentin and I thought it was a ploy to put to rest all the rumors about the daughter. Nothing wrong here, folks. All Claudia's fault wherever she ended up. There was speculation about her whereabouts for a while, and then some other scandal broke."

"Well, she was in a small town west of Boston that no one would have heard of except a student of obscure Revolutionary War history—Paul Revere made our bell, and it rang out the alarm for the skirmish on the green I look at every day."

Faith had been about to say Claudia was happy, alive, and well in the small town. Except she wasn't anymore.

"I think I'll go into the city today. Mostly to walk around, but maybe some distanced retail therapy," Faith said at breakfast the next morning.

"It's a beautiful day for it," Hope said. "I'd come with you, but I promised Quent I'd help him with a school project. We have to do something like measure the water temperature at different tides. But I could get Dad or Quentin to help him."

In the old days, the au pair would have done things like this, Faith thought. Things *had* changed.

"I'm free," her mother said. "I haven't been to the city for ages. Not since my last dental appointment."

Faith knew Tom had told her family that she was having trouble accepting Claudia's death as accidental or a suicide. Was having trouble accepting it in any form. They were dear, but she didn't want company today.

"I know it sounds selfish, but I'd just like to be on my own. Wander anonymously through the park, window-shop, get a nosh someplace."

"It's not selfish at all," her sister said. "You can just be Faith Sibley Fairchild, no one's daughter, sister, mother, wife. We've all been there!"

"That's it exactly."

Not exactly, she said to herself while masked on the off-peak train heading to Penn Station. She had a very specific destination and purpose in mind. She also had a small digital voice recorder in the pocket of the linen jacket she was wearing under her lightweight wool coat. The coat had pockets, too, but there was the chance it would be hung up. Zach had given her the recorder before she left, and he knew what she was planning. It was simple. Claudia's father didn't know of her death, and Faith, her good friend, would tell him. Knowing that Charles "Chip" Hamilton had hacked into a computer and knowing more about the new Mrs. Richards, Faith was sure she now knew what had happened—and who was behind the Zoom bombing. Just the jilted groom, or maybe mother and son were partners in crime. She wouldn't be able to prove it, she was sure, but at least she would see, and hear, Claudia's father's response to her death, hopefully with Bitsy Richards in the room.

Faith no longer wanted Claudia buried in the plot on Sanpere.

She wanted her to rest next to the grandmother and mother she loved so much. If there had been no other reason, this was enough to bring her to 113 East Seventieth Street.

She emerged from Penn Station into the sun and decided to walk over to Fifth Avenue before knocking at the Richards townhouse door. The city was in full bloom, more so it seemed than she recollected from previous April visits. At the New York Public Library, the stone lions, Patience and Fortitude, gazed down at beds overflowing with bright yellow tulips. The planters on the slope toward the Rockefeller Center skating rink, watched over by Manship's golden *Prometheus*, held red-and-purple parrot tulips in between masses of Stargazer lilies. Along the way, the sidewalks were filled with colorful planters. She wondered whether there had been some kind of horticultural surge in the fall of 2020—New Yorkers wielding bulb planters? Spurred by Pix's example, Faith herself had planted many more bulbs than usual, and the daffodils were starting to bud out. It had felt hopeful, that by spring there would be more flowers than Covid cases.

Ignoring the sight of all the stores that were closed, everyone masked, and concentrating instead on the day itself, she said hello to the Plaza Hotel, so changed—Eloise wouldn't recognize it—and crossed into Central Park, buying a hot dog from a vendor under the familiar blue-and-yellow Sabrett's umbrella. The fragrant cherry trees were flowering, and there were others: magnolia, redbud, dogwood. The daffodils were out here, drifts of them under the park's trees and along the paths. She walked to the bronze *Alice in Wonderland* statue and sat on a bench, feeling much like one of the inhabitants at the bottom of the rabbit hole. The lines from "Jabberwocky" inscribed beneath the tea party group made more sense than her life had for a long time. There would never be a "new normal."

She was tempted to just keep walking. Head to the West Side, ordering curbside from Zabar's to take back to Long Island. Not go to East Seventieth Street at all. Perhaps being in the city surrounded by this comforting renewal was the way to say a final good-bye to Claudia. She would have walked here, too. Yet Faith knew she had to go and go soon.

It was close to three o'clock when she pushed the doorbell at the imposing townhouse. Urns on either side of the door were planted with a tall, twisted juniper bush, nothing blooming. There was no answer. She tried again and the door opened immediately.

"Yes?" It was Bitsy Richards née Hamilton. Faith had expected the help, not the lady of the house herself, whom she recognized from the *New York Post* photo. Bitsy was wearing well-cut black pants, a turquoise silk tunic, several gold chains, and black Manolos with kitten heels. Her strawberry-blond hair was coiffed in a thick pageboy that did not move when she did, nor did her face—extensive work, Faith assumed. No mask.

"Hello. My name is Faith Fairchild, and I wondered whether I might speak to James Richards?"

"He is not available. I am Mrs. Richards. What is this about? I'm completely vaccinated, so you can take your mask off. I hate it when people try to talk through them."

She had not been invited in, but the door was wide open, so Faith took a step into the foyer. Hearing her voice, Faith realized it had been Mrs. Richards who had answered her call. She turned on the recorder in her pocket.

"His daughter, Claudia, was a friend of mine, and I'm afraid I have bad news for him."

"My husband does not have a daughter—"

Faith wasn't going down this road again, and interrupted. "I know about the wedding, or rather the wedding that didn't happen. Not from Claudia. She never mentioned it or anything about her family except that her mother and grandmother had died when she was a teenager. I need to talk to her closest relative. I recently found her father's information and came here to speak with him, and you. I live in Massachusetts. That's where Claudia lived."

"I suppose you'd better come in," Bitsy said irritably, and led the way upstairs to a large living room with a floor-to-ceiling bow window overlooking the street. The walls were deep ochre, the floor covered by the largest Aubusson carpet Faith had ever seen outside of a museum or stately home. An elaborate carved marble mantel dwarfed the fireplace, which was filled with birch logs and not a trace of ash. The furniture owed more to a Louis than to a later monarch. The walls were filled with artwork: impressionist landscapes, still lifes, and ancestral portraits dating back to New Amsterdam, with one recent exception. It was a young girl, perhaps seven or eight, seated with her hands folded, wearing a red velvet party dress. A green velvet headband, which held her dark curls back from her face, emphasized her deep brown eyes and their long lashes. Her mouth was closed, but a smile played at the corners. The sitting was a serious occasion, but the child was happy—her gaze straight ahead. Looking at someone who made her smile? Someone behind the artist in the room?

It was Claudia. No question.

Faith recognized the style and the signature—Aaron Shikler, the artist selected by Jacqueline Kennedy for JFK's posthumous White House official portrait. Shikler had painted hers as First Lady and later Nancy Reagan's. Were it not for the artist's fame, Faith was sure the image would be hanging in a broom closet if kept at all.

Aside from the other furniture crowding the room, there was a large cabinet, open to reveal a well-equipped bar. An empty martini glass on a table next to a sofa covered in crimson brocade hinted that Bitsy adhered to the notion that it must be five o'clock somewhere.

She sat down after refilling her glass from a cocktail shaker and motioned to a chair. Faith took her coat off and sat. She was not offered a libation of any kind.

"My husband doesn't know that Claudia is dead, and I don't intend him to. After what that little bitch did to him—to us—she was dead as far as he was concerned, so it doesn't matter now."

How does Bitsy know Claudia is dead? Faith started to ask the question, but Bitsy was on a roll. And well lubricated—the glass was almost empty.

"You have no idea what it was like to be the laughingstock of the whole city, the whole country! Did she think even for one second what would happen after her stunt? She left my Chip as the wedding was about to begin! Running out of the church never thinking how he felt, or me! Never thinking that for years every time he'd arrive at a gathering people would shout out, 'Claudia, get back here!' and laugh their heads off. She destroyed his life—nothing went right for him after that day, and he is very gifted. It was like she cast a spell. Law school, jobs, girlfriends, everything he did went wrong. I decided I wasn't going to let her get away with it." Bitsy drained her glass and got up, going to the liquor cabinet and bringing the shaker back with her.

Faith tried to say something, along the lines of "It must have been upsetting," but didn't get the chance. And she definitely didn't want to interrupt the Niagara of Bitsy's tirade.

Her cheeks were beginning to match the color of the fabric on the sofa. "Do you have children, Mrs. Fairchild? A son?"

"Yes, in fact I do. A son and a daughter."

"Then you understand." She waved the glass, spilling some of the drink on her sleeve. "A mother has to do what a mother has to do, and I did. Oh, it's taken long enough, but I got back at her." She laughed shrilly.

Faith couldn't believe what was happening. If she had come earlier, Bitsy would not have had as much to drink. Would her loosened tongue tell Faith what had really happened? Revenge. That hadn't been on the list of motives. The humiliation she'd suffered that day in front of people whose opinion meant everything to Bitsy had given birth to it.

Revenge. The dish hadn't been cold. It had been searingly hot.

Bitsy stopped laughing and the room was quiet. Faith thought it might be time to leave, but the woman started to speak again.

"All the gossip columns printed that stupid photo of me holding up traffic on Fifth for the wedding guests . . . but we still had a party that people continue to talk about," she said.

Faith was sure they did.

"Everything perfect, down to the rose petals in the centerpieces matching the color of the tablecloths. I had to do it all." Her eyes glistened, and Faith thought Bitsy might be at the weepy stage of inebriation. "The bride couldn't be bothered. Oh no, she had to finish college. Get some stupid art degree. She was never going to have to work a day in her life, and Charles wasn't, either. I gave them my beautiful house. She wouldn't have had to do a thing to it. The linen closet was full of Frette and Pratesi, and the kitchen had been remodeled in January." Bitsy was looking off to one side of the room, perhaps picturing the gem of a house Claudia had thrown back in her almost mother-in-law's face.

Faith ventured a comment. "Maybe living in Greenwich would have caused unhappy memories? Claudia's mother's illness?"

"Eleanor had no spine at all! James could have been very successful in politics. A senator if he'd married me, maybe higher office. That woman, and his daughter, too, didn't do a thing to move him along, especially after Eleanor's cancer. They have themselves to blame for their own deaths."

After this remark, it was more than time to go. Faith was about to stand up when Bitsy's next words, after she'd poured yet another drink, stopped her. "You can imagine how I felt when Chip showed me the photo he'd found on some Internet site. The little whore! Posing for porn! It was a gift from heaven, and we knew exactly what to do with it. She'd written to her father on some anniversary of her mother's death. Boo-hoo. I burned it, right there." She pointed to the fireplace. So, it *did* get used. "But not before I wrote down the postmark, and it wasn't hard to find out what she was doing in that place." Bitsy made it sound like a bordello. Faith would love to see her up against Millicent, Aleford's standard-bearer.

"The Zoom bombing was Chip's idea. He'd been having fun with it before, getting back at some of those professors in law school and at Yale who'd had it in for him. I watched the whole thing, watched her when we did it."

"How were you able to watch her?"

Bitsy shook her finger tipsily at Faith. "Now, that would be telling, Mrs. Fairchild."

Faith gave her what she hoped was an appreciative smile and said, "It sounds as if you or someone else has been very clever."

Keep her talking.

"Aha! And people said he wasn't bright. My son," she added for Faith's benefit. "True, I was the one who came up with the whole idea, but he did all the work."

Keep talking, keep talking . . .

"Except the end. I wanted to do that myself. That was my reward. I said I would see her dead, and I did!" She gave a triumphant laugh and settled back against the sofa cushions, a cat-who-got-the-cream expression on her face.

Talk some more, talk some more . . .

"But how did you see her? I mean, wasn't she far away from here in Massachusetts?"

"Maybe in miles, but not on my screen after Chip put those things in the alarm system. I knew the bombing would get to her, so I kept watch. It was tedious, but someone had to do it. I saw you once and some other woman. Man, too. Slut! I stayed in a Marriott nearby in some town. Waltham? And kept watch for days, parked in some woods near where she was living. It was her birthday that did it. She'd blacked out before, but I knew she was a goner this time." She gave a smug smile, kicked her shoes off, and stretched out, sipping from her glass.

Faith waited. And felt sick.

Just keep going, Bitsy.

"It wasn't hard. The house was open, but I knew where the key was. In case it was locked. Chip said she hid it in an urn, and he got the alarm code when he called about the battery problem. Battery! There was no problem! I wore gloves and used kitchen tongs to move the decanters, just in case."

She laughed again, and it was manic. Faith began to get scared. She had enough recorded, and it was time to get out. But first, one final question.

"You watched her pour the acid into the glass she'd been drinking from? Watched her drink it?"

"Oh, poor Claudia. Made such a face, and then such a mess. It was hard to leave, but I painted on her pictures first. X-ed her out and x-ed them."

Someone entered the room. The wheelchair had made no sound on the carpet, but the voice did. "You murdered my daughter?" James Richards shouted.

Bitsy sat up straight. "Oh, James darling, of course not. Faith here—it is Faith, isn't it?—and I were just talking about something that happened to someone else. Joking about it."

It was amazing how fast she had recovered her composure, and her speech wasn't slurred in the slightest. Years of practice.

He turned to Faith. "Is this true? A joke? I've been listening from the hall, and it hasn't sounded like a joke."

Bitsy was looking at Faith, her eyes filled with such hate that Faith flinched. The woman was both drunk and mad. She was gripping the cocktail shaker, pulling her arm back to throw the missile in her direction, Faith predicted. It was time to leave and take the next step, a complicated one. She took a deep breath.

"Your daughter was a dear friend of mine, Mr. Richards, and I came here from Massachusetts where she was living to tell you she died a little over four weeks ago. We were not able to find next of kin until recently. My husband, the Reverend Thomas Fairchild, and I have been making arrangements. I understand her mother and grandmother are buried at Woodlawn, and my intent was to ask you to have Claudia interred in their plot."

James Richards did not look like a high-powered New York lawyer. He looked like an old, ill man, and he sounded very tired. "I feel no guilt about what happened to Claudia. I never mistreated her in any way. I made sure she had everything she needed, including a suitable marriage. What she did shamed me, and the others concerned, but she made her choice. I hope she was happy with it, and I'm sorry she has died so young. If you give me your contact information, I will see to it. That's where she belongs. The three were very close. I wasn't, Mrs. Fairchild."

Bitsy lowered the shaker and filled her glass. She looked triumphant. "You can see yourself out."

Faith did.

Few people, she reflected, have a taped murder confession in a pocket and no clear idea how to proceed next. To start, she sat outside at an upscale bakery café on Madison with a view down Seventieth and the Richardses' front door. If Bitsy should make a run for it loaded down with Vuitton luggage, Faith would tackle her. The woman couldn't weigh more than a hundred pounds. If.

Choices. She could call Chief Pat and tell him everything. Play the tape over the phone. She could call the Massachusetts State Police Homicide Division. She could call Zach, even Tom—or Hope and Quentin, who were here in New York. In situ.

Or she could call the number she had on Favorites and had called periodically throughout the pandemic to check in. After a rocky start when she had discovered the body in the belfry, Faith and Massachusetts State Police Detective Lieutenant John Dunne had become friends, despite what he termed her "annoying interference" in several more investigations. He was originally from the Bronx and never lost the accent, which had immediately endeared him to her. They shared a love of the city and were exiles. After retirement he'd moved to southern Maine, where his wife was from, and then after her too-soon death moved to the place where everybody knew his name—or did at one time. Riverdale in the Bronx. She hit the number.

"Faith, how are you? I was just thinking about you," he said.

"And I you. Is there any way you could meet me at the corner of Seventieth and Madison as soon as possible? I need your help. I'm not in any danger. Or I don't think I am." She had a sudden vision of Bitsy going to her La Perla lingerie drawer for a small, lightweight but lethal Glock, maybe in pink.

"As it happens, I can be there sooner. My grandson is at Columbia, and we've just finished eating corned beef sandwiches we picked up for a walk in the park."

"I'll tell you all about it when you get here. It's a long story. The murder occurred in Massachusetts, but the murderer is here. Right here, across the street, and her accomplice may be, too."

"Of course, it would be murder," he said.

"I'm afraid so."

A cab pulled up in what seemed like only a few minutes, and Dunne got out. The years hadn't altered the initial impression he made on her—much larger than life. His tight curls, not the result of a perm, which had been salt and pepper, were now all salt. Age had not caused a stoop, and at six foot seven with a hefty body, he commanded attention. His face was still, charitably termed, homely. His smile changed all that, though, as did his clear blue eyes. He'd always dressed well, in contrast to Aleford's then chief Charley MacIsaac, who went for rumpled tweed jackets and baggy corduroy pants. Today Dunne was wearing linen trousers, a navy-blue Henley shirt, and a navy-blue N95 mask.

"Start at the beginning, unless you think something is going to happen here soon."

"That's the house. The one with the two twisted shrubs outside," Faith said. "I don't think anyone will come out. At least not for a while. The husband, James Richards, is the father of the woman who was murdered. A good friend." She had to stop for a minute. "The woman who murdered her, Elizabeth Richards, is there. She's always called Bitsy. I have her taped confession." She pulled the recorder from her pocket. "Her son, Charles Hamilton, was her accomplice. I don't know where he is, although he could be in the house."

She was kicking herself for not finding out. But Bitsy wouldn't be apt to get in touch with him to tell him what had just happened. That she had in effect set him up for twenty-five years to life.

They were the only ones at the café tables. "I'll get a coffee, although at these places it's not going to be my nabe's prices," Dunne said. "You want a refill?"

"I'm good," Faith said. Her flat white would have bought lunch and a bottomless cup at Aleford's Minuteman Café, where she'd often met Dunne.

He returned, and as instructed she started from the beginning. The very beginning—her friendship with Claudia, the Zoom bombing, the discovery of the body, her conviction that it had not been an accidental death or suicide, the disbelief of almost everyone, even Tom, her investigation with Zach, the suspects and their elimination, until finally today's unexpected confirmation. He sat quietly throughout, asking a question or two, and then said, "Give me the recorder." He took earbuds from his pocket, plugged them in, and listened. Twice.

"I know you're retired, John, but I couldn't think of any other way to handle this. No one listened to me before, and I don't know who would now, even with the recording."

"It always amazes me even after all I've seen what someone would kill for. Like being publicly humiliated, which is what it seems in this case. Although it was more about losing the money, I think. The money that would have set her son up for a luxurious life of leisure."

"Maybe money to be gained now. Claudia's father will inherit as next of kin. And he's quite ill. The humiliation of that day has haunted her and her son's lives, keeping them from what they assume are their rightful positions in their social world, but the prospect of inheriting what her son couldn't get through marriage but she can—maybe soon—may even be the stronger reason. She'd set him up and he'd be back to being the prince he was meant to be—never having to work a day in his life."

Dunne nodded. "I need to make a few calls. I'll take a walk. You stay put and keep your eyes on the prize. And, Faith, I may be retired, but once a cop, always a cop. You did the right thing, calling me."

When Dunne left, Faith phoned her sister and told her she might be later than she thought. That she had run into a friend, and they were having coffee. Which was true.

Dunne returned with an even bigger smile than she'd seen before on his face. "Now we sit and watch. Would you believe your friend's father, a Mr. James Richards, called the precinct to turn his wife and her son in for a murder they committed in Massachusetts? We should see something soon."

Two patrol cars and an unmarked one slid to a stop, double-parking outside the townhouse. Bitsy answered the door, immediately tried to close it, and after two more cups of coffee for Dunne and Faith, Mrs. Richards was escorted to one of the cars in handcuffs. A man who must be her son, looking barely awake, was led to the other.

"Never forget, my friend, 'the Wheels of Justice turn slowly, but grind exceedingly fine,'" Dunne said. He had kept the small recorder. "Now I'm going over to talk to the gentleman getting into the unmarked car, a lot nicer model than what we had, and I'll call you tonight. I'm assuming you can stay out on Long Island a while longer. They are going to want to hear what you told me and have you sign a statement. As we speak, the place in Aleford is being searched and sealed. Also her laptop, and they want her phone. Tell your friend Zach they'll be getting in touch."

"He didn't do anything illegal! I don't want him to be upset. He and his wife are having a baby!"

"Not this minute, I assume, and they are more likely to want to give him a medal. You, too. But don't be surprised if much is hushed up. Humiliation and revenge were what drove Mrs. Richards to kill."

"Powerful motives," Faith said in agreement.

"Exactly. But it's also got to be humiliating for your local chief and the rest up there to have missed finding the devices to start. Now, are you okay? Someone will be here soon to drive you to the bosom of your family, who will be more comfort than anyone else."

It was true, Faith thought. Only to be eclipsed by adding Tom, Ben, and Amy.

The news of Claudia's murder and the subsequent arrests reached Aleford before Faith did. She imagined the conversations in various households but didn't have to in hers. Tom was so contrite that she had to tell him to stop. That she knew he had only been thinking of her.

In another part of town there was a conversation she couldn't have imagined.

"I thought you did it," Margaret Kimball said. "I thought she might have been blackmailing you. I saw some of your texts back and forth. I thought she threatened to tell me about them when she wanted more from you, so you Zoom bombed her, got those photos somehow, and she found out, which meant you had to shut her up. Since then, you haven't really been yourself. Well, weren't before. I went to her to ask her to leave you alone. The door was open, but she must have been out walking, since her car was there. I saw the cup in her sink. The Russel Wright. I . . ." She started to sob.

"Oh my God, Margaret. I thought you *killed her," Brian said. "That you hated her. Thought we were having an affair and lost it that night. You knew what nitric acid is. I've used it. The cup. I told her one got broken. I didn't say how, and she found a duplicate on eBay. I never went to pick it*

up from her. I never told her how sorry I was she had been Zoom bombed. I thought my wife was responsible, and I didn't trust myself not to tell her my suspicion." He took her in his arms, and gradually she stopped crying.

"We've been idiots," she said.

Worse, *he thought.* I was a terrible friend, and I'll carry that burden with me the rest of my life.

Faith and Amy stood on the curb in front of Persis and Henry Wald's house, handing goody boxes through the open windows of the cars parading past. The boxes were filled with the cupcakes Niki had made, some with Henry's picture transferred, some with HAPPY BIRTHDAY, HENRY written on them, some simply with the number 80. Besides the large cupcakes, each box had one of the favors Persis had created in increasing numbers, as it seemed the whole town would turn out for the June 7 cavalcade. The favor was a small wire heart with Persis's yarn twisted around it, with a long loop attached for use as a decoration or a key ring. The Walds stood on their lawn waving and beaming.

Ben and Catherine led the parade in the van, a mixtape of 1941 hits playing—the big bands, Billie Holiday, the Andrews Sisters, and Judy Garland, as well as birthday songs. Claudia's banner was stretched across the front bumper. Another hung on the vintage fire engine bringing up the rear.

Catherine had come to meet Ben's family soon after her second shot, and all Tom and Faith's misgivings about how fast the relationship had developed vanished. She was a keeper, and when Ben met her family, their reaction was the same. The fact that, like his father, he could hoover up platefuls of pasta and other dishes while maintaining a tall, rangy physique especially appealed to Catherine's grandmothers, who were suspicious of picky eaters. "Who doesn't like calamari or garlic? Fuhgeddaboudit." Ben's professor was at long last back from France, and Ben had been commuting to Providence to the lab, also finishing the semester's classes. He was moving into Catherine's apartment.

Amy's graduation had been a socially distanced but very moving one on the football field. The graduation-cap drone event had occurred earlier, and the school had made postcards with all the names of the graduates on the back. This summer she planned to work in the kitchen at the new incarnation of the Sanpere Shores lodge before starting her college classes. Faith wasn't sure what she would do with herself, although Pix had plans for a joint vegetable garden so mammoth that she was joyfully envisioning trucking produce to farmers' markets all along the coast. Freeman, fully recovered from his coronavirus—"Think I'd let it keep me from hauling my traps?"—had already rototilled the space.

Having made sure her customers had alternatives, Faith suspended Have Faith Delivered with the hope that it wouldn't be needed again. Niki and she were catering a few small outdoor events in June. Niki had moved back to her house, and Eleni was selling hers, convinced by a Realtor friend after hearing what houses were going for in this Covid market. She was giving Niki and Philip some of the profit to expand their house, not that she was moving in. She'd give an equal amount to her son, and the rest would go for rent in a building in Watertown that was near friends, her church, and bingo.

Faith had called both Zach and Niki after leaving John Dunne. She expected things would drag on, especially given that Bitsy would hire barracuda lawyers, but it appeared it wouldn't play out that way. Chip had burned through the money from the sale of the Greenwich house, his mother's condo, and other funds she had. James had no intention of paying for their defense. They were both in custody awaiting trial, and Faith was sure Bitsy was complaining that orange wasn't her color. Faith made a point of avoiding the headlines. The *Post* and others dragged up the Runaway Bride story and photos.

Faith had not expected to hear from James Richards and didn't directly, but a week earlier she had received a note from Woodlawn Cemetery giving her the date of interment and plot number for Claudia Schuyler Richards. It was noted that a headstone had been ordered.

She would go visit her friend sometime. Woodlawn, four hundred acres in the Bronx at the end of the IRT from Manhattan, was a beautiful place, created in 1863 by the merchant princes and other notables as a convenient resting place to build temple- and castle-like monuments to themselves for all eternity, surrounded by lush landscaping. But Claudia would have Nellie Bly, Elizabeth Cady Stanton, Dorothy Parker, Duke Ellington, and others for company besides household names like Macy, Westinghouse, Penney, Woolworth, and Armour. Faith would go in the spring and remember another spring day when her friend was vindicated, providing sorrowful peace for them both.

Before she went to New York, Faith had given Claudia's last plate to the Clark Gallery, arranging for an impression, and the print was waiting for her. It *was* a self-portrait, her face superimposed upon a multitude of delicate lacy webs. The portrait was unexpected. It was a duplicate of the one Faith had seen hanging on the wall in the New York townhouse. Claudia as a young girl. There was one change, however. In the print, the smile that had lurked on her mouth in the other portrait was a broad one here. She was glowing with happiness. Happiness at what she had spun, created. Happiness at her life.

It was John Dunne who called to tell her about the disposition of Claudia's estate. Faith had assumed that without a will, the many, many millions would go to James Richards.

"I knew you'd want to know, and it may help."

"Help?"

"You can't fool me," Dunne said. "What happened is not something you will ever get over, although some of the impact will lessen, I hope. But Claudia's estate in its entirety goes to the

Schuyler Foundation. It was created by her grandmother and mother in case Claudia died with no heirs or, get this, intestate. They knew their girl pretty well, I'd say. After she left the city that day, she drew a sizable amount from her account and never touched any of her money again."

"She would have needed it for her tuition at MassArt, immediate living expenses."

"Another interesting thing is that her father was not designated as the estate's trustee before she turned twenty-one, which would have given him access to it all, *and* he is not on the Board of Trustees for the foundation. The list of grants run a broad gamut from art institutions, scholarships for students graduating from New York's public schools, cancer research, and a bunch of women's rights organizations."

"I wonder if Claudia knew about it. She said she didn't have anyone to leave something to, which suggests she was told what had been set up. She didn't need to make a will. Her grandmother and mother had taken care of everything."

"I think you should go with that thought," Dunne said.

"Egg creams, my treat, next time I'm in the city," Faith said, then added softly, "Thank you, John."

JUNE 18, 2022

The bride looked like a medieval princess, and the rich colors of the silken gowns her ladies-in-waiting wore swayed gently in the summer breeze. Her court, small in number, spread out in a circle around the altar, a trellis covered with white roses. Her prince, wearing a pearl-white suit of more modern design, carried a diadem, which he placed on her tresses before the priest began the service. The parents of both the bride and groom stood just behind them.

No rain had dared mar the day, and the sound of birds filled the air. The sound of first one baby crying and then another filled the air as well. The bride's mother hastened to take one of the babies, a newborn, from the winsome young woman who had been holding both. Returning to the paused vows, she placed the infant in the bride's arms and the crying stopped. The other child did the same. It was no fun to cry alone.

Faith was holding Tom's hand. She didn't know whether to laugh or cry. Weddings provoked so many emotions, memories of ones past, especially her own, and thoughts of future possibilities.

Tom leaned down and kissed the top of her head, whispering in her ear, "I guess it all worked out."

"I *guess* it did," she said.

AUTHOR'S NOTE

On March 9, 2020, I spent the day in Boston with relatives from Norway. My cousin's husband had been invited to attend a conference at the Harvard Business School starting the next day. Very worried about what was not yet the word on all our lips—Covid—I arranged to meet them downtown and stay outdoors. It was so sunny and warm, we soon shed our jackets. We walked the Freedom Trail, the Greenway, and along the harbor front, stopping to watch the seals in the New England Aquarium's outdoor tank. A happy, normal time. We tasted each other's ice cream flavors. The idea that I would not be in Boston again until January 29, 2021, and then only briefly to get our vaccinations at Tufts Medical, would have been unimaginable. As would the fact that I would not next see this family until June 24, 2022.

On March 10 the Massachusetts governor declared a state of emergency. It continued until June 2021.

What happened in between, to me personally, family, friends, and the world, became this book, which I began writing in the fall of 2021 and finished in the summer of 2022. I started keeping a daily journal a few days after being in Boston, when the pandemic became real with astonishing and terrifying speed. I jotted down notes on what I called "foraging," safely sourcing food and other supplies; where we went to walk—often driving to national and state parks in the state previously unknown to us; what was happening in the country, the world. How I was feeling. And more. The Norwegians left March 11, by the way, traveling in a rented car to JFK Airport to get one of the only flights back to Oslo and immediate quarantine.

Day by day the cancellations and closures mounted until March 20, when Massachusetts recorded its first death from the virus. On March 23 the governor's Stay at Home Advisory went into effect. Our son moved in and worked remotely from March 18, 2020, until May 20, 2021. We three were a pod.

At times it was difficult to write this book. I decided to begin the timeline in January 2021 when the hope vaccination offered became real, but as you have read, Faith looks back, as did I. Like millions worldwide, we lost someone beloved—a family member. It was April 9, only a month after my cloudless day in Boston. The inability to gather to mourn him, and for one of his sons, living literally minutes away, to be at his side, was devastating.

I saved many of the December 2020 holiday cards we received. The letters and notes were filled with the ways all were coping. A few had picked up stakes and moved to be near family or to hunker down in what had previously been a summer retreat. Many brought sad news, but all expressed hope for 2021. My favorite card was one from friends in Florida, a quote from Tennyson handwritten on a folded piece of construction paper: "Hope smiles from the threshold of the year to come." I looked up the poem, and the final words, "It will be happier," made it resonate even more.

A number of readers have mentioned going back to the Author's Note at the end of *The Body in the Lighthouse* in which I wrote about the aftermath of 9/11 and the difficulty of writing a book following the catastrophic event. I stopped for some months, as I stopped this time, too. Rereading the *Lighthouse* note, I've been struck by how I could simply have copied it, changed the date, several descriptive sentences, and it would apply—saying what I want to say to you now.

"There were no degrees of separation on September 11," I wrote, and that was true at the start of the pandemic. "We are all in this together." I am not naïve, and there are deep divisions in our country, but throughout the pandemic, and continuing as each new variant like the Hydra's head raises fears and causes a spike in cases, people helped one another. Acts of kindness were innumerable. The heroism of health care workers of all kinds, putting their lives on hold and on the line, will be remembered when the history of all this is written in the future.

The future. At the close of the *Lighthouse* note, I write, "Just as many of us date things from before the Cuban missile crisis and before the assassinations of the Kennedys and Martin Luther King, Jr., we now have another 'before.'" Now we have an even greater "before." "Pre-pandemic" has entered our daily conversations. "I saw someone . . ." "That was . . ." and so forth. After September 11, I mourned a world lost to our children, a place that had seemed safe from such an attack. Those children are adults now, many with children of their own, and I mourn the loss of the pre-pandemic world for them. The damage from remote learning, isolation, and loss in multiple forms can never be remedied.

As we enter into what is now "living with Covid," my wish for you, dear readers, is the same as I expressed all those years ago. That we hold on to hope—and in every way possible, each other. All together.

EXCERPTS FROM

Have Faith in Your Kitchen

by Faith Sibley Fairchild
with Katherine Hall Page

Sheet-Pan-Roasted Delicata Squash

2 medium-size delicata squash
2 tablespoons extra-virgin olive oil
1 teaspoon kosher salt
½ teaspoon freshly ground pepper
Parchment paper

Preheat the oven to 425 degrees F.

Cut the squash in half lengthwise and scoop out the seeds. Faith does this with the small end of a melon baller.

Slice into 1-inch crescents.

Toss the slices with the oil, salt, and pepper.

Line a sheet pan with the parchment paper and arrange the slices in a single layer.

Roast for 10 minutes, then turn the slices over. Roast for another 10 minutes. This caramelizes the squash and enhances its sweet, nutty flavor. When cooked, delicata's skin is tender and delicious. For a kick, add red pepper flakes to the spices, or toss the roasted squash with pumpkin pie spices and a tablespoon of maple syrup.

Serves 4 as a side dish.

Delicata is a winter squash. When spring comes, Faith uses this method to pan-roast fresh asparagus.

Sheet-pan cooking found a new and very wide audience during 2020, becoming popular as people found themselves cooking at home—and liking it! Faith paired various vegetables with fish fillets or boneless chicken, a meal on a sheet, starting the veggies, especially potatoes, sooner, and then adding the rest. High heat is the key.

Beer Bread

3 cups all-purpose flour
1 tablespoon baking powder
1 teaspoon kosher salt
2 tablespoons sugar
12 ounces beer (lager or ale is best)
2 teaspoons unsalted butter, melted

Preheat the oven to 375 degrees F.

Grease a 9 x 5 x 3-inch loaf pan with unsalted butter.

Combine the flour, baking powder, salt, and sugar in a large bowl.

Stir in the beer.

Spread the batter evenly in the pan and bake for 35 minutes, until golden brown. Test with a broom straw or cake tester.

Remove from the pan and brush the top with the melted butter.

Let cool completely on a rack before slicing.

The bread has a nice crumbly crust and is also good toasted.

Although Tom Fairchild is a Samuel Adams beer loyalist, Faith has made the recipe with other beers, including nonalcoholic beer. Ginger beer with 2 tablespoons of flaked ginger—Penzeys works well—stirred into the batter makes a sweet bread for breakfast or tea. Her favorite alcoholic brand for the recipe is Blue Moon Belgian White, a wheat ale with coriander and orange peel.

Amy's Cookies

- 1 cup almond butter
- 1 cup sugar
- 1 large egg
- 1 teaspoon baking soda
- ½ teaspoon vanilla extract
- 1 cup mini chocolate chips

Preheat the oven to 350 degrees F.

In a large bowl, mix the first five ingredients. Fold in the chocolate chips, stirring well. The dough will be sticky.

Form the dough into balls, a tablespoon each. Lightly moisten your hands to make this easier.

Place the balls 2 inches apart on an ungreased baking sheet and bake in the middle of the oven for 10 minutes. The cookies will expand and be soft to the touch.

Immediately transfer to racks to cool.

Makes 2 dozen.

Vanikiotis Baklava

Syrup

1 cup water
2 cups sugar
¼ cup honey
½ teaspoon cinnamon or 1 cinnamon stick (ground)
1 teaspoon lemon juice

Pastry and Filling

1 pound phyllo dough, thawed, in package, overnight in refrigerator
1 pound walnuts
2 teaspoons cinnamon
½ cup sugar
2–3 sticks butter, melted and clarified (start with 2, add another if necessary)

Prepare the Syrup

Combine the water, sugar, honey, and cinnamon in a saucepan. Bring to a boil, then cook on medium low for 20 to 30 minutes until thickened.

Add the lemon juice and cool in the refrigerator.

This should be done first, as it needs to cook and then cool, which can take an hour. You can also make the syrup a few days ahead and keep cool. It has to be cold when poured over the hot baklava.

Prepare the Pastry and Filling

Preheat the oven to 350 degrees F.

Bring the phyllo to room temperature. Leave the package unopened.

Butter the bottom and sides of a metal 9 x 3-inch pan.

Chop the walnuts finely in a food processor. Add the 2 teaspoons of cinnamon and ½ cup sugar. Mix together.

Open the phyllo and place on your counter, keeping it covered to prevent drying out. If the phyllo is too wide to fit the pan, cut it in half. You should have between 36 and 40 layers.

Lay one layer flat in the bottom of the pan. Brush with the